COMMANDER WILLIAM RIKER WATCHED THE VIEWSCREEN IN HORROR . . .

. . . as Dr. Starn was hurled backward by the explosion that shattered his office.

Then there was the sound of scuffling, and something moved across the shuttlecraft's monitor. "What's going on?" Riker demanded. The figure whirled, leveled a weapon of some kind at the camera lens, and fired. The screen went dead. "Lieutenant," Riker growled to the shuttle's pilot, "tell me you can get some more speed out of this thing. . . ."

Look for STAR TREK Fiction from Pocket Books

Star Trek: The Original Series

Star Trek: The Next Generation

Star Trek: Deep Space Nine

Star Trek: Voyager

THE DEATH OF PRINCES

JOHN PEEL

POCKET BOOKS

New York   London   Toronto   Sydney   Tokyo   Singapore

An *Original* Publication of POCKET BOOKS

POCKET BOOKS, a division of Simon & Schuster Inc.
1230 Avenue of the Americas, New York, NY 10020

STAR TREK is a Registered Trademark of Paramount Pictures.

A VIACOM COMPANY

This book is published by Pocket Books, a division of Simon & Schuster Inc., under exclusive license from Paramount Pictures.

ISBN: 0-671-56808-6

First Pocket Books printing January 1997

10 9 8 7 6 5 4 3 2 1

POCKET and colophon are registered trademarks of Simon & Schuster Inc.

Printed in the U.S.A.

This is for Rachel Sapienza

THE DEATH
OF PRINCES

Chapter One

"HE'S GOING TO BE ASSASSINATED!"

Starn's lean face stared back at Maria Wallace as she leaned across his desk, her face flushed with frustration and anger. His only concession to any form of emotion whatsoever was the slight arching of his left eyebrow. "I understand that," he replied.

"Do you?" It was impossible for her to keep her temper. No matter how long she worked with Vulcans, she would *never* understand why they considered a dispassionate nature a virtue. "Then what are we going to do about it?"

For a moment, Starn did not reply. Finally, he blinked. "I believe we are simply retreading the same ground we have already explored, Observer," he commented. "If you have no further information to impart, then you are dismissed." He gestured at his desk, which was so clean it looked sterile. Knowing his penchant for cleanliness, it might have been. "I am very busy, as I am sure you must realize."

Maria took a deep breath and tried to control her temper. Blowing her top wouldn't win any arguments with a Vulcan. "What I realize is that a man will die if we don't do something."

Starn inclined his head slightly. "At this moment in time, many men are dying, and we do nothing, Observer," he pointed out. "Our function here is not to interfere but to observe. Hence your designation. I would suggest that you return to your duties."

"Doesn't his death *mean* anything to you?" she cried, wishing that she could kick or smash something.

"Of course it means something," Starn answered. "I do not relish the death of any living creature, much less that of a sentient being. And I know that First Citizen Farra Chal is, by any account, an insightful and intelligent leader. I will regret his demise, if it should occur. But we are forbidden by the Prime Directive to interfere in any way with this native culture. You knew this when you became a member of my team. I would appreciate it if you returned to your former objectivity."

How could she make him understand? He was so close, and yet so utterly far away at the same time! "But Chal is the one person who could unify Iomides. You *know* that! If he lives, he'll make this planet a prime candidate for Federation membership."

Starn nodded slightly. "I agree with your summation of the political situation here. Chal may well do as you suggest, should he live. This assassination attempt on his life, if it succeeds, may well set back their unification by decades, and perhaps longer."

"Then surely you can see why we *have* to stop it?" Maria cried, exasperated. "Not just for the sake of Chal, but for the sake of the planet!"

The Vulcan shook his head minutely. "Surely you must see that we cannot do this. Allow me to posit an analogy. What if we were to learn that he had a brain tumor, inoperable by current Iomidian technology but easily corrected by a laser scalpel? Should we then kidnap him and perform this operation on him to save his life?"

Maria hesitated barely a moment. "I think we should, yes."

"And suppose he elects to go mountain climbing?" Starn continued. "A dangerous sport, and one where he might easily break his neck. Should we then stop him from climbing for the sake of his planet?" Starn spread his hands. "Observer, you must see that interference, once begun, has no foreseeable ending." When she was about to protest again, he held up a hand. "Enough. You clearly have a faulty understanding of the significance of the Prime Directive. You appear to view it as an impediment to action, when it is in fact a preventive against disaster. We will do nothing to alter the course of this planet's events. If the assassination takes place, then we will mourn the passing of a good and wise leader.

"Meanwhile, I believe you should reread Morgan's *The Prime Directive in Action* to correct your faulty perceptions of it. That will be all."

Maria started to protest, but she could see from the look on Starn's granite face that there would be absolutely no point to it. With a frustrated growl, she whirled and stormed out of Starn's office.

When she had agreed to join the Federation observation team here on Iomides, it had seemed like a dream posting to her. It was a world on the rim of known space, where ships had only recently explored. Only two planets in this sector had so far joined the Federation, and Iomides was poised to become the third. It was standard practice for the Federation to establish an observation post on possible member worlds, one that was hidden from the population of the planet. There a team of experts would monitor the progress of the race, and evaluate them. The two prime requisites for membership in the Federation of Planets was knowledge—no matter how rudimentary—of warp drive technology, and a planetary government.

At this point, Iomides had neither. However, there was a supposedly top-secret laboratory in the city of Mellim where a team of experts was on the verge of either discovering the first warp inversion field or of blowing themselves and their small island base halfway across this solar system. The scientific experts were pretty much split on which would occur first.

As for a planetary government . . . Chal was the brightest hope for this. He had been pressing for this dream for decades, and now that he was First Citizen of Tornal, he was in a strong position to achieve his dream and unify Iomides.

Unless he died first.

Maria's specialty was economics, not politics, but she'd been studying all of the team's reports on the planet. Like almost everyone else on the observation team, she didn't view this assignment merely as a job but as a mission. They all desperately wanted Iomides to succeed and to become a part of the Federation. The people here were, on the whole, pretty decent and friendly. The observers were able, with a minimal amount of cosmetic surgery, to go out from time to time and walk among the people here. It was a standard procedure, because more information could be gathered by informal personal contact than by any amount of scanning. Maria had a small apartment on Tornal, and she had assumed an identity there that she masqueraded under about once a standard month. She went out among her neighbors, shopping, eating, talking—and she thoroughly enjoyed it. They were decent folk, who reminded her of her neighbors from her hometown in Iowa, back on Earth.

She *wanted* these people to be a part of the Federation. But if anything happened to Chal, the unification movement would be dealt a potential deathblow.

She ignored her co-workers as she stormed through the corridors of the observation post, heading for her small cubicle. She knew that Dr. Starn was right, and that the Prime Directive was, on the whole, the best law on the Federation's books. But Starn didn't seem to understand that there were times when the Directive had to be set aside. In special cases only, she knew, and not just when the whim struck you. But she knew her history: Many starship captains had made judgment calls and deliberately ignored or subverted the Prime Directive when the occasion called for it. True, in some cases the people involved had made horrible mistakes and been reprimanded or even punished for their actions. But in many cases, the Federation—and Starfleet in particular—had commended the actions of the captains involved. In fact, some of those men and women were now legends at the Academy. Who hadn't heard of Kirk, Sulu, T'Shaar, Belak, or Gardner? They had made judgment calls and defied the Prime Directive when they knew in their hearts that this was the right thing to do.

And Maria Wallace was absolutely convinced that, despite all his logic, Starn was wrong here. Allowing Chal to be assassinated would not only be the worst possible thing to happen to the planet, it would also be morally reprehensible.

She had reached her room now and entered it, locking the door behind her. She took a good look around the tiny, cramped space and sighed. What she was about to do would certainly get her into very serious trouble, but she had no choice. She moved to the closet and started to pull a few of her local clothes out of it.

Maybe the Federation as such couldn't get involved. Maybe Maria Wallace couldn't. But Galia Wade—the Iomidian identity she'd built up—could. All she had to do was to warn First Citizen Chal of the details that she knew, and then fade away again. He could take it from there. And she was certain that she could get to him. One of the lovers she'd taken while she was posing as Galia had worked for Chal's party, and he was highly placed enough to get a message to Chal that would be believed.

She stripped off every vestige of her Federation-issued clothing, with a wry smile. It seemed to be symbolic. Then she dressed in her local clothing. She slung her bag over one shoulder, checking that it still contained her keys and credit chips, and that her credit was still good for the amount she'd need to draw on for this venture. One of the nice parts about being an economist was that she could . . . transfer . . . any funds she needed in absolutely untraceable ways.

It would be nice to see Jamal again. She had pleasant memories of evenings and nights that she spent with him. Though it was frowned upon to get involved with the locals in romantic relationships, it wasn't actually forbidden. And, unless she'd been monitored—which was very doubtful—nobody knew about it, since she didn't talk about her private life in the observation post. Sooner or later, even Starn was going to get suspicious of her behavior, but she was certain that she'd have plenty of time to carry out her plan before he could do anything to stop her. For all of his Vulcan brains, he wasn't really a very creative person. It would be a while before he'd even miss her, and even longer before he suspected what she was doing.

Feeling better now that she had made her decision, Maria strode down the corridor and to the outer security door. She nodded amiably to the guard on duty, a woman whose name she couldn't even recall.

"Your turn again, Maria?" the guard asked.

"Yes," Maria answered. "Lucky me, eh? A short break before another round of number crunching."

"Better you than me," agreed the woman cheerfully. "I'd hate all that analysis. I like things simple." She tapped in the code to dephase the outer door. "Okay, you're all set."

"See you in a few days," Maria lied, as she stepped through the electronic curtain. The last thing she saw was the guard's casual wave, and then she was through the phase shield and standing on the hillside overlooking a small wood.

The post was completely invisible behind her now. It had been constructed into the side of this hill, out in the wilds. It was sufficiently far from the nearest town so that it wouldn't be stumbled upon, but close enough to be able to catch local ground transportation into the city center. No matter how much a local might search for the post, it was completely secure behind the electronic shields that disguised it.

Not, of course, that anyone on this planet even suspected that aliens were actually here. Well, aside from the local flying saucer nuts that every pre-spacefaring world seemed to spawn, and nobody much took them seriously.

Maria hitched her bag over her shoulder and started down the hill toward the road about a mile away. She'd made her decision now, and she would go through with it. Whatever Starn or the Federation might say, she couldn't simply sit back and do nothing. She had to help Chal.

She had to break the Prime Directive—and let the future decide whether she was a heroine or a fool.

Chapter Two

"TEA. EARL GREY. HOT."

As soon as his specified brew had materialized, Captain Jean-Luc Picard walked across his ready room sipping at it. Its creation was one of those daily miracles of life aboard the *U.S.S. Enterprise* that he sometimes had to force himself not to take for granted. The perfect cup of tea at precisely the correct temperature at any time that he desired it was definitely something to savor and appreciate.

He sat down at his desk and started to glance through the reports. It was a routine task that had to be done, but one that he knew would all sum up to one sentence: Everything was in order on this ship of his. If everything hadn't been in order, he would have been informed of it in person. "Of the writing of books, there is no end," he murmured, quoting the

9

Book of Proverbs wryly. "Or reports, either, it seems." Taking another sip, he then placed his cup down and started to read the first of the reports.

As he had known, it boiled down to the fact that everything was fine.

The same applied to the next seventeen reports that he gamely plodded through. By this point, he'd finished his tea and was contemplating having a second brew. It would be an indulgence, but he needed help in getting through the pile of papers.

His desk communicator chimed. With a sigh of relief, he called out: "Picard here." He didn't much care what it was, he was sincerely glad of the interruption.

"There is an incoming transmission for you from Starfleet Command," came the gravelly tones of Worf. "It is marked as most urgent."

Picard straightened up in his chair. "Put it through to me here, please, Mr. Worf."

"Aye, sir."

A second later, the communicator panel on his desk lit up with the Starfleet logo blinking to show a transmission was being received. Then Admiral Halsey's face blinked into existence. She looked tired and more than slightly irritated—pretty much how she always looked, whether she was declaring disasters or handing out commendations. "Captain," she said, nodding slightly. "I trust your crew would not be averse to fresh orders at this moment?"

Picard suppressed a smile. They had been mapping protostars for eight days, and most of the crew was getting bored of the constant views of gassy clouds.

Worf, for example, had been holding practice drills for his security team and demanding a five-percent increase in reaction times. He was driven by a frustration that most of the crew probably shared. "Well, Admiral," he answered carefully, "I suspect that stellar cartography would be the only department aboard that wouldn't exactly bless your name."

"It's always hard to keep them happy," Halsey answered, with no trace of humor in her tone. "And they won't like this either, I'm afraid. The *Enterprise* is ordered diverted immediately to the Buran System, Captain. Coordinates are being relayed as we speak. You are to head there at maximum warp and prepare to render all medical assistance possible."

Picard raised his eyebrows. "May I ask what, precisely, we will be heading into?"

"A plague, Captain." Halsey sighed, and ran a hand through her short, graying hair. "The Buran are suffering terribly from a highly virulent plague that is apparently one hundred percent lethal to anyone infected. The death tolls are staggering, and Starfleet has promised all possible assistance in this situation."

"Of course." Picard nodded slowly. "I'll have my medical staff begin work, and head for Buran immediately."

"There's one more thing, Jean-Luc."

He narrowed his eyes and stared at the admiral's image. There was *always* "one more thing." "Yes?" he prompted.

"I don't know if you know much about the Burani," she replied, and waited for an answer.

Thinking hard, Picard shrugged. "They're a relatively new race to have joined the Federation, I believe," he answered. "Within the last two years, if I recall correctly. Nothing more than that, I'm afraid."

"You've hit on the salient point," Halsey informed him. "They were inducted eighteen standard months ago. An Andorian trader recently stopped at their world, and the plague began immediately after this visit. The Burani vote to join the Federation was almost evenly split, Captain, and there seem to be a lot of them who feel that it was a bad move. Some of the more vocal opponents of Federation membership are claiming that the plague came from the Andorians, and they're screaming for Buran to pull out of the Federation."

Picard frowned. "Is that possible?" he asked.

"That they might pull out? Yes. That the Andorians somehow transmitted the disease?" She shrugged. "That will be up to you and your crew to discover, Captain." She paused. "As you probably know, Starfleet is actively seeking footholds in this sector to strengthen our borders. Buran is quite important to us, since there is only one other world already in the Federation in that area of space. And three others under scrutiny. If Buran should pull out—or worse, decide to ally itself instead with the Romulans—it would weaken our presence in the sector severely." She paused. "Not to mention, of course, the terrible consequences of this plague from a humanitarian perspective."

"I understand," Picard said softly. "We will, of course, do everything in our power to address both aspects of the situation."

"I know you will, Jean-Luc," Halsey answered, a

faint smile showing. "You have a good crew and a fine reputation. All relevant files are being transmitted to you now. Good luck. Halsey out." The screen reverted to the Starfleet logo, and Picard tapped it off.

He strode immediately to the door, and then onto the bridge. Despite the routine nature of their current mission, it was a hive of activity as always. "Mr. Data," he called as he marched across to his command chair. "You should be receiving new coordinates from Starfleet. As soon as they are in, set a course for the Buran System at maximum warp."

Commander Riker moved swiftly from the captain's chair to his own as Picard approached. "Trouble, sir?" he asked.

"Yes indeed, Number One." Picard checked the displays in the chair arms, noting that everything was still copacetic. "Plague." He tapped the communicator panel. "Bridge to sickbay."

"Crusher here," came the reply a moment later.

"We're receiving data from Starfleet at this moment," he informed her. "As soon as it's complete, download it and examine it. We're heading for Buran and a plague situation. There will be an officers' meeting in an hour."

"I'll be ready for it," Beverly promised, and then signed off.

Picard glanced up at his android officer. "Mr. Data, please stand down and review all current files on Buran and prepare a presentation."

Data rose smoothly from his seat. "Certainly, Captain." He nodded as Lieutenant Van Popering took his place. "I shall begin immediately." He headed for the science station.

Sighing, Picard sat back in his command chair. "This isn't going to be very pleasant, Number One," he commented. "The plague is apparently highly infectious and almost inevitably fatal."

Riker nodded, a slight frown on his face. "Will any of our personnel be at risk?" he asked.

It was the same question that Picard had been asking himself. "We'll have to wait for the briefing and hear what Beverly's opinion is," he admitted. "We can only pray that it's a very specific disease. It won't do anyone any good if our relief teams were to come down with this thing as well." He stared at the starscape on the main viewer, and then called out: "How long until we reach the Buran System?"

"At present speed, three days, sir," Van Popering replied promptly.

"I wish it were sooner," Picard muttered. "Who knows what hell those poor people are going through?"

There was death everywhere. J'Kara stared about the ward, his eyes peering through the contamination suit with difficulty. The suit was designed to protect its wearer from infection, but that was about all. It had been a rush job, and the designers had evidently not taken into account humidity from the wearer's breath. The supposedly clear plastic lenses over each of his eyes were fogging over already. It made the nightmarish sight all around J'Kara look blurred and even worse.

This was simply a temporary hospital—if "hospital" was the right word. It was little more than a waiting place for the dead-to-be. There were over three hundred patients here, all in terminal stages of the plague. Their sore-encrusted bodies oozed puss from their joints. Their feathers had molted, leaving glaring, palid patches of infected skins. Their eyes were rheumy and milk-white where the disease ate at their corneas. Each breath was a labored, long, painful wheeze.

His heart felt as though it would burst. Three hundred of his nestlings in here, all of them dying. And this was only one of forty temporary hospitals set up in the capital. The overall numbers of the infected were appalling.

J'Kara walked slowly into the ward, trying to avoid breathing too much. It was partly to avoid steaming up his mask's lenses and partly a foolish but strong revulsion against smelling the air in here. Since his suit had its own self-contained air supply, that was stupid, but he couldn't prevent the thought. He *knew* the place must reek horribly from the open sores on the victims.

"My prince," came a crackling voice over his radio link, "again I tell you that you really should not be here."

"Where else should I be?" asked J'Kara bitterly. "At home, feasting and pretending that all is well with my world? Doctor, when my people suffer, I suffer with them." He sighed. "This is appalling."

"We do the best we can," the doctor beside him assured him hurriedly, wringing his hands together in despair. "It is just that—"

"I meant no accusation against you or your staff," J'Kara interrupted. "I can see that you are doing all that you possibly can. More, in fact, than anyone has a right to expect. It is the situation that upsets me, not your treatment. It is appalling that anyone should have to suffer and die like this."

The doctor nodded, relief showing even through his smoky mask. "It is dreadful, my prince," he agreed. "We should never have joined that cursed Federation. This is all their fault."

That angered J'Kara. "You are an educated man," he said sternly. "I had not expected to hear such foolish speculation from you. This plague cannot be connected in any way with our decision to join the Federation. In fact, a starship has been dispatched to help us and will arrive in a few days. With their technology, they should be able to help us to recover from this plague."

The doctor didn't immediately reply. J'Kara could see that he wanted to do so, but that he was racked with indecision. "Well," the prince said with a sigh, "out with it. What is it that you don't like? Don't worry, this won't go any further than the two of us."

"Are you sure," the doctor asked slowly, "that the Federation will be coming to help us? They may simply be intending to check up on how well their work is progressing. They may only be pretending to offer us aid."

"Don't be such a fool," J'Kara snapped. "Why should the Federation have caused this plague? I don't know how that stupid rumor ever began, and I don't know why anyone believes it to be true. What possible motivation would our allies have to inflict such terrible devastation upon us?"

"Forgive me, my prince, for saying this," the doctor

answered. "But you must hear it, obviously. There are many who believe as I do, that the Federation is not our friend. They covet our world because we are on the border between them and their enemies, the Romulans. They wish to fortify our planet and turn us into a war zone."

"That is ridiculous," J'Kara said coldly. "First of all, we have a treaty that states the Federation will import no weapons to our world unless we specifically request them. And, second, you know that my father would never allow our world to be so used."

"Precisely," agreed the doctor, triumphantly. *"That* is why the Federation has caused this plague. They hope to either wipe us out completely and then resettle our world with their own soldiers, or to devastate us to such a great degree that we will have to allow them to *help* us to rebuild—in their image."

J'Kara felt his feathers rising as his anger grew. "Is this nonsense what passes for logic nowadays?" he cried. "If the Federation wanted to wipe us out, they need never have contacted us first to offer us their friendship. They could have performed all of this"— he waved his hand about the death ward—"while hidden in orbit waiting for us to die. They could have completely hidden their existence. You and others like you are victims of foolishness and paranoia. The Federation is our friend and will prove itself when their *Starship Enterprise* arrives."

The doctor nodded and bowed slightly. "I can only pray that your belief in their goodness is correct, my prince," he said unctuously. "Because I must tell you frankly that the medical community of Buran cannot stop this plague. The rate of infection is growing, and those who are infected will die. In a month or less, every last living Burani will be infected. In two months, our entire race will no longer exist."

Two months . . . J'Kara stared around the ward in horror. In two months or less, his whole world would be like this, without exception. Only pain, suffering, horror, and then, finally, death to look forward to.

It was Hell indeed.

Chapter Three

THE MOOD IN THE BRIEFING ROOM was grim. Picard nodded for his senior staff to be seated as he took his place at the head of the table. "I'm sure that you've all heard by now that we have abandoned our charting mission and rerouted to the Buran star system," he began, looking at the serious faces around the table. Data appeared as attentive as ever. Worf, the Klingon security chief, was as always grim. Very little made him smile—and when he did, it was often a prelude to battle. On the other hand, the rest of his senior staff tended to be pretty lighthearted as a rule. It was impossible to feel that way in the present circumstances.

Deanna Troi, the ship's counselor, was frowning. Beside her, Will Riker scowled at the padd in front of him that he'd been studying. Chief Engineer Geordi La Forge's face was tight, his eyes invisible behind his omnipresent VISOR. Grimmest of them all—aside from Picard himself—was Beverly Crusher, the ship's chief medical officer. She had very good cause to be so serious.

"Doctor, could you fill us all in on what you know about the plague?" Picard inquired.

"Of course." Beverly was all business. She glanced occasionally at her own padd as she spoke, but she'd memorized most of her presentation. "Most of you won't know a lot about the Burani, since they're very recent members of the Federation. They're basically an ornithoid species, having descended from avian ancestors." She tapped the padd and a small hologram sprang into being above the conference table, showing a typical Burani. "They're about two meters tall," Beverly explained. "Body structure is similar to Terran bird-forms, though their legs are more humanoid than avian. They're light-boned and large-brained. Their wings are functional—Buran has a surface gravity only about point four Earth normal and a thick atmosphere. They don't fly well—they glide, mostly. Their wings end in a three-fingered hand with an opposable thumb.

"On the whole, they're a pretty robust race, even given their light body structure. However, they are being ravaged by a plague that has sprung into existence only in the past few months. I have virtually no details about it except for some news footage of victims. The disease is proving to be very difficult to trace for the Burani, and impossible to treat. Their medical knowledge is fairly advanced, though not yet up to Federation standards. I understand that there has been some resistance from the population to assimilating Federation technology, and that resistance is undoubtedly hampering their medical efforts.

"No cause or origin for the disease has yet been discovered. We don't know how it's transmitted, or if it is even possible to cure it. Once we arrive, we're going to have to take down several medical teams immediately and begin scanning for everything we need." She glanced back at Picard.

"I have to ask," he said gently, "whether there is any risk of our people becoming infected once we reach Buran."

Beverly chewed at her lip. "I don't have a lot of data about Burani biochemistry," she said finally. "They're a very insular race and haven't allowed much probing by outsiders. What I have seen, though, suggests that their biological makeup is quite different from humans. It is my belief that any disease that affects them will not be transmittable to humans, or to most of the other species on this ship." She tapped the table beside her padd. "There are, however, thirty-four crew members of avian or near-avian descent. I would advise that none of them be allowed to beam down to the planet or to contact anyone who has until I can be certain. I'm also recommending that the initial teams who beam down for contact wear biohazard suits until we can be absolutely certain that there will be no cross-contamination."

"Understood," Picard said with some relief. Even if there were a danger of infection, he still would have proceeded with the mission. It would have been unthinkably inhumane to have done otherwise. But his first responsibility was the lives of his crew, and he wanted them to be as protected as possible during this errand of mercy. "Data, could you give us some background for this mission?"

"Certainly, Captain." Data looked about the table. "The Burani have evolved a highly technical and intricate civilization, which is slowly unraveling as this plague strikes. Their cities tend to be vertically planned, with access to the skies from all buildings, and many high points for gliding takeoffs.

"Their world was discovered by the Vulcan Starship *Sarek* three standard years ago. The Burani were even then united under a single ruler, named T'Fara. They had limited space travel within their own star system, and were experimenting with warp technology. As a result, the usual period of observation was waived and contact made almost immediately. What followed was a yearlong debate and then a vote by the Burani on whether their world should join the Federation.

"Their world contains a number of large and sometimes very deadly predators. Some of these the Burani had wiped out, but others still exist. It would seem that there are conservationists who argue that to wipe out the predators would be unethical, while their opponents believe that it is better to annihilate them all, for safety reasons. The Federation has remained neutral on the issue, naturally. However, the Burani are, as a result of historic predator attacks, an insular and suspicious people. Though there were evident advantages to be gained from Federation membership, many of the Burani strongly favored isolation instead. In the end, the vote was very close, but with a 52.745-percent majority, the world did become a member of the Federation eighteen standard months ago.

"There still remains a great deal of discomfort with this decision, and there would appear to be an upswing in membership of isolationist groups. If the plague continues much longer, this group may force a revote and then retract Buran's membership."

Beverly leaned forward slightly. "If this plague continues, Data," she observed, "then that will be the least of their worries. Their figures on the plague indicate that it will infect everyone on their world within two months. The Burani won't be isolated— they'll be extinct."

Picard winced at this news. "So," he summed up, "we seem to have a very volatile situation on our hands here. We have to offer medical assistance to a race that does not really trust us. It isn't going to be easy."

"There is more, Captain," Data said. "I regret that it complicates the issue further."

"Proceed, Mr. Data."

The android nodded. "The plague's outbreak began some two days after an Andorian trader stopped off at the world. From the video broadcasts that I have scanned, it would appear that many Burani ascribe the plague to the Andorian visit."

Beverly scowled. "You're saying they think they caught the plague from the *Andorians?*"

"That is one interpretation they appear to be favoring," Data agreed cautiously. "Those who favor this belief appear to be in two camps: one believes that it is an accidental infection; the other believes it was deliberately induced."

"Deliberately?" Riker leaned forward, his scowl intensifying. "You're saying that some of the Burani believe that the Andorians *intentionally* caused this plague?"

Data nodded. "It would appear that this is a view held by approximately twenty-four percent of the population, if the video broadcasts are to be believed."

"What is your opinion on this subject, Doctor?" Picard asked Beverly.

"You mean about the feasibility, I assume," Beverly replied. "The idea that anyone would be low enough to deliberately begin a plague is repugnant." She shrugged. "Accidentally—well, until I get more data on the Burani physiology, I can't really be certain. But it's highly unlikely. Andorian diseases tend to be pretty specific to Andorians alone. Humans can't catch even diostrophic fever from an Andorian host, and offhand I can't recall many races who can be infected by them. As for *deliberate* infection . . . well, it's always possible to create biological weapons, Captain. You know that. But why would the Andorians do that? They value honor in battle, and they outlawed biologics centuries ago. Besides, to create a biological weapon, they would need to know a fair amount about Burani biology, more than the Federation records contain. I can't absolutely rule out the possibility, of course, but it strikes me as being pretty ludicrous."

"I agree," Picard said. "But if it is a popular view on Buran, it's one we shall have to consider. Mr. Data, do you have the name of the Andorian ship that paid this highly unfortunate call on the planet?"

Data shook his head. "It is not in our records, Captain. There are many Andorian traders plying this sector, and it would take a while to track them all down. However, I assume that the Burani would have a record of the vessel and probably a flight path in their logs after it left their world."

"Assuming they weren't involved in starting the plague," Riker commented, "then they should be pretty easy to find. On the other hand, if I can play devil's advocate for a moment, what if the Burani are right? If the Andorian trader *deliberately* infected the planet, they would hardly have been likely to stick to any flight plan on record."

"That would then complicate matters," Picard agreed. "But we'll take this one step at a time. When this meeting is concluded, Mr. Data, contact the authorities on Buran and find out what you can about that ship. We're going to need to speak with the captain at any rate. Now, is there anything further that we should know? You had mentioned this theory of the Andorians as being only one of several favored on the planet."

"That is correct, Captain," Data agreed. "Another, in favor with twelve percent of the population, is that joining the Federation angered their people's gods."

Deanna managed a wry smile. "That's only to be

expected, I'm afraid," she observed. "There are always some who accredit any disaster to divine intervention. As long as it's a minority, it isn't likely to harm us, is it?"

"That might be the case," commented Data, "if there were not another complicating factor. The Burani are highly religious, and even those who do not believe this theory respect it. One who does subscribe to this belief—and quite vocally—is their ruler, T'Fara. Naturally, his own conviction sways a lot of his people."

"I don't get it, Data," Geordi objected. "If he's their ruler, why is he against the Federation? Didn't he vote to join us?"

"No," Data replied. "It appears that until about fifty standard years ago, Buran was divided into various warring nation-states. It was T'Fara's father and then T'Fara himself who managed to unify them into one peaceful community. This was partly by force of arms, but mostly due to T'Fara's powerful charisma and personality. His son, Prince J'Kara, has pressed for democratic reforms and was the one who suggested the referendum on joining the Federation. T'Fara agreed to the vote because he is very emotionally attached to his child and heir. He did not take the result very well. I believe that the best expression to describe his actions might be *temper tantrum.* Though he acquiesced to his peoples' choice, he has been rather vocal in critiquing the treaty."

"Sore loser, eh?" asked Geordi thoughtfully. "Well, it makes sense, then, that he's advocating the belief that the gods are irritated. It vindicates his own opinions."

"And it doesn't make our task any easier," Picard observed. "It becomes more important than ever to determine the real source of the plague. Though, of course, our primary concern must be to halt its spread and effect a cure." He looked back at Beverly. "That, I'm afraid, means that the burden of this mission will fall on your shoulders, and those of your medical staff, Doctor."

"We'll do our best, Captain," Beverly replied with confidence. "Once we can get established and start running tests, I'm optimistic that we should be able to help contain the disease. Then we can begin work on a search for a cure."

"Other comments?" Picard asked his staff.

"Only that we're going to have to proceed with caution on this mission, Captain," Deanna replied. "The Burani are suspicious of outsiders, and if they perceive us as either not helping or, worse, as exacerbating the situation, we may not be allowed to finish helping them. They may ask us to leave."

"That possibility had crossed my mind," agreed Picard with a sigh. "We're certainly laboring under a handicap here, but I have every confidence in my crew."

"So do I," Deanna commented. "It's not our teams I'm worried about. It's the Burani. All of our teams should bear in mind their volatility. We can't afford any incidents that might serve to make the Burani more hostile."

"I agree," Picard said, pushing back from the table

and standing up. "Unless anyone else has anything to add at this moment, I believe this meeting is over." There were no further comments. "Well, I'm sure you'll all have plenty to keep you occupied until we reach Buran. Dismissed."

Data headed for the door promptly, eager to begin his information search for the Andorian vessel. Worf followed with Geordi. Beverly moved to join Picard.

"A private word, if I could, Captain?" she asked.

The two of them moved away from Riker and Deanna. "What is it, Doctor?"

Beverly said gently: "I'm worried about Deanna coming into contact with the victims of this plague," she admitted.

Picard's eyes narrowed. "You think she may contract it? But you just said—"

"No, it's not that." Beverly ran a hand through her hair and sighed. "Captain, there will be thousands of people on Buran, all dying in extreme agony. Their thoughts will be uncoordinated and filled with despair and pain. It's difficult enough for us. But to expose an empath to emotional overload on this level . . ."

That hadn't occurred to him. "It could be pretty devastating," he agreed, concerned. "But you know the counselor—she'll insist on doing her duty, come what may."

Beverly nodded. "Deanna is very responsible. She's also very strong. But I can't help wishing she was not along for this mission," she said frankly. "Perhaps I could give her medication or something that might dull the pain she'd feel. But it's likely to leave her unable to function at full capacity."

"I see." Picard mused for a moment. "And she might very well refuse to take the medication, out of her sense of duty." This was a thorny problem. "Well, let's just hope for the moment that it doesn't come to that, shall we? But if it does, then I shall have to order her to take medication. Will that do?"

"It will have to." Beverly flashed him a grateful smile. "I'd better get busy now." She hurried from the room, dictating notes into her padd.

Picard moved back to the table, where Riker and Deanna were conspicuously hovering. He recognized the symptoms. "Something on your mind, Number One?"

"Worst-case scenario," Riker admitted. "What if we can't help the Burani?"

"I'm not willing to entertain such speculation yet, Will," Picard said softly. "It would mean standing by helplessly and watching an entire intelligent species die out."

"Not necessarily," Riker stated. "Since there are uninfected sectors of the population, shouldn't we at least start thinking about evacuating them to a safer planet?"

Picard rubbed his chin thoughtfully. "It's worth taking a logistic look at it," he agreed. "But you heard Data. They're a very insular people and are already suspicious of the Federation. How will they take it if we start offering to move them off their home planet for safety?"

"Probably not too well," Riker agreed. "But we can't afford to overlook any possibilities, can we?"

"No," agreed Picard readily. "We can't. Number One, why don't you start working on a proposal? See what other vessels we have in the area that might be diverted to help out. If we do have to run an evacuation, it will probably involve millions of people, and we couldn't possibly manage that alone."

"Of course, Captain. I'll begin at once."

Picard nodded. "I'll—" He broke off as the communicator beside the table sounded. "Picard here. What is it?"

"Sorry to disturb you, Captain," came Van Popering's voice. "But we're receiving a transmission from a Dr. Starn on Iomides. He says that it's vital that he speak with you."

Picard frowned. "Iomides?" He had only a vague knowledge of the name. He'd seen the planet marked on stellar charts of this sector, but that was all. "You'd better put it through, Lieutenant," he ordered. Crossing to the wall viewer, he arrived as it lit up. The face of an elderly Vulcan stared back at him. Naturally there was no sense of urgency about the Vulcan—such a display of emotion was considered unseemly and abhorrent. By the same token, a Vulcan didn't cry "emergency" without good cause. "Dr. Starn," Picard greeted him. "I'm Captain Jean-Luc Picard of the *Starship Enterprise*. What can I do for you?"

"You can divert your vessel immediately to Iomides, Captain," Starn replied. "We are in immediate need of your assistance."

Picard stared at the screen, his face darkening. "I'm afraid that isn't possible," he replied with concern.

"We are already on a medical emergency alert. We cannot divert."

"Captain, I am sorry to hear that," Starn responded. "But I must insist that we are in need of assistance on Iomides. The fate of the planetary civilization here is in grave danger."

Chapter Four

Picard shook his head slightly. "I'm sorry, Dr. Starn, but I really don't believe that I can divert from my mission. Perhaps if you could explain a little more about your problem I might be able to come up with a compromise that would not involve my diverting from my mission."

Starn inclined his head slightly. "I perceive that you have your first officer and a ship's counselor with you."

Picard had almost forgotten about Deanna and Riker. "We can speak privately, if you prefer."

"By no means necessary, Captain," Starn decided. "They may be able to offer valuable advice. You may prefer to be seated," he added, "as it may take a while to explain the nature of our emergency."

Picard nodded and led the way back to the conference table. Here, the three of them called up Starn's message on individual screens. "We're ready," Picard announced.

Starn began immediately to fill them in. "Iomides is an isolated world, Captain, and we are a Federation observation team, here to evaluate the planet for possible entry into the Federation. As matters stand, there is a strong possibility of first contact occurring within the next several years."

"I understand," Picard commented.

"One of our observers, monitoring what were supposed to be routine financial transactions, uncovered an assassination plot against one of the planetary rulers here, a being named Farra Chal. He has been elected First Citizen of the continent of Tornal, and it is quite likely that he will succeed in unifying Iomides under a single world government should he survive this assassination attempt. If he should perish, this might well set back political stability on this world a hundred years or more. Of course, such projections are highly speculative and should not be taken by any means as inevitable."

How like a Vulcan to hedge his predictions! "I understand," agreed Picard. "It's a nasty mess, by the sound of things."

Starn nodded silently and then spoke again. "The observer who reported this plot came to see me three days ago and requested permission to alert the First Citizen of this conspiracy against him."

Riker's eyes widened at this news. "Oh."

"Naturally I refused," Starn added. "It would be a gross violation of the Prime Directive to do otherwise. I had no option but to refuse. The observer, however, was extremely vocal in her requests for me to reconsider. Naturally I could not, and she left my office apparently subdued.

"One of the perimeter security operatives reported that the observer then dressed in local costume and left the post, claiming she was leaving for authorized business in the local capital. She has not returned since and cannot be contacted."

Picard leaned forward in his seat. "You believe she has gone to attempt to warn this . . . First Citizen of the plot against him?"

"It is the most logical explanation for her behavior," Starn agreed, inclining his head slightly.

"And your people haven't been able to find her?" asked Riker.

"No. She had taken an apartment in the city under the guise of a Galia Wade. My chief of security investigated and discovered that she spent the first night there, but has not subsequently returned. My officer declared her a missing person with the local constabulary, but without result. She does not appear to have taken her communicator with her, and we have not been able to find her."

Deanna leaned forward, frowning. "But wasn't she ever fitted with a subcutaneous transponder?" she asked. "Surely you could detect her through that."

"The transponder was discovered in the hygiene unit at her apartment," Starn replied. "She must have removed it to prevent us from tracking her movements."

"Ouch," muttered Riker. "She seems to have planned this well."

"Indeed." Starn lowered his head slightly. "I am at

fault for not predicting that she would behave in this fashion."

"Don't blame yourself, Doctor," Picard said encouragingly. "It's a very rare thing for observers to subvert their duties this seriously. This woman must have become far too emotionally entangled, and unable to divorce her duty from her emotions."

"It is one of the problems of working with humans," Starn agreed. "No offense intended."

"None taken," Picard replied. Had the situation been less calamitous, he might have smiled. "I assume you called us to ask us to help in recovering this observer?"

"Indeed, Captain." Starn spread his hands helplessly. "Most of my people here are observers, and not trained in fieldwork. We have only three security officers and can spare but one for the search. With your facilities and staff who are trained and experienced, you stand a far better chance of recovering my errant observer."

"I agree," Picard mused. "There may be a compromise possible here. You wouldn't need my starship for this mission, merely an away team. And, in fact, probably a small one at that. We wouldn't want to gather too much suspicion around this search." This could also provide a solution for the problem of Deanna that he and Beverly had discussed. Not only could he keep her away from Buran, he could assign her an equally vital mission. He looked up at Riker. "Number One, I think that you'd probably be the perfect person for this assignment. And you, too, Counselor. Your particular talents could prove invaluable."

Riker nodded. "I agree, Captain. I'm sure that a small team could track her down fairly swiftly. I hope before she's caused too much damage."

"Excellent," Starn replied. "That would be most acceptable. I will ensure that all available information on this world is transmitted to you to help in your preparations. You will be able to go out among the Iomidians with minimal surgical alteration," he added. "They are very like humans, which will make your task considerably more comfortable. Their level of culture is approximately that of the late twentieth century on Earth, though there are, of course, some significant differences." He paused for a moment. "There is, additionally, one important factor that may indeed make Commander Riker the perfect person for this assignment. The name of the missing observer is Maria Wallace. I believe that you know her."

Riker's brow furrowed as he concentrated on the name. "Maria Wallace?" Then he grinned. "That's right! She and I were at the Academy together. She was in a few classes with me."

"Is that all?" asked Deanna, with the slightest trace of a smile.

"Yes," Riker told her, his own lips twitching. His fondness for the fairer sex was well known, especially to Deanna. "She was a little too intense for me. As I recall, she majored in xenobiology, so after the first few semesters we had only a class or two in common." He paused reflectively. "She certainly had the brains to do well as an observer, but I have to admit, I always had a few doubts about her stability."

Starn raised a single eyebrow. "Interesting. Until

this lapse in her judgment, she was an exemplary worker," he said. "I had praised her work highly in my reports. I confess that this was one reason why I was reluctant to believe at first that she had attempted to break the Prime Directive." He stared straight out of the screen at them. "I am sure that I do not need to stress the urgency of this matter to you."

"No, indeed," Picard agreed. "I'll contact you again when we know precisely when my away team will arrive on Iomides. *Enterprise* out." He tapped the command to end the transmission and then swung about to face Riker and Deanna. "Well, Will?"

Riker managed a faint smile. "To be honest, Captain, I wasn't sure how much use I'd be fighting a plague anyway. This mission sounds a lot more in my line of work."

"It may not be as simple as you think," Deanna cautioned. "It sounds as if this Maria Wallace has been covering her tracks very well."

"Oh, I never said I thought it would be *easy,*" Riker answered, grinning. He turned back to Picard. "But still, I think you're right about a small team being best, Captain," he mused. "A couple of security officers and perhaps one other person should be enough."

Picard nodded. "That sounds about right," he agreed. "However, I don't think I can afford to let you have Mr. Data. He's going to be invaluable to us on Buran by the sound of things. At the very least, he's the one person on the ship who I can guarantee will be immune to this plague."

"I understand." Riker stroked his beard. "Actually, I was thinking that in this case what we could really use is someone who is really imaginative. It seems to call for some lateral thinking, and I know just the perfect person for that. . . ."

The noise was almost deafening when Riker stepped into holodeck three. It hit him physically, making him shudder from the vibrations as well as the taste—or, rather, lack of taste—involved. It was hard to believe that some people considered this sort of thing to be music. Gritting his teeth, Riker moved throught the swaying holographic crowd to the concert stage ahead.

There were six members of the group onstage, all in various degrees of what looked like death paroxysms. Most of them were lacking at least portions of their clothing as they belted out the raw sound from their instruments. Riker stared in astonishment as some alien he couldn't identify managed to get a cacophonous rift out of a Vulcan autoharp. He'd never heard it played quite like that before, and sincerely hoped he never would again. Finding the steps up, Riker bounced onto the stage and headed for the clavier performer. He was lost in a world of his own, eyes closed, sweat pouring from his brow, his receding hair plastered against his skull. He appeared to be jabbing at random chords, but in the general din it was hard to be certain. Wincing, Riker strode across the stage and tapped the player on the shoulder.

The man almost had a heart attack. He leaped upright, jerking out of his state of ecstasy, and his eyes widened as he saw Riker. He obviously tried to say something, but nothing could be heard above the violent level of the rest of the room. Instead, he tapped a microphone on his collar and his amplified voice yelled out: "Computer, freeze program."

Then came blessed silence, as everything and everyone but Riker and Barclay came to a sudden stop. Riker sighed. "Thank you."

"Uh, you're welcome, sir." Barclay struggled to look dignified in his tight synthleather jeans and torn fluorescent orange shirt. "Uh, is there something I can do for you?"

"You've already done the important part." Riker waved about the stage. "What *is* this anyway?" he asked, intrigued despite his ringing eardrums.

"Oh, it's a reconstruction of a concert by my favorite group, Commander," Barclay explained. "Ebenezer Todd and the Sky Monkeys."

"Ebenezer Todd and the Sky Monkeys?" repeated Riker slowly. "I don't believe I've ever heard of them."

"Really?" Barclay looked amazed. "They were incredibly popular about eighty years ago. Had sixteen pressed-latinum albums in a row. Their tours and concerts were mobbed."

"Oh." Riker's own tastes leaned more toward Dixieland jazz. "I hope they finally made enough money to take music lessons."

Barclay smiled politely at the weak joke. "It's not exactly to everyone's taste, I know," he admitted. "But you get a terrific workout just playing backup for them."

"So I see." Riker couldn't resist a smile. Reginald Barclay was a rare individual who threw himself heart and soul into anything he did. Most of those things tended to be at least mildly eccentric, but the man was a very competent engineer, and once you got to know him, quite a personable individual. You simply had to dig a little under the surface layers to get to understand him, which was why he tended to be something of a loner. "I'm sorry to interrupt your exercise session, Mr. Barclay," he apologized, "but I did try calling you first. Unfortunately, given the ambient sound level, you didn't hear the message."

"Sorry, Commander."

"No, you're off duty." Riker waved the problem away. "Anyway, this was . . ." He groped for a polite description. "An experience. Still, I came to see if you'd be up to being a part of an away team I'm assembling."

"Of course, sir." Barclay straightened up and glanced at the ceiling, where the strobe lights hung suspended. "Computer, end program." The frozen concert about them faded back to the basic black with yellow lines of the holodeck.

"It should be interesting, as well as urgent," Riker explained.

"Buran, sir?" asked Barclay, as they headed toward the door together. He winced slightly. "I'm not terribly keen on plagues, but if I'm needed . . ."

"No, not Buran," Riker said, and saw the relief on Barclay's face. "The *Enterprise* is heading there, but we're being dropped off en route on a planet called Iomides." He handed Barclay a padd. "All the current information is here, Mr. Barclay."

"I'll study it right away," the engineer promised eagerly. "Umm, isn't that a Federation observation posting?"

Riker raised an eyebrow. "You've heard of it?"

"Oh, yes. I saw it listed a few years back, before I was assigned to the *Enterprise*. I'd considered applying for a posting there." He looked apologetic. "It's at a stage in its history that sounded kind of interesting," he explained. "I thought it might be fun to go there. Not that the *Enterprise* isn't more fun," he added hastily, to avoid creating the wrong impression. "I'm really glad I came here instead."

"Fine," Riker answered with a smile. "Now you'll get to see if you made the right choice, Mr. Barclay. We're going to be looking for a missing observer."

"Missing?" Barclay looked quizzical. "Missing as in what, sir?"

"Missing as in probably trying to break the Prime Directive," Riker replied.

"Oh." Barclay paused for a moment. "That could be a real problem," he agreed. "I'll get on this right away, sir. When do we assemble for the away team?"

"Oh-eight-hundred hours," Riker informed him. "There's a list of everything you'll need to bring with you on the padd. You'll have to report to sickbay an hour earlier for a little cosmetic surgery. The Iomidians are fairly standard humanoid, but their noses and ours differ slightly, and they have a couple of extra ribs. Simple stuff; it won't take long."

"No problem." Barclay's eyes lit up. "So, we're going to be going undercover, then?"

"That's right," Riker informed him. "We have to track down the observer, preferably before she interferes with the local culture. Otherwise, we'll have to try and hide anything she's done. We can't afford to have anything interfere with Iomides's progress."

"Understood, sir." The engineer looked slightly

nervous, as usual. "I'm right on it," he promised, and hurried off down the corridor toward his room. He was already humming a tune to himself.

Riker winced again. This wasn't one of that weird group's songs, but a piece of classical music that Riker recognized. The James Bond theme . . . it looked as if Barclay's fertile imagination was already hard at work and play. Riker only hoped that he wasn't starting to fantasize too much about this mission. It was complicated enough already without Barclay seeing himself as a secret agent off on a dangerous mission to save the world. . . .

Chapter Five

"THERE WE GO," BEVERLY SAID, replacing her plastic laser applicator and studying Riker's face. "A rather good impression of an Iomidian, if you ask me."

Riker studied his face critically in the mirror she offered him, and grinned. His nose now rose straight halfway up his forehead, a thick ridge that looked and felt quite solid indeed. The two extra cosmetic ribs that Beverly had added to his chest felt a little odd, but he'd get used to them. "It does make me look distinguished, don't you think?"

"As long as nobody gets an internal look at you, you should be fine," Beverly informed him. "So don't plan on an appendectomy, okay?"

"I'll bear that in mind." Still grinning, Riker donned his shirt. The styles on Iomides were quite relaxed, according to Starn's notes. This bright purple shirt, ruffled about the neck and sleeves, was comfortable to wear, if a little flashy. The darker purple trousers were slightly tighter cut, and the knee-length boots were quite swashbuckling. "I feel like a pirate," he commented.

"I'll see if I can find you one," Beverly joked. "Now, out you go. I've got quite a lot of work to do."

Riker sobered up immediately. "It's going to be rough," he commiserated.

"It would be a lot rougher for Buran if we don't get there," Beverly replied. "So don't hold us up."

Riker nodded quickly and left sickbay. He grabbed the nearest turbolift down to the launch bay.

The *Isaac Newton* was already prepped, the door open and waiting. Riker hurried over and saw that he was the last to arrive. Barclay gave the commander a self-conscious grin as he stowed his own gear in the shuttle's locker. He looked uncomfortable in his coordinated yellow outfit. There were two security officers checking off their equipment packages at the rear of the shuttle. Riker knew from Worf's memo that the man and woman were Lieutenants Vanderbeek and Kessler, respectively. As with any of Worf's officers, they both looked alert and ready for action.

Deanna was there also, finishing packing her travel bag. She wore a long skirt and a blouse with even more ruffles than Riker's, both items in a cheery red. Even her knee-length boots were the same shade of red.

"Maybe we could start a flamenco-dancing team?" Riker suggested to her. "You look very good in that outfit."

"I'll keep that in mind," she promised him, smiling. She had the same nose ridge as they all did, which made her look even more exotic than normal. "You look as though you've got a Spanish galleon somewhere."

"I feel rather like that," he admitted.

There was a slight *harrumph* from the doorway, and Vanderbeek snapped: "Captain on the ship."

"At ease," Picard replied as he entered the shuttle. He looked the party over with a tinge of amusement in his eyes. "Well, you seem to be a very jolly bunch. I assume everything's in order?"

"Yes, Captain." Riker glanced forward at their pilot. Lieutenant Porter caught the glance and nodded back, a slight twinkle to her eye. "We'll be ready to depart in a few minutes."

"Excellent." Picard inclined his head slightly and led Riker back out of the shuttle again. "I'm sorry we can't take you closer, Will. You'll still have a ten-hour flight from here."

Riker nodded. "I'm sure we'll keep busy, Captain."

"I know you will." Picard frowned again. "I don't like being unable to help if matters get rough down there. I've alerted Captain Kintu of the *Agamemnon,* and she's taking a detour toward this sector in case you need assistance. But she won't be able to make it for four days at the very least. As for the *Enterprise . . .*" He spread his hands helplessly. "There's simply no way to tell until we reach Buran and assess the situation."

"I understand," Riker said gently. He knew how frustrated the captain had to be at abandoning the away team like this. He hated not being able to render further assistance. "I'm sure we'll be fine."

Picard gave a short barking laugh. "I sound like a worried parent, don't I?" he asked with a rueful smile. "Of course you will be. I know there's no one better suited for this mission. I have every confidence in you, Number One." With a final nod, he spun on his heels and marched away.

Smiling, Riker reentered the shuttle. "All right," he called. "Final checks. Let's get this show on the road, shall we?" He sealed the air lock behind him and then moved forward to take his place beside Lieutenant Porter. "How are we doing?"

"Looking good," Porter reported. She brushed a length of long blond hair from her eyes. "We're ready to launch as soon as you give the word, sir."

Riker nodded and looked back over his shoulder. "Report."

Deanna sat closest to him. She smiled slightly. "Ready, Commander."

Barclay, looking tense and nervous as usual, nodded his head. "All systems go."

Vanderbeek and Kessler both nodded. "Ready, sir," they said in grim unison.

Turning back to the communications panel, Riker raised the bridge. "Shuttlecraft *Isaac Newton* ready for launch," he reported.

"Acknowledged," came Data's reply. "You are cleared for immediate launch." There was a slight pause, and then: "Good fortune, Commander."

"That's *luck,*" Riker replied, grinning. "And thanks, Data." He nodded to Lieutenant Porter, who immediately engaged the power systems and drivers.

The twin bay doors at the end of the hanger slowly slid open, and the great expanse of space beyond began to appear. Porter tapped her panel, and the shuttle started to move slowly forward toward the growing gap. Anticipation made Riker lean forward slightly, watching as the small craft gently lifted from the bay floor and slid easily through the open doors. As soon as they were clear of the *Enterprise*'s hull, Porter engaged the maneuvering thrusters and kicked the craft away from the parent ship.

"All clear," she reported. "All systems showing green."

Riker nodded once. "Impulse," he ordered, tracking their passage on his own instruments. *"Isaac Newton* to *Enterprise,"* he reported. "We're clear of hanger bay."

"Acknowledged," Data answered.

There was a slight kick as the inertial dampers came on-line, and the stars began to rush past the main windows of the shuttle. Riker kept an eye on his instruments. As soon as they were a safe distance from the *Enterprise,* he ordered: "Warp three."

"Aye, sir." Porter tapped in the appropriate commands, and the familiar whine of the warp core powering up sighed through the shuttle. There was a brief feeling of movement—mostly psychological, Riker knew—and then the stars streaked furiously as he watched. "Warp three," Porter announced. "Time to destination . . . nine hours forty minutes standard."

"Good." Riker leaned back from his panel. There was nothing much that they could do until they arrived in orbit around Iomides except to check their gear and consider possible courses of action. Once they were closer to the planet, he'd contact Dr. Starn and see what the Vulcan could tell him. Meanwhile, he had several hours with little more to do than study what information Starn had already sent them about the planet and its culture.

It was going to be a long flight.

It was going to be a long flight. Picard sat straight in his command chair, staring at the main viewscreen. There was nothing to see but stars, now that the *Isaac Newton* had passed beyond scanning range. True, Will Riker was a more than competent officer, and Picard had the utmost confidence in him. But each away mission was potentially dangerous—if not lethal—and he hated not being able to back up his officers.

Picard shook his head briskly in an attempt to shuffle all further doubts out of his mind. "Mr. Worf," he called. "Please contact Dr. Starn and alert him that the shuttlecraft has been launched, and inform him of their ETA. Then contact the *Agamemnon* and inform them of the same."

"Aye, sir."

That was about all he could do for the moment in that direction. He tapped his communicator panel in the chair arm. "Bridge to Crusher," he called. "How are your preparations going?"

"As well as can be expected," came the reply. "They would be faster if you didn't keep asking me that question every ten minutes."

Picard smiled. "I'm sure that's the case," he agreed.

"I'll try to keep my queries down to every twenty minutes in the future."

"I'd appreciate that." There was warmth in the doctor's voice. "Actually, Captain, there is one thing that you might be able to do to help me out."

"Of course."

There was a slight pause. "I'm having trouble with my database," Beverly informed him. "I've scanned for all Burani medical data, and they're pretty meager. But when I contacted the planet, they informed me that this was all they could let me have." She sounded worried now. "Captain, it's simply not enough for me to work with. I'd hesitate even to try to set a broken bone with such scant records, let alone try to cure a plague."

"Odd." He snorted. "Probably just some bureaucratic red tape. You know how these things can be. I'll see what I can do to help expedite matters."

"I'd appreciate that, Captain. Sickbay out."

Getting to his feet, Picard called out: "Mr. Data, you have the bridge. I'll be in my ready room."

"Aye, sir." The android moved to assume the command chair as Lieutenant Van Popering took over the helm.

Picard nodded and left the bridge. Within his ready room he crossed to his desk and tapped up the communications function. Worf's slightly scowling face came on-line.

"I have sent both messages you requested, Captain," he reported.

"Good. Please patch me through to the Burani authorities, Mr. Worf."

"Aye, sir." Worf's face vanished and the Federation

of Planets emblem momentarily replaced it. This then faded to a view of a worried-looking Burani.

At least, the alien *looked* worried. It was hard to be certain. Picard tried to avoid imbuing alien faces with human emotions, but it was a natural conclusion. This was the first Burani Picard had seen face-to-face, so he took a second to examine the being's appearance.

That this person had evolved from an avian stock was quite clear. What was visible of his body was covered with thin bright feathers, including several very lengthy ones cresting from his head. The Burani's chest was large, necessary for the flight muscles, and the wings long and graceful. There were thin hands close to the tips of each wing, clear of feathers.

From the doctor's head, Picard assumed that the Burani had come from a predator stock. The head was large, with forward-looking eyes—binocular vision being a requisite for a raptor. The beak was hooked, another indication of a predatory background. Small nostrils were placed just above the beak, and there was no sign of external ears.

The Burani's color was almost pure white, the only splash of color being in his crest. There was no way of knowing whether the bright magenta was natural or whether it was simply a fashion statement. There were no other possible signs of adornment, though the doctor was visible only from the midchest up. He was wearing some kind of medical gown and a band of some sort about one bony wrist.

"Captain Picard." The alien spoke without inflection. It was an acknowledgment, not a greeting. Picard chose to ignore this poor beginning.

"Doctor . . . ?" Picard prompted.

"L'Tele," the Burani replied with a note of reluctance.

"Dr. L'Tele," Picard said warmly. "I'm glad that you've taken the time to answer my call. We're all looking forward to helping you as much as possible."

The ice was still present in L'Tele's voice. "As you say," he replied noncommittally. "Is there something that you desire?"

"Well, yes," Picard admitted bluntly. "My chief medical officer is attempting to ready her team of specialists to help out with your plague, and she has just informed me that we have as yet received no medical files on the plague from your world. I'm sure that this is a simple oversight, due to either bureaucracy or the fact that you're so dreadfully busy right now." He spread his hands. "So, if you could just—"

"It is no oversight," L'Tele answered brusquely.

Picard frowned. "I'm sorry, Doctor," he said carefully. "I'm afraid that I do not understand."

"It is no oversight," L'Tele repeated, as if speaking to a child. "No medical data have been sent to you, and no medical data will be sent to you. If that is all, I *am* rather busy."

"That is *not* all," Picard snapped, ice tingeing his own voice in turn. "How do you expect us to be able to help you if we do not have medical data on your people?"

L'Tele stared at him, fire in his eyes. "I do not

51

expect you to help us at all, human. I did not request your assistance, and would not trust it if you offered it. My suggestion is that you go back to your Federation and leave us in peace. You have done more than enough to harm us already. We require nothing more from you." He moved to cut the connection.

"Stop!" Picard snapped in his most authoritative tone. The startled doctor did pause. "We have done nothing to harm your people, Dr. L'Tele," he continued sternly. "And we have been asked by your rulers to aid you. Now if you have a problem with that, I'm afraid that it's your own personal problem. You are being asked for simple medical information, and for the sake of your sick and dying people, you had better supply as much as possible."

"That is out of the question," the doctor answered. "And my own personal animosity toward your Federation has nothing to do with my refusal to comply with your abhorrent request." His eyes narrowed. "Since you clearly do not understand my race, I will explain. We are a very private people, human. We do not share with others. We certainly would not offer such personal information as our medical records to a non-Burani species. It is unthinkable."

Oh, marvelous . . . Picard stifled a sigh and leaned forward. "Dr. L'Tele, we have resources that you cannot imagine. I am certain that we will be able to aid you, but we cannot fulfill our mission if you will not let us assist you."

"I am not interested in your fulfillment," L'Tele answered coldly. "I did not request your aid and do not want it. We will discover the cure for this plague without your interference."

"And if you do not," Picard pointed out, "then your entire race will die. Is that what you want?"

"Of course not!" snapped L'Tele. "But if it is a choice between my people dying and being forced to strip ourselves of dignity and privacy before aliens, then I know I speak for all of my people. We would sooner die." He shook his head. "You will not find any Burani who will agree to share our medical data with you, human. You might as well turn back." He reached forward and the screen went dead.

"That might have gone better," Picard muttered. He tapped the panel again. "Picard to sickbay." Beverly's image lit up quickly. "Bad news, I'm afraid." He outlined the gist of his conversation with L'Tele. "I'll speak with T'Fara, of course," Picard finished, "but it doesn't look to be too promising."

Beverly growled with frustration. "How can I possibly help these people if they won't let me?" she complained. "Jean-Luc, I desperately need information on the healthy state of the Burani, and a comparison with the plague victims in various stages. If I don't get it . . . well, L'Tele is right. We might just as well turn around and leave the Burani to die."

Picard nodded. "I'll do what I can," he promised her. "And we're not turning back, whatever the Burani might say. Our assistance has been requested and it will be delivered, come what may."

"Over their dead bodies?" Beverly asked. "Jean-Luc, I'm afraid it might just come to that."

So am I, Picard thought. But he wasn't going to

discourage Beverly any further. "I'll get back to you," he promised, and cut the line. Then he sighed. How could the *Enterprise* do anything to help these people if they didn't want to cooperate?

This wasn't going to be an easy mission, that much was certain.

Chapter Six

THIS WAS GOING TO BE an easy mission, Riker decided, as he leaned back in his seat, studying Starn's information. Iomides was quite similar to the way Earth had been in the mid-twentieth century—split into semibelligerent nations that sniped at one another without causing too much devastation, all told. This was sparking their industrial and technological progress, and raising the general social conscience of the natives. There were peace marches, protests, and foreign aid. There were also rising crime statistics and social tension.

The planet was ripe for a major change, and he could see precisely why Starfleet had an observation team down there. With the research they were doing on static warp fields, it was merely a matter of time before someone stumbled onto whatever they would end up calling the Cochrane drive, and then the Iomidians would be out in interstellar space. Right now, they had scientific probes exploring their own solar system and had managed to launch and recover several dozen orbital missions.

All that they lacked to become nominated for Federation membership was a unified planetary government, and that clearly wasn't too far off. This Farra Chal was a fascinating character—part revivalist preacher, part charismatic politician. He'd galvanized Tornal already and was influencing other countries with his integrity and brilliant policies. Riker could believe Maria Wallace's summary that showed an eighty-percent chance of his unifying the planet in twenty years.

If he lived, of course . . .

"I'm not so sure I like this culture," Deanna murmured.

Riker raised a quizzical eyebrow. "How so?" he challenged. "I was just thinking how decent they seem to be."

"Really?" Deanna answered, a slight curl to her lips. "Don't tell me that you haven't noticed that Iomides is a chauvinist's idea of paradise?"

Blinking, Riker studied his padd again. "Actually, no, I hadn't," he admitted. "What makes you say that?"

"Well, just look at the statistics," she answered. "There are exactly two elected officials on the entire planet that are women. *Two!* Women have only been given the vote in most countries in the last ten years, and there's still almost a third of the planet where they can't vote. Even in Tornal, the most advanced country on the planet, they don't have the right to instigate divorce proceedings, but they can be divorced. Almost all property is passed along to the males, with women's rights to own even the land they live on only being granted within the past thirty years. Ninety percent of the journalists are male, and the other ten percent cover flower arranging and pet shows. They have television news, and there's exactly one female anchor on the planet. Ninety-three percent of their best-selling books are written by men. Women write mostly for children. The only professions where women outnumber the men are teaching and nursing. Women make up only eight percent of registered physicians, and—"

Riker threw up his hands in protest. "Okay, I get the picture. They haven't come to appreciate women like I have." He grinned.

"They don't appreciate women at all," Deanna said. "They're very much second-class citizens."

"It *is* pretty difficult to keep the Prime Directive in mind under such circumstances," Riker replied, frowning thoughtfully.

"Um, maybe Maria Wallace felt the same way?" Barclay offered. "I mean, I've been studying her record, and she's really quite remarkable, isn't she?"

Riker realized abruptly that though he'd been reading up on the planet, he'd not really been examining Maria Wallace's record at all. "She was in several classes with me at the Academy," he said slowly. "She was certainly something special there."

"I'll bet," joked Deanna.

"I meant in class," Riker said patiently. "She had one of the most brilliant analytical minds I've ever known. She could simply look over a list of dull statistics and then start spouting all sorts of information that nobody else ever noticed. She loved to dig into things. I guess that's why she ended up in the observers."

Barclay nodded eagerly. "I've been studying her reports on Iomides," he agreed. "Some terrific stuff in there. There are eight observers on the team, but almost half of the reports were filed by Wallace."

"It sounds like that poor woman was working herself half to death. Maybe she had some sort of breakdown," Deanna said.

"You think so?" asked Barclay, frowning. "I just can't see why she'd do anything so crazy as to break the Prime Directive like this. Maybe she *is* crazy?"

Deanna shrugged. "We could make any number of guesses, Reg," she replied. "But these reports aren't the work of someone who's really broken down. On the contrary—they read to me as if she was inspired by the Iomidians." She glanced at Riker. "What do you think, Will? After all, you're the only one of us who knows her."

"Knew her," Riker corrected. "It's been a decade since I last saw her. Still . . ." He considered the point. "I think she's had an attack of idealism. She was always very passionate about issues. I remember one semester when she led a protest on the Narsican Embassy, to protest their treatment of the Dovinian League. She managed to get six demerits, which she worked off in a month without any regret at all. She was simply on fire with wanting to help people." He tapped the padd. "And from the look of things, she

was convinced that this Farra Chal was the best thing ever to hit this planet. I'd say she really believes that he can unify Iomides, and that without him the planet might degenerate for a couple of hundred years back into near anarchy."

Deanna nodded slowly. "So she decided that she simply *had* to save his life?"

Barclay was shocked. "But . . . to just flout the Prime Directive like that! It's . . . it's totally crazy."

"Not exactly," Deanna replied. "I know the Prime Directive is supposed to be sacrosanct, but sometimes it has to be bent a bit."

Riker smiled. "Captain Picard has dented it a few times himself," he commented. "Reg, the point is that the Prime Directive is a *directive*. It gives direction to our dealings with alien races. But it's not a law, as such. Its purpose is to prevent anyone from interfering in situations that they probably don't understand, even if they think it's for the best. But sometimes it simply has to be worked with or around. The problem is having the maturity and good judgment to make those kind of calls."

"And it's one of the most difficult and dangerous calls we may ever have to make," Deanna amplified. "That's why it's only done in very exceptional circumstances, and generally either by fools or very exceptional people."

Barclay was clearly trying to assimilate all of this. "So, which is she?" he finally asked.

Riker sighed. "That's what we're going to have to determine," he said. "The problem is that on the face of it, she's likely to be right. Chal is really the best bet these people have for unity. If he dies, Iomides might just fragment again. The question is, though, whether interfering might cause even more damage. We're none of us omniscient in this business, so we can only go by our best guesses. And that's when the Prime Directive is expressly meant to kick in. When in doubt, don't interfere. And Maria *has* interfered."

"Actually, we don't know that," Deanna pointed out. "Yes, she's vanished, and it looks like she *means* to interfere, but we've got no proof so far that she's going to go through with it. She might just have a change of mind and return to the observation post instead."

"Which would simplify our mission a great deal," Riker said with a sigh. "But I'm not counting on that possibility for the moment. We have to work on the assumption that she's not going to come to us, and we have to go to her. So, let's get back to the files and see if we can figure out the best places to look for her."

Tormak checked his chrono again and then glanced around the woods. To an untrained eye, it looked like almost any of the woods about the town. Trees, the odd pond or stream, and lots of plants whose names Tormak had never bothered to learn. His life was organized on a need-to-know basis, and he never concerned himself with anything irrelevant to his profession.

Half a unit to go.

His hooded eyes scanned the trees. He could see only two of his men, which was as it should be. Had he been able to see more, there would be severe reprimands when they returned to base. And people had been known to die from Tormak's reprimands.

He readied his handgun. This was one raid where he'd reluctantly left his rifle behind. It was going to be fought in close quarters. Tormak vastly preferred the almost anonymous style of a simple assassination. It left more time for a clean getaway, and was overall much less complicated. But for this mission he had no option.

A quarter unit left.

He pulled the small device he had been given from his field pouch and readied it. He had no real idea of what it was or how it operated. He didn't care. Need to know, again. As long as it did the job he'd been promised, that was all that concerned him. It was his key, and that was enough. He moved forward now, low and silently, to the target rock. It looked like any rock that lovers might sit on, or a *durka* might pause upon to eat nuts. If his information was correct, though, it was anything but a normal rock.

And he was certain that his information was correct.

Time . . .

He pressed the "key" to the rock and tapped in the numbers he'd been given. There was a brief pulse of light and then the side of the hill started to open up.

Anyone else might have been startled by this, but Tormak was well briefed. You didn't live long if you were constantly surprised like the startled guard behind the door. Her eyes widened as she realized that he wasn't one of the authorized personnel.

His bullet caught her between the eyes, slamming

her back inside the hidden room. Tormak followed the bullet as fast as he could, sweeping the rest of the small room. Aside from the dead guard, it was empty.

As Tormak headed toward the door to the rest of the underground complex the first two of his men followed him in, their own weapons at the ready.

"Our information was accurate," Tormak said briefly. "Proceed as planned."

They nodded, signaling back over their shoulders. Tormak took in the incredible technology about him with the barest of glances, and then concentrated on the mission at hand. The man—if that was the word!—he was after had offices deep in the hillside. At the moment he had the advantage of surprise, but it couldn't last. It was essential to make this extraction work as swiftly as possible. Stepping over the corpse of the first casualty, he keyed open the security door and dived out into the corridor.

There was a startled gasp, and he fired almost by instinct. Another body thumped to the floor, and he vaulted it without a second glance. The clock was running.

"I'm getting an emergency signal," Porter snapped suddenly from the pilot's chair. "It's from Iomides."

"On screen," Riker snapped, coming fully alert again from his study slouch. He fastened his padd down and hit the communications controls. He could feel everyone's eyes focusing in on the screen also.

Dr. Starn's face, impassive as ever, came into view. "Commander, the observation post is under attack by an armed force. We are in serious danger."

"Can you hold it off?" Riker demanded. He glanced

at Porter, who understood without words. "One hour," she mouthed.

"Given time, I am sure we can, Commander. However, this appears to be a very well-planned raid by the local people of this planet."

"Iomidians?" Riker was astonished. "There's no way they could have broken into an observation post, surely?"

"There are many questions for which I have no satisfactory explanation as yet," Starn answered. "That is one of them. How long will it be before you are able to render us assistance?"

"An hour," Riker said grimly. "But we'll get out and push if we can make it any sooner." He felt so powerless. "Can you hold out until then?"

"We will have no choice," Starn answered simply. Abruptly, there was a shaking of the image and then a muffled noise. Starn glanced over his shoulder. "They appear to have brought along explosive devices."

"Maybe you'd better head for cover," Riker suggested.

"There is nowhere else," Starn replied. "This is as secure as an observation post ever gets, Commander. I shall simply have to—"

The explosion that shattered his office door was perfectly audible over the link. Smoke and debris sliced across the picture, and interference cracked the image further. Still, Riker could plainly see Starn hurled backward by the blast. Then there was the sound of scuffling, and something moved across the camera lens.

"What's going on?" Riker demanded, frustrated and scared for Starn.

The figure whirled, leveled a weapon of some kind at the screen, and fired.

The screen went dead.

"Porter," Riker growled, "tell me you can get some more speed out of this thing."

"I'll do my best," she promised, equally grim. "We'll be there in forty-five minutes or less."

"It's not good enough."

"It's the best I can do, sir." Porter sounded offended as well as worried.

"I'm sure it is." Riker slammed his fist down on his knee. "Damn! There's nothing we can do. What the hell is going on down there?"

Tormak fired a fresh burst down the smoke-filled corridor as his two aides half-dragged, half-carried the unconscious alien behind him. This phase of the operation was over. They had located and captured— almost intact—their main objective, the alien creature that ran this hidden place.

Now it was time to retreat.

There was the sound of another explosion as team four sealed another corridor, preventing further reprisals from these aliens. Everything was proceeding precisely on schedule. Maximum results with minimum loss. He led the way back to the wrecked entrance. There was movement down a crosscorridor, and he whipped his handgun around. It was team two, so he held his fire. The three men moved to join him, their backpacks depleted, their weapons hot and smoking.

Tormak nodded acknowledgment and they headed back together. There was no opposition. The corridors should all have been sealed, locking the aliens away from the line of retreat. Dead bodies littered the floor, but they could all be ignored. Tormak sprinted on, knowing his force would keep up with him. He entered the security room where the first corpse now lay in a large pool of her own blood. Team three was waiting there. One man had a badly burned arm, but other than that there were no casualties.

"Team four?" he asked, softly.

"No sign."

"Then we go, now." Tormak waved his men forward as he removed the final explosives from his own pack. "Twenty seconds." He primed the detonator and tossed it into the equipment behind him. Then he sprinted outside into the crisp, clear air and joined his men as they made their way down the slope and away from the alien installation.

Fire howled through the gap behind them as his pack detonated. That would seal in the creatures and give the team plenty of time to get back untraced to their transport. Their captive, still only semiconscious, was dragged along.

The whole mission had lasted five units and was successful.

It was a bit of a shame that he'd been forced to leave team four behind. Still, they had their instructions. They had known what would happen if they didn't make it out in time. They were both dead by now—either by enemy fire or by their own hands. Tormak knew his men. Had they survived the raid and his explosion, they would have killed themselves to prevent interrogation.

The enemy had been identified, raided, and beaten,

and was left without a single clue as to who had done it.

A very successful mission.

Tormak allowed himself a slim smile of self-congratulation. His masters would be very pleased indeed.

Chapter Seven

PICARD LISTENED TO THE NEWS in stony silence. Only the hardness in his eyes betrayed emotion as Riker finished his hasty report. "That's appalling," he said softly. "Will, I'm afraid I can't bring the *Enterprise* to your assistance, much as I'd like to. I can send you further security forces in shuttles, though, if you require them."

"I'd rather wait and see if that's necessary, Captain," Riker replied. "We don't know how the raiders broke in yet, but they seem to have had a specific objective in mind. There are survivors, but they're trapped in sealed-off corridors. Once we arrive, I'll have a better idea of what's happened there, and I'll report in again."

Picard nodded. "I trust your judgment, Number

One. And I'm sure I don't need to tell you to be careful."

"Yes, sir." Riker nodded and then cut the line.

With a sigh of frustration and anger, Picard swiveled his seat around to stare at his fish tank. His lion fish was swimming unhurriedly about his aquarium, and the gentle, relaxed rippling of his fins served to calm Picard, as they always did. This attack on the observation post was a nasty fresh twist in the problems that Riker faced. But Picard had to put it from his own mind and concentrate on the mission at hand. Will would have to handle Iomides, and he'd call for backup if he required assistance. The deaths of the members of the Federation team angered Picard, but there was nothing at all that he could do about it right now. There were other people dying whom he had to help first.

The communicator sounded again, and Worf's voice reported: "Prince J'Kara is now available to speak with you, Captain."

"Ah. Excellent. Please put him through, Mr. Worf." Picard leaned forward in his seat, staring intently at the screen. The image of the heir apparent to Buran materialized. In general, his appearance was similar to Dr. L'Tele—a tall white-feathered being, with a prominent beak and intent eyes. His crest, however, was a deep purple and longer than the doctor's had been. A sign of his greater status, or simply the evolutionary luck of the draw? Picard filed it away for future comparison.

"Your Highness," Picard greeted him warmly. "Thank you for taking time from your busy schedule to speak with me."

"Captain," J'Kara acknowledged. "Please do not thank me; it is I who owe you thanks for coming so swiftly to our aid. My people are very grateful."

Really? thought Picard. *Some of your people are not as grateful as you.* Aloud he said as tactfully as possible, "I've been speaking with Dr. L'Tele, and he informs me that we are not to be allowed any medical data on your race that might enable us to work on a cure."

"Ah." There was a pause and then the prince nodded. "I understand your quandary, Captain. But you must realize that my people are very private. We do not like to share unnecessary information with outsiders. That is one reason why it took our planet so long to become united. We have a very strong flocking mentality, and it has taken us a great deal of time to overcome our fragmentation."

"I appreciate that your people have strict and perhaps understandable taboos against sharing information on your private lives," Picard replied. "But you must surely understand that we can do very little to help you if we are not granted even basic medical information on your people."

J'Kara nodded. "Of course, Captain." He considered the matter for a moment. "What, precisely, would be the minimum information that your medical officer would require?"

"As many medical logs as you could spare," Picard informed him.

"Captain." J'Kara looked pained. "There is no way that I would be able to get all of our medical files released to you. If such an action were taken, there would be a public outcry at my betrayal."

"Ah." This was evidently a very touchy subject. "Well, then, I believe that Dr. Crusher would need a comparison file of sick and healthy individuals. The minimum to be of help would be one male, female, and child each that are healthy and the same that are infected, so that comparisons could be made."

J'Kara considered the matter for a moment and then nodded. "I will see if I can . . . persuade five individuals to give their permission for such data to be released to you."

"Five?" prompted Picard.

"I shall, naturally, supply my own medical records for the healthy male data you require." J'Kara ruffled the feathers of his wings. "How could I ask my subjects to dishonor themselves if I were not prepared to set an example myself?"

"That's very commendable of you," Picard murmured.

"It is my duty," J'Kara stated simply. "We must both lead by example, must we not? We cannot give orders that we would not ourselves obey."

Picard felt himself warming toward the feathered alien. "Quite right," he agreed.

"And, Captain—a request." J'Kara winced slightly. "I would appreciate it if my medical records were scanned only by absolutely essential personnel. Preferably only by your chief medical officer. I am not above the . . . distaste my people feel for others knowing their intimate details."

"Of course," Picard promised. "I will ensure that as few people as possible see the data that you send me. Thank you for your help in clearing up this small matter."

J'Kara inclined his head. "And thank you, Captain, for everything you are doing for my people. I hope to be seeing you in person shortly, and I will ensure that the medical records are transmitted as soon as possible to you."

As the screen blanked, Picard sat back, feeling somewhat relieved. Thanks to J'Kara, they had cleared the first hurdle in Burani relations. The probability was, however, that this was simply the first of many such issues that could crop up. It was likely to be a very nerve-wracking mission. He could only hope that Riker's mission was a little less complicated. Though from what he'd heard so far, it didn't sound like it.

Porter brought the shuttle into standard orbit about Iomides. "Full screens," she reported. "The planetary defenses aren't tracking us at all, Commander."

"Good." Riker moved toward the transporter pad. "Maintain orbit and remain hidden. We'll contact you from the ground, and then at least every thirty minutes. If we fail to make any contacts, call in help from the *Enterprise* immediately. And under no circumstances are you to beam down to the planet at all. Understood?"

"Perfectly, Commander."

"Fine." Riker took his place beside Deanna and unholstered his phaser. He set it to stun and glanced around. Deanna had a tricorder at the ready, as well as her own phaser. Barclay had the same. Both Kessler and Vanderbeek held phaser rifles at the ready. "Energize."

There was a brief tingle and the air sparkled about

him as the beam took hold of him. A moment later, the away team was standing on a small hillside on the planet's surface, with a light breeze ruffling Riker's hair. He scanned the surroundings, his phaser at the ready. The only movement, however, was of a small bird hopping across a rock.

"Looks like they've gone, Commander," Kessler called.

"Affirmative," Deanna agreed, studying her tricorder. "No humanoid life out here at all. I'm picking up . . . twelve signs from within the post, though."

Riker nodded, and turned to study the gaping hole where the entrance to the post had once stood. "This can't last, though. Someone must have heard or seen the explosion that took this out. The local security force will probably be along shortly. Our first priority is to get the screens up again." He headed for the entrance. "Barclay, that's your task."

"Aye, sir." Barclay moved to pass Riker and then hesitated as they both came across the body of the guard. She'd been shot through the head, and blood stained the floor and equipment behind her. Barclay swallowed and looked pale.

Riker gestured to the security panel. "To your post," he said roughly. He felt as sick as Barclay, but there was no time for that. "See how much of that's still operational." Barclay nodded and shot across the room.

It was a mess inside. The explosives had torn out one wall panel and broken part of the main lock. Debris was scattered about the room. The doorway leading further into the post was halfway across the room, crushing a stand-alone unit of some kind.

The two security guards moved carefully through the room and into the corridor beyond. Riker knew they were scanning for any booby traps that the invaders might have left behind. He felt a touch on his arm, and glanced down into Deanna's disturbed, liquid eyes.

"The poor woman," she murmured.

"She's not the only one, I'm afraid," Riker replied. "If there are only twelve people left alive, then that means there must be thirteen more dead in here." He rubbed at his beard. "We'll have to get them all into stasis tubes until they can be taken out."

Deanna nodded. She followed Riker as he stepped into the corridor beyond. The two guards were out of sight, but their path was clear from their prints in the dust. The corridor was littered with further debris. Riker tapped his communicator pin.

"This is Commander Riker of the *Enterprise* to anyone who can hear me. Report in."

"Commander!" exclaimed a happy female voice in return. "This is Lieutenant Garth, sir. I'm in corridor C with six others. We've almost finished phasering our way out."

"Good. Two security officers should be with you in moments, then. Anyone else there?"

"Yes, Commander," came a dry male voice. "This is Dr. Saren. There are four others trapped with me in corridor B. We are without phasers and have been endeavoring to dig our way out, without much success."

"Understood. Are you short of air?"

"Negative, Commander. We will be fine until you can reach us."

"Okay. Sit tight and we'll be with you shortly."

Deanna caught his look. "I'll go and see what I can do," she replied, hefting her phaser.

"Good." Riker nodded as she moved off down the corridor. With rescue well in hand, he returned to the main entrance where Barclay had restored some power to the main systems. "How's it going, Reg?"

Barclay shrugged and then returned to his work under a panel. "There's a lot of burned-out systems," he reported, "and many of the remaining ones have considerable damage." There was the smell of smoke, and he yelped. "But I'm not gonna let that stop me. I'm draining power from anywhere I can, and should have the shields up and running again in a few minutes."

"That's good news," Riker answered. "Let's just hope that the locals give us that long before they arrive to investigate." As Barclay worked away, Riker crossed to the exposed entrance and scanned what he could see of the park. There was still nobody visible, thankfully, but this luck couldn't last. Unslinging his own tricorder, he scanned the area about the post. Three life-signs registered. They were about a kilometer off in the trees, and heading this way. "Company's coming," he called.

"And I haven't baked a cake," muttered Barclay. "But I have . . ." He leaped to his feet and started to tap commands into the battered panel. "I think . . ." When nothing happened, he thumped the casing of the console.

Immediately the sheen of the protective screens sprang into being. From the inside they appeared dull gray in color, but the exterior should look like normal grass and soil. They were hidden again from prying eyes, at least.

"Good work, Reg," Riker said warmly. "Perfect timing." He turned to the security panel next. "Now, we'd better see about changing the codes to this place. See if you can discover how the raiders got in while you do it."

"Yes, sir," Barclay replied, moving to work again with his tool kit.

Now that they were secure again, Riker moved back into the corridor. There was a noise from the left, and Kessler rounded the corner with two other people, obviously station personnel. "Lieutenant," Riker called. "You'd better start getting the dead together. Find a spare room somewhere where they can be stored and identified for transportation."

"Aye, sir." Kessler turned to one of the men with her and began conferring on a suitable site. Riker moved off down the corridor to the right, where he found Deanna phasering away at the fallen rubble that had blocked the way ahead. Using his own weapon, Riker helped her to finish cutting through, freeing the last of the observation post personnel. At their head was a Vulcan, but obviously not Starn.

"Dr. Saren?" Riker asked.

"Yes, Commander."

"Dr. Starn isn't with you?"

Saren managed to restrain himself from stating the obvious. "I believe he was in his office when the attack commenced," the Vulcan replied. "We should seek him there."

Riker nodded and allowed Saren to lead the way. As they approached the wrecked office, Saren paused and looked down at two corpses. "These are not our personnel."

Frowning, Riker bent to examine them. They were clearly Iomidians and dressed in what obviously passed for local combat fatigues. Both men carried handguns and had backpacks stuffed with equipment. Both of them were dead, each from a shot to the temple. "That's not phaser fire," Riker muttered. "These men shot themselves."

Saren raised an eyebrow. "Death before capture," he suggested.

"My guess, too," agreed Riker. "Well, we'll see what information they can give us after we've checked on Starn." Rising to his feet, he entered the office.

The room was wrecked and the communication screen had been put out of operation by a bullet. Riker scanned the room but it was obviously empty. "He's gone," he informed Saren. "Is there anywhere else he might be?"

"He might be anywhere," Saren answered. "But it is not likely. He was here when the raid began."

Riker nodded, recalling what he had seen before communications had been severed. "It looks as though he was the target of their raid," he replied tightly. "This was the only corridor not blocked by the attackers. They needed to get him out."

Saren concurred with a slight nod. "But how did they know where he was?" he pointed out. "And why would they do all of this to capture him?"

"I don't know," Riker replied. "Yet. But I will.

Whoever planned this went to a great deal of trouble to kidnap Dr. Starn. It at least suggests that they've kept him alive." His communicator beeped and Riker slapped it. "Riker."

"Commander," came back Barclay's voice. "I think you'd better get down here, sir. I've accessed the security logs and there's something you should see."

Riker sprinted back to the main entrance where he found Deanna already waiting with Barclay. They both glanced up from the electronic log as he arrived. "What is it?" he growled.

"I've pulled up the records of the security station right before the attack," Barclay replied, displaying the records. "The raiders got in using a Federation access code and an authentic password."

Scowling, Riker examined the record. "How could they do that?" he demanded. "Where would they get one from?" The answer came to him as Barclay spoke it.

"From Maria Wallace, Commander. It's her access code they used."

Riker's face went taut and he stared down at the incriminating information. "That would explain how they knew where to look for this place," he mused. "And the layout, so that they could go straight to Starn's office and kidnap him."

Deanna shook her head, trying not to believe what he was saying. "You think *she* was behind this?" she asked incredulously.

"It makes sense," Riker replied, bitterly. "She's not simply broken the Prime Directive—she's switched her allegiance to the Iomidians for some reason." He stared coldly at Deanna. "This changes our mission considerably. We may not be here now simply to recover Wallace. We may be forced to prevent her from aiding these newfound terrorist friends of hers any further. I just hope we can do it without more violence."

Chapter Eight

PICARD ROSE TO HIS FEET as the *Enterprise* took up standard orbit above Buran. It was an inviting-looking blue-green world on the main viewscreen, very reminiscent of so many worlds that Picard had visited. Naturally there was no sign of the plague from this safe distance.

"You have the bridge, Mr. Worf," Picard snapped. "Data, you're with me for the away team. Signal Dr. Crusher to meet us in transporter room two." Knowing that he didn't have to check to see that these orders were carried out, Picard spun on his heels and marched for the elevator shaft. Data moved to join him. "Did you have any luck tracing that Andorian trade ship?" Picard asked him as the elevator began moving.

"Some," Data replied. "I have narrowed the possibilities down to two craft. Minor assistance from the planet would resolve the question. The natives may also know where the trader was heading next, which should help us to locate the vessel."

"Good." He saw that Data looked thoughtful. "Is there something else, Mr. Data?"

"Possibly a foolish point that has occurred to me, Captain," the android confessed. "Lacking emotions, I am often very naive about human reactions. However, it seems to me that this mission might well produce a great deal of stress for the crew. It is likely that we shall all see much of illness and death."

"That's not a foolish notion at all," Picard informed him. "It had occurred to me, too. It's a shame that the ship's counselor isn't on the *Enterprise* right now, because I'm sure Deanna would be a great help in this matter. All we can hope is that Dr. Crusher's team can come up with a cure quickly, so that optimism might be the prevalent feeling."

The elevator doors hissed open, and they walked down the corridor to the transporter room. Dr. Crusher and Dr. Margolin were already there, loaded down with medical tricorders, sample boxes, and other equipment.

"It looks as if you're ready," Picard murmured. "How has the research been going, Doctor?"

Beverly sighed. "The information that J'Kara sent us has been very useful, Captain, but tracking down whatever is causing the disease is proving difficult. The Burani have a fascinating and delicate biology, and the plague seems to be playing havoc in many different places at once. I've been trying to isolate direct effects from secondary ones. And not being allowed to share the data with my colleagues isn't exactly helpful." She brushed the hair from her eyes and took her place on the transporter pad.

"I'm sorry about that restriction," Picard apologized, "but it was the only way I could obtain anything at all for you."

"I know that, Jean-Luc, and I'm grateful." Beverly grimaced. "It's just that it's so frustrating working under these constraints. The Burani seem to be going out of their way to make it harder for us to help them. I know it's not intentional, but it is a problem."

"I'm not so sure that it's all unintentional," Picard told her. "The anti-Federation sentiment seems to be growing on the planet. This visit of ours might provoke a prejudiced response." He nodded to the technician on duty. "Do you have the coordinates?"

"Yes, sir," he replied. "The Burani have supplied them, and they're locked in."

"Very well," Picard answered. "Energize!"

In a sparkling haze the transporter room vanished, and a large airy room formed about the small party. As soon as his vision cleared, Picard glanced about their destination.

It was certainly some kind of formal greeting room. The room was large and very tall. It had elongated windows, all with light, pastel drapes. At the far end of the room was a dais with three—well, *thrones* was the only word for them, Picard realized. These were artfully crafted, carved from some dark native wood, with elaborate pictorial designs that seemed to represent foliage on them. One of the three was a foot higher than the two that flanked it, and clearly belonged to the king, T'Fara.

There were perhaps thirty or forty Burani in the room with the away teams, all standing at a distance and watching the new arrivals warily. Picard discovered that his lines of thought seemed to be correct about the race. All of them were very similar, with basic white plumage. Only their crests of different styles, lengths, and colors seemed to mark them apart. Their clothing was flamboyant and bright, but also loose and nonconstricting. Their wings were perfectly free of adornment of any kind, of course.

The air, as Beverly had warned him, was a trifle thin. He felt as if he were standing on the slope of a small mountain. It was slightly uncomfortable. There was the strong scent of incense in the air.

"Captain Picard!" The greeting came from the Burani seated at the right hand of T'Fara. Picard recognized by the crest and seating that this was Prince J'Kara. "Please, come closer."

Inclining his head slightly, Picard led the team across the room to stand before the triple thrones. There was still no sound from anyone else in the room. Was this due to deference to the prince, or simply hostility? There was no way to determine this yet. At the foot of the steps leading up to the dais, Picard stopped. He bowed slightly in the direction of the king.

"Your Majesty," he greeted T'Fara. "It is a great pleasure for us to be here."

"I'm sure it is," T'Fara replied formally. He eyed Picard with some reserve. "Though many of my race would rather you were not here at all."

Picard studied the king thoughtfully for a moment. He was an older version of J'Kara, with a slight yellowing to his feathers. His crest was the largest, longest, and deepest purple of anyone in the room. He wore a loose robe that was patterned about the hem and sleeves with intricate golden stitchwork. He also wore a thin golden chain about his neck, with a medallion of some kind. Presumably this was the royal ensemble. "I am aware that some of your people blame the Federation for this terrible plague you are experiencing," Picard said carefully. "And I understand why they might think that. But we are here to offer you all the help that we can give. I am certain that nothing that the Federation has done could have caused this dreadful misfortune, but I promise you that we will help you to track down the cause of it."

"We already know the cause of it," said the third person on the dais. "It was those Andorian traders who brought it to our world."

Picard studied this individual. This had to be one of the Burani females. She was taller and more slender than the males. She also possessed a ruffle of feathers about her neck that was of a lilac tint, instead of the crests of the males. "I find that difficult to believe," Picard admitted. "But if it should prove to be true, then you have my word that the appropriate actions will be taken."

"Appropriate?" the woman sneered. "And who will decide what is *appropriate,* human?"

"That is something I am sure we can agree on when the time comes," Picard replied smoothly. *"If* it should turn out to be necessary. Meanwhile, my medical staff are eager to begin work to help you." He gestured to his side. "This is Dr. Beverly Crusher, who is in charge of this part of the mission."

"We are pleased to meet you," said J'Kara quickly, before the female Burani could speak again. "I, for one, am certain that your gracious help will be invaluable." He gestured to the female. "This is my bride-to-be, S'Hiri, daughter of D'Raka, one of our world's greatest merchants."

Ah . . . Picard began to understand. S'Hiri was the queen apparent, then. "This is Dr. Margolin, one of our experts in xenobiology," he said, completing the introductions, "and Lieutenant Commander Data, who is attempting to track down the Andorian trader. Any assistance your authorities might be able to give him could make that part of the task simpler."

The king leaned forward, studying Data with a frown. "You would appear to be quite ancient," he observed. "Does this mean that you are wise—or senile?"

Data inclined his head slightly. "I am not ancient," he replied. "You are mistaking the pigmentation of my skin for age. I have always been this color. I do, however, have a great deal of information on file that I can access."

"We shall see," T'Fara growled. "Very well, I suppose you had better begin. L'Tele!" he called.

The Burani doctor with whom Picard had spoken earlier emerged from the waiting crowd. "Your Majesty?" he responded, with an ornate and courtly bow.

"You'd better take these alien physicians and let them see some of your patients." His eyes narrowed. "Watch them *very* closely, of course."

"Naturally, sire," agreed L'Tele. He stared distastefully at Beverly. "Follow me. And touch nothing— especially me." He strutted off.

Beverly gave an almost imperceptible sigh and then a slight nod at Picard before following him. Picard suspected that this was going to be a very tough tour for her.

T'Fara leaned forward. "I am sorry if I sound . . . hostile, Captain," he said in a gentler tone. "But you must know that I did not favor our union with the Federation. My son"—he gestured toward J'Kara— "spoke strongly in favor, and he persuaded my people that his views were right. While I am not entirely certain that I yet agree with him, I am trying to be as open-minded as possible about all of this."

"It can't be very easy for you," Picard replied sympathetically.

"It is not," agreed the king. "But . . . I am doing my best. If I should falter from time to time, I would take it as a kindness if you would correct me."

"I will endeavor to do so," Picard agreed. *"Gently."*

That brought a smile to T'Fara's face. "Thank you, Captain. But, while I try to be . . . understanding, I will also have to be cautious. There are many who suspect the worst of the Federation, and it would not do to have them think I am unconcerned with their beliefs. I will offer you all the help that I can, but it may not be all that you would desire."

Rising from his throne, Prince J'Kara moved to join Picard and Data. "I shall look after you and your companion, Captain," he offered. "We can check the flight logs at the spaceport from my offices, and that may be of assistance. Also, I look forward to the opportunity to talk with you. You must have been to so many worlds and seen so much that is fascinating."

Picard smiled. "I think that's quite accurate," he

agreed. He turned back to T'Fara and gave a slight bow. "With your permission, Your Majesty?"

"Go, go," the monarch growled, waving a wing in dismissal. "But stay with my son. You do not have permission to walk freely on my world yet. It may be forthcoming, but I will have to speak with my ministers."

Nodding his understanding, Picard followed the prince from the reception room and into a wide corridor. Statues, sculptures, and other works of art lined the long walkway. J'Kara managed a slight smile—the edges of his beak were really quite mobile, Picard noted.

"My father is not quite as grim as he may sometimes sound, Captain," he said. "He worries greatly about his people, and this concern makes him sound harsh."

"I can't blame him for that, Your Excellency," Picard replied. "These are terrible times for anyone to live through. And he sounds as if he's genuinely trying to keep an open mind."

"We're not in the Royal Audience Chamber now," the Prince informed him. "So, please drop the formality and call me J'Kara, Captain."

"Then I am Jean-Luc," Picard responded.

"Agreed." The prince considered for a moment. "You have already experienced the reaction of Dr. L'Tele. My fiancée, S'Hiri, also does not place her trust in the Federation, as you no doubt noticed."

"She was rather vocal in her opposition," Data concurred. "She seems to have already passed judgment on the Andorians as being the guilty parties."

"Yes," J'Kara agreed. "I am not so sure myself.

They were the first off-worlders ever to visit us since the initial contact by the Federation. It doesn't seem logical to me that they would be so hostile as to attempt to murder us before they got to know us."

"An admirable point," Picard commented. "Also, their biology is very dissimilar to your own—at least, as far as I can tell. I haven't had the opportunity to study your race, of course, but Dr. Crusher assures me that the possibility of an accidental cross-infection is remote, to say the least."

J'Kara looked thoughtful. "So, then, am I to assume that there are only two plausible alternatives? Either that the Andorian presence here shortly before the plague started was a coincidence, or that they must have deliberately begun the plague for their own unknown reasons."

"There is a third alternative," Data offered. "That they are indeed innocent, but that their arrival may have been the opportunity seized by a third party to disguise the cause of this plague."

"A third party?" J'Kara looked puzzled. "But who would do such a thing?"

"Who indeed?" agreed Picard. "We shall have to investigate to determine any plausible guilt—*if* this plague was somehow started artificially. But we are close to Romulan territory, so I cannot yet rule out the possibility that they or their agents might have wanted to create a panic situation on Buran in order to get you to withdraw from the Federation."

J'Kara gave a hearty sigh. "As interesting as this conversation is, Jean-Luc, it isn't really getting us anywhere, is it? We can speculate forever. What we need are hard facts." He gestured toward a doorway.

"And here is where we can begin to search for them. My office."

It was a room almost the size of Ten-Forward, dominated by a massive desk. Like the thrones, this had been carved from some dark wood. The elaborate scrollwork was present here, too, making the desk both functional and artistic. There were cabinets of similar styling in the same wood scattered about the room. A huge window open to the world beyond allowed plenty of illumination into the room.

J'Kara gestured at the desk. "Data, that is a standard Federation padd built into the surface. I'm sure that you will be able to utilize it to discover whatever information you need to know."

"Thank you." Data went to work immediately.

"Meanwhile," J'Kara suggested, leading Picard to a side table, "perhaps you would like to try a little of our local refreshment, Jean-Luc?" He gestured to several small crystal decanters. "These are our best fruit wines, and I'm rather proud of some of them. I believe they will be safe for you to sample." He unstoppered one bottle. "This is a blend I make myself, in fact. I grow the vines for it in the palace gardens."

"Really?" Picard studied the pale turquoise drink with interest. "My family owns a vineyard back on Earth. My father always wanted me to follow in his footsteps."

"Then you should be able to appreciate this properly, Jean-Luc." J'Kara poured him a small glass, taking one for himself. "It should provide us with a diversion while I explain to you as fully as possible the situation in which you have arrived. Even without the plague, these are troubled times."

Picard sniffed gently at the wine's bouquet and raised an admiring eyebrow. Then he sipped gingerly at the liquid. It was full-bodied, with a pronounced and not unpleasant fruity taste unlike anything he had quite tasted before. There was a very warm afterglow in his mouth and throat as he swallowed. "Excellent," he pronounced. "A remarkable wine. Would it be presumptuous of me to ask if I might be able to talk you out of a bottle or two of it for my own cellar? I could repay the favor with several from the Picard line."

J'Kara smiled again. "Jean-Luc, I suspect we shall get along very well. Of course, you are welcome to several bottles. And I look forward to trying your family wines." He gestured at the table. "And there are plenty for you still to sample yet. And now," he pointed to two comfortable-looking seats away from the desk, "perhaps I should explain to you something of our recent history and misfortunes."

Chapter Nine

BEVERLY CRUSHER STARED about the hospital ward and felt as if her heart would break. The place was crammed with as many beds as it could hold, and then most of the space was filled with sleeping mats. There had to be almost two hundred Burani in here, crammed together tightly. Even through the isolation suit that Dr. L'Tele had insisted she wear, Beverly was certain she could smell the stench of death. There was a low background hum of pain and several individuals who were contributing far louder cries. There were four other Burani in isolation suits like the one L'Tele wore, and they were obviously trying to minister to the needs of the dying.

"This is appalling," Beverly whispered, shocked and despairing.

"It is the best we can do," L'Tele said rather sharply. "This crisis has overwhelmed our resources."

"No, that's not what I meant," Beverly replied. "I can see that you've tried, and I can empathize. What shocked me was the number and condition of these poor people. And you say that every hospital on the planet is like this?"

"Not every one," L'Tele corrected her. "But most, yes." He stared at her and seemed taken aback slightly by what he saw on her face. "You really do have concern for these patients," he said almost in wonder.

"Of course I do!" Beverly snapped back. "I'm a doctor—how could I not feel for the sick and suffering?" Her fingers were twitching and she was dying to begin diagnosis and treatment. But she had been very strictly warned not to do anything or touch any patient without absolute permission. "Isn't there anything that you will let me do to help them? *Anything?*"

L'Tele hesitated. Obviously his antagonistic attitude about the Federation was taking a beating when he could see so plainly how she felt about this place. "Perhaps we could talk to one of the more coherent patients," he suggested finally, "and ask permission to examine him or her." He examined a small computer he held in his hand, and then led the way slowly down the ward.

Beverly almost wished she could blot out what she was seeing. Most patients showed clear symptoms of disease. Many were molting, and there were dry, discolored feathers all over the room despite obvious efforts to clean them out. The sick had body sores and lesions. Most had medication or bandages on them, but each patient had dozens of sores, clearly more than the overwhelmed staff could treat. Sanitary conditions were virtually impossible. It tore at her to see patients in this state, but she knew that the Burani were doing the best they could.

"I . . . understand that the disease is almost invariably fatal," Beverly said softly, trying not to disturb the patients.

"You understand incorrectly, then," L'Tele said sharply. "It is inevitably fatal. Once contracted, no one has ever survived it."

"That's incredibly virulent," Beverly answered. "And almost unprecedented, in my experience. There are always a few people who survive even the deadliest of diseases."

"Not this one," L'Tele replied brusquely. "Ah, here we are." He stopped by one of the mats on the floor. It couldn't have been easy to tell which patient was which, but he had obviously managed. "M'Riri," he said, bending low over the diseased female. "How do you feel today?"

The female Burani coughed and managed a very weak smile. "Better, I think, Doctor," she answered. She stared at Beverly with interest. "Is this one of the Federation people who've promised us aid?"

"Yes, I am," Beverly answered. "I want so desperately to help you all, M'Riri."

"We could certainly do with all the help we can get," M'Riri answered. She broke off as she coughed again.

"Well, I need some help in return," Beverly said cautiously. "I can't do very much until I know how the disease works. Your people are hesitant to allow strangers to examine them, I know, but I would greatly appreciate the chance to do so."

M'Riri shuddered slightly and managed to ease herself up on one wing. There were fresh sores on her that were leaking a clear liquid, and others raw with blood. "Will this help others?" she asked, clearly disturbed.

"Yes," Beverly promised. "And it may even be able to help you."

The woman tried to laugh but it became a cough. "I am already dead," she said simply. "But if I can help others to live, then I can endure the indignity of being examined." She lay back on the mat again. "You have my permission, Doctor."

Beverly felt like giving a cry of triumph but she restrained her emotions to merely smiling. She had her tricorder out and scanning in a second, taking in every last item of data that she could manage. With luck, this information from a patient with an advanced stage of the disease would provide her with a clue as to what the damned thing was doing to the Burani.

"Thank you, M'Riri," she said finally. "You really have been a tremendous help to me. Would you mind if I came back later, just to see how you are?"

"Of course not," the Burani answered. "I hope you'll keep me informed of your progress, too. I was one of the contacts for the Federation and I want to see this work out for all our peoples. This mistrust has to end."

L'Tele touched Beverly's shoulder. "We should try

another patient," he suggested. "The more samples you can obtain, the easier it should be for you."

"Yes," Beverly agreed. She gave M'Riri another smile and then stood up. "You picked her deliberately, didn't you?" she asked as they moved off down the ward. "You knew she was the most likely to grant me permission to examine her."

"Yes," agreed the doctor.

"That's something of a turnaround from your earlier attitude," Beverly said frankly. "I was expecting you to obstruct me, to be honest."

L'Tele halted and turned to face her. "I had intended that, if we are being truthful," he admitted. "I am still not entirely certain that I trust you people. But I am first and foremost a doctor. These people"— he waved his wing about the room—"are my patients. Even if there is only a slight chance that you are telling the truth and are concerned and wish to help, I have to take that chance for them. Besides," he added, starting to walk again, "I saw your face when you witnessed this room. Your compassion was evident. I cannot deny that you genuinely wish to be of help."

"I'm glad that you understand that," Beverly said.

L'Tele snorted. "That doesn't mean that I think you'll be effective, mind you," he snapped. "But, as I said, I have to take every chance I'm offered in seeking a cure."

"I'm sure that together we can deal with this thing."

"Maybe." L'Tele gestured. "There's someone over here who might be able to help you next," he said. "Come along."

* * *

Pointing to a computer-generated map of the planet, J'Kara said proudly, "My father's father united our people for the very first time, Jean-Luc. Before that, my world was fragmented into many nests. He convinced them by persuasion and example that more could be accomplished by our coming together than by our staying in small fragmented communities."

Picard examined the map, which showed the single main continent of Buran and the archipelagoes of island strings that bordered the continent. "He sounds like a remarkable man."

"He was," J'Kara answered. "I only knew him for a few years, but he was so . . . *focused.* He wanted the best for our world and he knew that this was unity. He fought against the stubborn desires of our peoples to stay isolated and independent. He made them change what until then had been almost instinctual, and made them work together." He gestured at the large picture window. "Almost everything that you see out there has come about within two generations, Jean-Luc, thanks to his vision and drive."

"Astonishing," Picard murmured, honestly impressed. To come from a virtually tribal society to the stars in such a short time was indeed an achievement.

"Yes." J'Kara smiled again. "And it is my grandfather's example that inspires me. My father felt that we were moving too swiftly when I wanted to join the Federation. He pleaded for time to consolidate our people and to wean them away from old habits into new thought processes. I know that he means well, of course, but I disagreed. As we had unified our planet and grown stronger and wiser, I knew that by joining the Federation we would be able to do the same—only with far greater effects. This is why I argued so passionately for membership, even against my father's wishes."

"Your grandfather is clearly not the only one with vision and drive in the family," Picard observed.

"I wish to be as great in the service of my people as he was," J'Kara said simply. "It is my birthright and duty to do my best to improve their lot. We must continue to strive for the best. I know that with your help we shall achieve greatness, and I am grateful for it."

"The first thing we have to achieve is a cure for this plague of yours," Picard said practically. "Has there ever been anything like this before in your history?"

"No," the prince answered. "Of course, since my race was so fragmented, plagues never had much of a chance of establishing a foothold, did they?" He frowned. "Perhaps this is a downside to progress after all. We are now so close to one another that disease spreads more easily."

"And cures can be discovered more easily, through united efforts," Picard argued. "But that theory is worth exploring." He thought for a moment. "Were you at that reception for the Andorians when they arrived?"

"Of course," J'Kara said. "As the prime mover for unity with the Federation, I knew it was my place. I attended with S'Hiri and several others. It was quite a reception. I found the Andorians to be a fascinating people, and it looked as though we should have had a great deal to trade."

"Interesting," Picard mused. "Yet neither you nor

your fiancée have contracted this disease, though you must have had the most intimate contact with the Andorians."

"That is true," J'Kara agreed, surprised. "Then it means that the Andorians are innocent of any complicity in this plague."

"We can't go quite that far yet," Picard said. "But it does look better for them. What we need to know, then, is whether those who *did* come down with the plague after the reception had anything else in common. Anything that you and S'Hiri don't, for example." He rubbed his chin thoughtfully. "Do you think you could generate two lists for Data? One of those who were at the reception and later contracted the disease, and one of those who didn't?"

"Of course," J'Kara replied. "And then we can cross-reference any connections between members of either group. It may give us a clue as to where the disease may actually have originated."

"That's the idea," Picard agreed as J'Kara moved to another computer panel to begin work. It looked as if they might be able to get somewhere with this line of reasoning. His love of detective novels often paid off in the real world.

"Captain," came a voice from the doorway. Picard spun around and saw T'Fara standing there, an unreadable expression on his face. "May I speak with you for a moment?"

"Of course, Your Majesty." Picard hurried over to the doorway. "Is there something I can do for you?"

"If many of my people had their way," T'Fara said, "they would have you off my planet and heading back to your own world as soon as possible. I do not believe that we need be so extreme, and I am willing to be open-minded for the sake of my people. But J'Kara . . ." He sighed. "J'Kara is a good son, but he is moving too fast for the good of our people."

"I understand your concerns," Picard said politely, "but I naturally feel that your son is right."

"I understand that. But you must understand that other forces drive me." The king gestured behind him. "My people are out there right now, dying by the thousands, and it may possibly be because of you."

"I assure you—" Picard began, but the king cut him off with a growl.

"I *know* what you assure me," he snapped. "And you may even, gods know, be telling the truth. You may have nothing to do with this plague at all. But it is still a punishment on my people for their obstinacy and foolish optimism. If they had not rejected my opinions and demanded this unity with you, the plague would never have happened. Now they are being punished for their foolishness."

"You can't possibly know that," Picard answered. "This plague may well have happened even if you had not joined the Federation."

"Perhaps it might," T'Fara said with a shrug. "Who can say?" He shook his head. "Of course, it is always possible to see afterward what one should have done. Whether it was a correct decision or not, we *did* join the Federation, and it is important to work from here. Captain, I would urge you to act quickly and discover who or what is behind this plague. My ministers are not all as liberally minded as my son, nor as patient as myself. There is talk of throwing you all off this planet. A speedy solution to this issue would help matters considerably."

"We're doing our best, Your Majesty," Picard assured him.

"I'm sure you are," T'Fara agreed. "But—alacrity, eh?" He spun about on his heels and left the room.

J'Kara shook his head. "Hasty decisions and discoveries are often the wrong ones," he said with a sigh. "I fear my father is too eager for answers to be bothered about where they are found. He seems to think he can order the universe to obey his every whim."

Picard managed a reassuring smile. "When he was a child," he pointed out, "his father was the sole ruler of this planet. Your efforts toward democracy have loosened the reigns a little. I suspect your father is thinking about the good old days."

"Probably," agreed J'Kara. "I know he wanted me to inherit a world that I would rule from strength, as he did." He smiled. "He does not understand that my world will be far freer and stronger than his was. The more people are involved with their own government, the better it is for all."

"Remarkable," Picard observed. "Especially considering what you stand to lose."

"I stand to lose nothing that is worth keeping," J'Kara said. "And I shall keep the honor and strength of my people, which nothing can take away. I am content."

"Captain," Data called from the desk. "I am sorry to interrupt you, but I am sure you will want to see what I have discovered."

Picard and J'Kara moved to look over the android's shoulders. "What is it, Mr. Data?"

"I have traced the Andorian trader who called here, Captain." He pulled up one of the computer log entries. "It is the *Tivela*. She stayed here for four days and then left three weeks ago. Her captain listed Artax Four as their next destination, which is only two days away at standard warp. I have checked with the authorities on Artax, and they confirm that the *Tivela* never arrived there."

J'Kara looked puzzled. "What does this mean, Captain?"

"Two possibilities," Picard decided. "First, that the captain of the *Tivela* deliberately filed an incorrect flight plan, and that his destination was not Artax Four. If that was the case, it would suggest strongly that your plague was indeed spread by the Andorians, who did not wish to be found afterward.

"The second possibility is that something may have affected the crew of the *Tivela*, and they were not capable of reaching their destination. Perhaps something at this meeting with your representatives."

J'Kara inclined his head. "That makes sense. So, now what is to be done?"

Picard tapped his communicator. "Picard to Worf."

"Here, Captain."

"Mr. Worf, prepare a shuttlecraft for launch as soon as possible. I want you and an away team to immediately begin tracing the route of the Andorian freighter *Tivela*. Mr. Data will supply you with the course. You are to track the ship and contact the captain." He paused. "Be aware that there is a possibility that the ship may either be in difficulty—or potentially hostile. Understood?"

"Aye, sir." There was no mistaking the satisfaction in Worf's voice. The prospect of battle always brought him to life. "I will begin preparations immediately. Worf out."

Picard sighed and stared at the prince. "I'm sure that Mr. Worf and his team will find the *Tivela,*" he said. "But I can only wonder what they will find when they make contact."

Chapter Ten

ADMIRAL HALSEY PURSED HER LIPS and scowled out of the screen at Riker. "Please pass my condolences along to the surviving staff," she said sincerely. "I'll ensure that the relatives of the deceased are notified. I'm reassigning the *Powhaten* to collect their remains for return or burial in space. Are all the staff now accounted for?"

"All but Dr. Starn," Riker responded. "This raid seems to have been staged for the sole purpose of capturing him."

"I can't imagine why," the admiral said.

"Maria Wallace had an argument with him the day that she disappeared," Riker commented. "Perhaps she still bears him a grudge for his refusal to help Farra Chal?"

"It would have to be a very strong grudge," Halsey

said, shaking her head. "No, I'm sure there's some other reason. But that's not the main issue here. It's quite clear that whoever these raiders were, they had help from Maria Wallace. Either wittingly or unwittingly, it doesn't really make much difference."

Riker nodded. "She's obviously already made contact with someone on this planet and revealed her origin to that person. Since she was concerned about Farra Chal, the logical assumption is that he's behind this."

"Perhaps." Halsey scowled. "From his dossier, though, I'd have hardly expected something this . . . crude from him. He appears to be a very moral person."

"He wouldn't be the first politician to lead a double life," Riker pointed out.

"True," agreed the admiral. She leaned forward in her seat. "As of now, your orders are modified as follows: Your primary goal is still to retrieve Maria Wallace. If that is not possible for any reason, then she must be killed to prevent further contamination. Is that understood, Commander?"

Riker nodded tightly. "Yes, admiral," he agreed. "Otherwise this situation could get further out of hand." He stared at her. "But I have to tell you that I don't like it."

"I don't like it, either, Commander," Halsey snapped back. "But we can't let one foolish, misguided person wreck this planetary culture by premature contact and contamination."

"I understand that, Admiral."

"Good." She sighed. "I'm sorry to place such a burden on your shoulders, and *anything* that you can do to avoid harming Wallace has my full approval—short of leaving her to continue this insanity. Now, your second goal must be to locate and retrieve Dr. Starn. This is just as vital."

"You don't think that he'll cooperate with his kidnappers, surely?" Riker asked, amazed.

"I doubt it." Halsey sighed again. "But we don't know that Wallace voluntarily cooperated with these thugs, either. She may have been coerced into helping them. And while Vulcans can withstand a lot of . . . persuasion, I don't want to risk finding out just how stubborn Dr. Starn can be. And that's aside from the fact that the faster you find him, the less time there's likely to be for him to be harmed."

"Understood."

"Good." Halsey nodded. "I'm sure you'll be able to handle this, Commander. The *Powhaten* will be with you in five days. Dr. Saren is to assume command of the observation post immediately and continue with as much work as he can. I'll see about getting him replacements as soon as possible. The post is now fully secured again, I take it?"

"Yes, sir," Riker replied. "Lieutenant Barclay has the screens up, and all access codes and links have been recoded. Only he, Dr. Saren, and I possess these new codes. All personnel have been forbidden to leave the post until further notice. Only my away team will be going out, and we'll be very careful to ensure we're not spotted by any Iomidians." He paused. "You're going to be leaving the observation post open, then, even after what has happened?"

Halsey considered for a moment before replying. "Iomides is in a very delicate stage at present, Commander. They are very close to discovering warp technology. They are also extremely prone to violence. This sector is vital to the security of our perimeter with the Romulan Empire. I'd hate to see them expanding into space without a Federation affiliation. We *must* monitor their progress. If the post is secure, then I'm willing to leave it for the moment. As soon as it is up to staff again, they will have to transfer to a new location and destroy the current post." She sighed. "It'll take time. I'm hoping that you'll shortly report that we will have that time, Commander."

"Understood, Admiral."

"Excellent, Commander. Halsey out."

Riker sighed, ran his hand through his hair and spun around from the communications panel. Dr. Saren, Deanna, Barclay, and Kessler were in the command center with him. "I assume you all heard that?" There were four nods in reply. "Good. Dr. Saren, I'll leave the post in your capable hands, then. As soon as we're ready, my team will be leaving. Have your security officer check the area constantly for any sign of native intrusion or monitoring. We don't want to be caught when we leave here."

"Of course, Commander." The Vulcan bowed slightly and left the room.

Riker glanced from Deanna to Barclay. "Okay, any thoughts from you two?"

"I was just wondering," Barclay offered, "if maybe Starn did go willingly?"

"What do you mean, Reg?" asked Deanna, puzzled.

"Maybe this whole business about him disagreeing with Wallace was a setup," Barclay offered. "They could have worked out this whole scenario as a plan for him to go over to the rebel side and make it look like he's an innocent captive."

"That's a little far-fetched," Deanna objected. "I don't think a man of Dr. Starn's reputation and skills would do that."

"You've been playing too many spy holos," Riker added with a slight smile. "No Vulcan would agree to any kind of plan that involved injury or murder as a part of it. No, I'm sure he really is an innocent captive, and that this whole raid was staged just to get him out of here. But why, and by whom?"

Barclay shrugged, but he had a gleam in his eyes. "I can't answer the first, but I've got a couple of suggestions as to the second. And, if you'll pardon me, sir, you're wrong: The raid wasn't solely staged to grab Starn."

"Oh?" Riker raised a surprised eyebrow. "What else were they after, then?"

"Wallace's computer files," Barclay responded. "One of the packages of explosives took out a good deal of the computer memory. Since Wallace had left all her reports here when she went AWOL, whatever had caused her to think that Farra Chal was going to be assassinated must have still been on records. I tried accessing them, but this was the portion of the computer records that was destroyed. Several other nearby records were destroyed as well, but it's obvious to me that her research was what they were after."

"Damn." Riker scowled. "So we've lost the whole thing?"

Unable to restrain a smug grin, Barclay shook his

head. "No, I've recovered about eighty percent of it intact."

"How did you ever manage that, Reg?" asked Deanna, impressed.

"Well, I realized Dr. Starn had to have accessed her records when she requested that interview with him. He's very methodical, so I figured he might well have kept his own copy of her research to go over. And with her disappearance, he might not have gotten around to wiping those files. The explosion that took his desk apart ruined some of the records, but I was able to reconstruct a lot of them with a little guesswork." He looked like a dog waiting to be complimented for doing a particularly difficult trick.

"Nicely done, Reg," Riker said approvingly. "So, have you had a chance to scan the records yet and see what she was doing?"

"Some of them," Barclay answered. "Maybe enough, though I'd like a little longer just to check what I've deduced. Anyway, Wallace was assigned to do some economics scanning. The Iomidians have an interesting computer system. It's nowhere near as sophisticated as ours, of course, but it's pretty decent. Anyway, Wallace had tapped into their financial records and was studying several of the planet's tycoons, to see how the wealth was distributed and being used.

"One of them was of great interest to her—a financier and factory owner named Tok Grell. He seemed to have come out of almost nowhere about fifteen years ago and has his fingers in a lot of pies. Most of them are innocent enough, though Wallace's records seem to suggest that he was less than ethical about what he's been doing to make his fortune. One of his holdings—and one of his major sources of income—is a gigantic munitions plant. He manufactures everything from handguns to atomic warheads. He's also big into playing politics and supports the opposition party to First Citizen Chal.

"And he's the ringleader of this assassination plot against Chal."

Riker nodded. "That makes sense, I guess. He's tried financing opposition players, none of whom work out, to try and get rid of Chal. Now that that's failed, he's getting a little more direct."

"And he's against Chal's politics of peace," Deanna summed up, "because it would cut into his profits. No wars, no new weapons needed. No new weapons, no profits for Grell. It's nasty and quite logical."

"Right," Barclay agreed. "Anyway, he's trying to set up the assassination in such a way that attention won't be drawn to him. After all, it wouldn't be exactly hard for the police to figure out he'd have a stake in the killing."

Riker rubbed at his beard thoughtfully. "If he's as smart as this sounds, he's going to come up with a plan, I'm sure. Still, all of this is irrelevant to our mission, isn't it? We have to leave this business to the Iomidians to settle, one way or another."

Kessler moved slightly and spoke up for the first time. "With respect, sir, I don't think it is quite that far offtrack."

"Oh?" Riker prompted her. "What do you mean?"

"Vanderbeek and I examined those two dead raiders, Commander, as we'd been instructed." She grimaced. "They had plenty of weaponry on them, all of it apparently untraceable—at least, by Iomidian technology."

Riker smiled. "But not by ours, I gather?"

"No, sir." Kessler smiled back. "I did a metallurgic analysis of the guns and a chemical determination on the explosives that were on them. I even did a thread count on their clothing. I'd say that there's absolutely no doubt at all that the weaponry came from one of Grell's factories. The metallic contents were identical, for one thing. And the clothing was manufactured by a firm he owns in the local capital."

"So you're saying that these raiders were Grell's men?"

"It's logical," argued Kessler. "Of course, they *might* be someone else's, and whoever that someone is may have used Grell's stuff to frame him. We can't rule out that possibility."

"Maybe," mused Riker. "On the other hand, that's getting a little subtle. They covered their tracks as well as they knew how, obviously. And they're not really used to thinking that there may be someone on this planet with superior technology. I'd say your first guess is probably right, and that Grell was behind this raid for some reason."

"I can think of an obvious one," Barclay offered. "He's likely to lose his profits without manufacturing all those weapons. If Chal unifies the planet, there'll be no on-world enemies left. . . ."

"So Tok wants to finger an *off*-world one!" Deanna exclaimed. "If he can prove that there are aliens, hidden, watching his race, he could use that to create xenophobia and another round of weapons-building."

"Which might explain why he'd snatch Dr. Starn,"

Riker added. "He's very clearly alien, by any standards."

"Everyone here would be," objected Deanna.

"But not as much as Starn," Riker pointed out. "Humans are a little too similar to the Iomidians, remember? But Starn is physically very different. Green blood, for one thing."

"Maybe," agreed Deanna. "But we're getting a little carried away on a theory here, after all. All right, it looks like Grell *may* be the mastermind behind this attack on the observation post. But, even if he is, *how* did he find out about the place? Wallace wanted to prevent the assassination of Farra Chal. She'd hardly have gone running to the man who was behind the killing, would she? Surely she'd have gone to Chal?"

Riker nodded, thinking hard. "That's probably true," he agreed.

Barclay shook his head. "She's an idealist," he objected. "Maybe she thought she could go to Grell with proof of his intentions and blackmail him into stopping?"

"That sounds a little bit too naive for the Maria Wallace I knew," Riker objected. "Trying to blackmail a would-be killer isn't the safest game on any world."

"It would explain how Grell found out about this place, though," Barclay countered. "And why he was taking such trouble to eliminate her research."

"Maybe," Riker agreed. He winced. "Well, it looks to me like there are two possible alternatives here. Either Grell is behind this attack on the observation post, or he's being framed for it. If we assume the former, then that logically means that he's holding

Dr. Starn and most likely Maria Wallace—but where, and why? If we assume the latter, then we have an unknown party who's doing the whole thing and wants us to waste our time chasing after Grell, while he or she conducts their own plans."

"It's more likely to be a *he*," Deanna pointed out. "There aren't a lot of women in many positions of power on this planet, and this whole affair smacks of power to me."

"And the logical candidate for this unknown mastermind is, sadly, First Citizen Chal himself. If Wallace went to him with her warning, he'd obviously be interested in knowing where she got this information from. If she talked—willingly or otherwise—she'd have revealed her secret about this post."

Deanne nodded, eagerly. "And then, perhaps Chal could have seen the chance of killing two birds with one stone: getting proof of alien interference on his world, and setting us against his enemy Grell at the same time."

"Maybe," agreed Riker. "It holds together as a conspiracy theory. The problem is, why would Chal want Starn? Of what benefit is it to him?"

"Maybe he's after Federation technology?" suggested Barclay. "He may be trying to force it out of Dr. Starn. Or maybe he's a hostage, and we'll be contacted for terms of release?"

Riker shook his head and sighed. "It's all speculation," he decided. "There are too many *maybes* in this whole thing for my liking. What we're going to have to do is to split up and try approaching this from several different fronts. The logical place to begin from would be Wallace's apartment in the city. Maybe she left some clues there as to where she was heading next—communications records, or something. She can't simply have walked into Chal's office—or Grell's, either—and simply demanded to speak to the boss. If we can trace—"

He broke off as Dr. Saren returned to the room. For a Vulcan he looked almost agitated. "Yes, Doctor? Is there a problem?"

"I am not absolutely certain if it is relevant," the Vulcan replied. "However, we have begun monitoring the airwaves of this planet again for their news programs. And one of these has just made a startling announcement. A politician named Brak Norin has attempted to impeach the First Citizen, Farra Chal."

Barclay's eyes went wide. "Norin's the politician that Grell has in his pocket," he explained.

Riker whistled. "Then it looks as if Grell's making some kind of power play. I think this is one news report we'd all better sit through. . . ."

Chapter Eleven

PICARD STOOD looking out over the city at night from J'Kara's picture window. There were few lights, and fewer travelers now. Occasionally he'd see one of the local people soaring across a patch of sky, but far less than by day. Now and then a lumbering ground vehicle rumbled through the streets. There wasn't much road traffic even by day, since the Burani had their own built-in transport systems.

On a hill overlooking the town, Picard could make out a dark shape of some building. This was the only one lit up. A small column of fire was visible from behind the building.

J'Kara, at his side, sighed and said, "That is where the bodies are being burned, Jean-Luc. It used to be used only once a week. Now it operates continually."

Hearing the pain in the prince's voice, Picard said, softly, "It must be terribly hard for you."

"Not as hard as it is for my people," J'Kara answered, anger tingeing his voice. "My father occupies his time with cursing the Federation and vowing revenge for what has been done to our people. In one way I envy him his belief. At least he has a foe he can rail against. I have nothing to pin my own pain upon. I must simply endure, and pray, and hope."

"We will beat this thing," Picard promised. "I know Beverly and her team. They won't rest until they've come up with the answer to this plague." That was all too likely to be literally true, Picard knew. He had considered checking up on Beverly to make sure she was getting sufficient rest, but he knew it was a pointless exercise. If he ordered her to bed before she decided to go, she'd never sleep anyway and would simply be frustrated at the time she was wasting.

"That is good to know," J'Kara replied. "But every minute of every day before we find a cure, there are deaths. Every second that passes reminds me constantly that people are dying." He slammed his fist against the wall and then winced with pain. "I can't stand doing *nothing.*"

"We're not doing nothing," Picard answered gently. "We're working very hard on this."

"No," J'Kara contradicted him. *"You're* working hard on this. Your Dr. Crusher is. Your security team is. L'Tele and his physicians are. *I'm* just standing here feeling guilty and helpless. That's all I'm doing."

"You're doing more than you may realize," Picard reassured him. "You are giving hope and confidence to your people. There's very little panic, you know, all things considered. I recall a plague situation once on Rigel Seven. When we arrived with vaccines there was wholesale looting, murders, and anarchy. Your people are taking this very well. I think a part of the credit for that is that they see you bearing it well and doing everything in your power to help them."

J'Kara managed a wan smile. "My people are generally well behaved, Jean-Luc," he replied. "Well, most of them, at any rate," he added. "We're a private people, as I've said before. We try to keep our emotions and our fears to ourselves and not share them." His smile grew almost wistful. "I must be atypical, then, because I'm sharing my emotions and fears with you."

"Sharing emotions is a good way to work them out," Picard answered. "Sharing pain helps to lessen your own burden. Shared joy increases pleasure."

"Then let us hope that we soon have something to rejoice over, my friend," the Prince replied.

Picard's communicator sounded. "Crusher to Picard."

Not wanting to let his hope get the better of him, and yet feeling a surge of anticipation, Picard tapped his badge. "Picard here, Doctor. Do you have good news for us?"

"I'm afraid not, Captain." Picard's heart sank again as Beverly continued. "I'm going to take a break now before you order me to, but I thought you and Prince J'Kara might like to hear a little bit about what progress we've made so far."

"Progress is a good word," J'Kara interrupted. "I would dearly love to hear some news of it."

"Dr. Margolin and I have managed to isolate a sample of what we believe is the active agent in this plague," Beverly informed them. "It's a very virulent microorganism, something I've never seen before. Since Dr. L'Tele has given us so few records, we can't really compare it to any other virus or bacteria from Buran. I've sent him information on what we've discovered, though, so he can try and do a medical search. This is clearly some sort of a new strain of an old disease, so if we can find its ancestor and see what helped to cure that, then we may have a weapon against this new breed."

"That sounds hopeful," Picard ventured.

"Be hopeful," Beverly replied. "It's not much, but it's a start." She paused, and then there was a note of frustration in her voice. "Captain, I have to tell you this disease bothers me."

"It worries us all," J'Kara commented.

"No, not in that sense," Beverly answered. "There's a lot about it that doesn't seem right to me."

Picard scowled. "What do you mean?"

"Well, it's just too darned efficient at killing people, for one thing," she answered. "As far as I can see, the organism attacks the membranes of the Burani lungs, so that oxygen can't be transferred to their blood. The patients essentially drown in their own saliva. But if they don't, for some reason, die of that, then the organism attacks the nerve sheaths. That causes a disruption in nervous activity, and eventually a stroke."

Picard's scowl intensified. "But that doesn't explain those horrendous lesions on all of the patients," he objected.

"No, it doesn't," she agreed. "They appear to be where the organism breeds. It feeds on the lymphatic tissues, breaking them down for food. That causes the pustules, and when they burst it spreads the disease."

"Then treating the pustules should help prevent the spread of the plague," Picard said, puzzled. "And it looks to me that this is what the doctors have been doing."

"Of course they have," Beverly snapped rather sharply. "But the plague is still spreading anyway." Then she caught herself. "I'm sorry, Captain," she apologized, pushing the hair back out of her eyes. "I guess I'm getting more than a little tired."

Picard nodded. "I understand. You're also very concerned."

J'Kara inclined his head and twitched his beak. "Then what is it about all of this that distresses you so?" he asked.

"It's *too* lethal," she replied promptly. "Look, infection and disease are generally caused by organisms invading another living being and then using that being as food for their own reproductive needs. The disease breeds within the patient. This makes the patient ill for one of several reasons. Simplifying a bit, it's either due to poisons created by the invader, countermeasures the body itself takes to get rid of the invader, or disruptions of the body's functions because of the depletion of the body's resources. Now, the best organisms are the ones that cause the minimum amount of damage to the host. That way, they can continue to breed almost indefinitely while taking what they need. Many times with those kinds of infections, the victims often don't know they even have the disease.

"The worst case is when the invader kills the host. It's not merely bad for the host, it's also bad for the infiltrator. Killing off your food source isn't an efficient way to live. Eventually you'd starve to death. So it's not really in the interest of the organism to kill the host. If it happens, it's generally accidental. Plagues occur because a virulent strain of some disease comes into contact with a population of hosts that's never faced it before. The new hosts' bodies can't respond in time, and they die before their body can beat off the invader."

"So much I can see," J'Kara replied. "That is what has happened here with this plague."

"Not exactly," Beverly objected. "For one thing, I can't discover a similar situation in recent history on your world. Where, then, did this disease originate? If it's a new strain of an old disease, *what* old disease? And how did it get started? And finally, I've been reliably informed that there are no survivors of this plague. If you're infected, you die. That's not logical, either. There are always *some* individuals who are immune or recover from any plague. Even the notorious Black Death on Earth in the Middle Ages killed only a third of the population. Two-thirds survived it. Here, *nobody* survives."

"What are you getting at, Doctor?" Picard asked.

"This organism isn't acting like a proper disease, Jean-Luc," she replied. "It's definitely a biological agent, and a living one. Otherwise, I'd say it's acting more like a poison than a disease. Poisons are inevitably lethal."

"A poison?" asked J'Kara, stunned. "Do you understand what you are saying?"

"I understand it only too well," Beverly answered grimly. "If there's a poison, then there has to be a poisoner." She sighed. "I could be wrong, of course. But I think your father is at least half-right, J'Kara. This isn't a natural plague at all."

Worf hunched over the panels of the shuttlecraft *Hoyle* with his usual dark scowl on his face. Beside him, Ensign Ro shuffled, scratched the back of her neck, and then tapped her screens again.

"Nothing," she repeated for the third time.

"That is unacceptable," Worf snapped.

"With respect, sir, I can't *invent* a trace that isn't there," Ro replied. "Let's face it, the trail's gone dead."

Worf glowered again but didn't speak for a moment. This mission had looked very promising as they had followed the *Tivela*'s warp wake across two star systems, only to lose it completely here in the third. They were close to a gas giant, but sensors showed that the trader hadn't approached it. "It does not make sense," he complained. "The trail led here, and it simply stops. There is no wreckage and no sign of the ship. This is not possible."

"Maybe it was cloaked," suggested Ro. "If they *were* working with the Romulans, they could have been given a cloaking device, you know."

"Possibly," conceded Worf. "But why would they have waited until this distance to utilize it?"

"Why not?" countered Ro. "Maybe they wanted us to simply get frustrated. As we are doing."

Worf growled in the back of his throat. "It does not feel right," he objected. "There is something we are missing here." He turned to the pilot. "Could some other ship have intercepted the trader and then taken it aboard?" he asked.

Lieutenant Benares shrugged. "It's possible," he agreed doubtfully. "But that would have had to be a cloaked ship. I'm not picking up any further warp signatures."

"In which case," Ro argued, "why not simply assume that the *Tivela* was cloaked? Instead of inventing some kind of Trojan horse scenario . . ." She broke off, her eyes lighting up. "Trojan horse!"

"What are you talking about?" Worf grumbled.

"It's an Earth legend," Benares offered helpfully. "Soldiers invading an enemy town hid inside a large wooden horse. The Trojans thought it was an offering to the gods and dragged it into their town. At night, the soldiers came out of the horse and sacked the town."

Worf nodded. "It is a sound strategy," he said approvingly. "But what does it have to do with our situation?"

"Absolutely nothing," Ro said, grinning in triumph. "It was the word *Trojan* that set me thinking. Several large gas giants have captured asteroids at their Lagrange points in front and behind their orbits. They're named for the Trojans and the Greeks, as in the case of Earth's Jupiter. This one ahead of us is no exception. And two weeks ago, when the

Tivela passed through this system, the asteroids were here."

Worf's smile was quite intimidating. "Then they could have hidden in the asteroids," he finished. "An excellent notion." To Benares, he added: "Take us within sensor range of the group."

Alert, Ro bent over the scanners as Benares piloted them to catch up with the retreating asteroid cluster. There were thirty or so rocks in the group, but spread out widely over their orbit. Visually only one at a time could be detected through the shuttle's large forward window. The sensors weren't as limited, of course.

"Got it," Ro announced. "Course one-four-two mark three. Range, thirty-thousand kilometers. I'm reading the *Tivela*'s power cells all right." She frowned. "But it's very odd."

"What do you mean?" asked Worf.

"If they're hiding in the asteroids, why did they switch off their warp drive but leave their power cells radiating like crazy? It's not the most efficient way of playing hide-and-seek."

Considering the matter, Worf replied, "Perhaps they are not hiding. Perhaps they are bait." He turned to the six security officers who shared the ship with them. "Ready your weapons," he ordered. "Yellow alert." As they reacted smoothly to his instructions, Worf turned back to the panels, scanning for any sign of a second ship.

"You really think that this is an ambush?" asked Benares, worried.

"I do not know," Worf answered. "But it behooves us not to take a risk. Be prepared to raise shields on my command. If there *is* a second ship, it may well be cloaked. We will not have very much warning if they attack."

Ro hunched forward, looking almost eager for a fight. "There are other possibilities, you know," she suggested.

"I know," agreed Worf. "But we would be foolish to discount any possibilities until we know for certain."

The asteroid they were approaching was growing bigger. To Ro, it looked like a dirty pockmarked peanut. A faint glint of light briefly flashed.

"That must be a reflection off the *Tivela*," Benares commented. "They really aren't hiding very well."

Bending back over her screen, Ro said softly, "They're really not hiding at all. They've crashed. The bows of the ship are wrecked. They must have collided with the asteroid and crashed."

"Maintain yellow alert," Worf ordered. "And scan for other craft. They may have been forced down." He bent to his own screens. "I am reading no life-forms aboard the vessel at all."

The shuttle was drawing closer, and Ro could make visual contact now. The Andorian trader must have hit the asteroid at an angle, because it had gouged a deep trench into the surface before coming to a rest.

"The engines are still on-line," she reported. "That's why we're picking up their trace. But the warp field has collapsed and gone out."

"It has been there for two weeks," Worf stated. "The collision must have killed the crew."

"I don't think so," argued Ro. "That asteroid doesn't have much mass and it's pretty visible. The *Tivela* should have been able to avoid it easily even if their sensors were down. It doesn't make much sense."

Worf scowled his agreement. "Stand down from yellow alert," he decided. "Whatever has happened, it does not look as if the Romulans were involved." He rose to his feet. "I shall beam over with three security guards," he decided. "You," he told Ro, "will remain here and monitor the away team. Also, scan the area . . . in case."

Ro nodded. Sometimes Worf's paranoia was pointless, but it often paid off. "Understood."

Worf had the away team suit up, since there was a good possibility sections of the Andorian craft would be airless, and the artificial gravity field had collapsed. Then Ro beamed them across to the *Tivela*.

"We are aboard," came Worf's flat report. "Internal power is operating sporadically. We are in the control center. There are bodies all around us. It looks like . . ." There was a slight pause. "Sixteen bodies. All of the crew is here," he reported. "And they are all dead." She could almost hear the scowl in his voice. "It would appear that they died *before* the ship impacted on the asteroid."

Ro chewed at her lip. "Was it the disease that killed them?" she asked. "The one that's affected the Burani?"

"I do not think so," Worf replied. "There is no evidence of any pustules on their corpses. But the bodies will have to be returned to the *Enterprise* for autopsy. Stand by to receive coordinates."

"Standing by." Ro grimaced. She disliked intensely having to handle corpses. She'd been forced to do that too often in her life, and frequently the bodies were of those she loved. This was one task she'd prefer to pass on to others, but she knew that she had to do it herself.

Transporting sixteen corpses back to the *Enterprise* would not make for a cheerful return.

Chapter Twelve

"IT LOOKS AS THOUGH we're finally getting some-where," Picard remarked with a sigh. "But every road at present seems to lead to dead bodies." He tapped his fingers against the china teacup positioned on the table in front of him.

"Are you going to drink that tea?" asked Guinan. "Or shall I take it away from you to prevent you from making that irritating noise any further?"

Hastily drawing in his hand, Picard apologized. "I'm sorry, Guinan."

"I should think so." Her smile belied the rough tone of her voice. "Death is a given, Captain," she added more sympathetically. "You of all people should know that."

"I do," he agreed. He stared down at his green tea that she had insisted on fixing for him, and then took a hasty sip of the scalding liquid. "It's just the prospect of watching people die and being unable to help them that frustrates me so much."

"You're doing your best, and nobody can ask for more than that. Not even you."

Picard nodded glumly.

Guinan's eyes narrowed. "Pardon my bluntness, but why are you here, anyway?" she asked. "Why aren't you checking on Beverly's progress?"

With a rueful smile, Picard admitted, "She threw me out of sickbay while she finished the autopsies."

"Ah," she said, getting to her feet. "I'm no doctor, of course, but I'd suggest that you finish your tea and then get some rest."

"Will that make me feel better?" he asked, smiling slightly.

"I don't know," Guinan replied. "But it'll make *me* feel better if you stay out of my hair." She laid a friendly hand on his shoulder. "I'm sure that you'll find a way to help the Burani. From what you tell me, they're a pretty nice bunch of people on the whole."

Picard smiled fondly as he watched her serve other customers. She somehow always left him feeling better for having talked to her. He wasn't absolutely certain how she did it, because she rarely dispensed sympathy directly, but she lifted his spirits with her mixture of wisdom and nonsense. He sipped at the tea again, and did feel more relaxed. As for sleeping, though . . . he couldn't, just yet. There was too much on his mind.

His communicator beeped at him. "Crusher to Picard."

"Here," he replied eagerly. "Do you have news for me?"

"Yes," came back her crisp reply. "I think you'd better get back to sickbay as fast as possible. I've finished three autopsies, and that's enough for me to become very, very worried."

He was on his feet and heading for the door briskly as he continued speaking. "What is it?" he asked, anxiously. "Did they die of the plague?"

"No, Captain, nothing like that. As far as I can tell, they weren't infected at all." Beverly paused slightly. "These three Andorians were murdered."

Riker, Deanna, and Barclay all followed Dr. Saren into the monitoring room. This was the heart of the observation post, with several stations. They all looked slightly battered in the aftermath of the raid, and three of the screens were still dead. The other seven were up and running, though, with observers at two of those posts. Saren led the way to one of the monitored screens. A Bajoran operator nodded to his supervisor as they arrived.

"The fun's just starting," he announced, gesturing to the picture of the flat screen. "That's the Citizen's House in Tornal," he explained. It was a large, obviously venerable building, with tiers of seats facing several small thronelike podiums. "The First Citizen, Farra Chal, is on the left of the podium. Beside him is their equivalent of the presiding officer. He keeps order in the assembly and tags speakers. Brak Norin is in the third row toward the left. The presiding officer's been trying to avoid giving him the floor, but he's run out of excuses."

Riker nodded his understanding. "Is this being broadcast all over Iomides?" he asked.

"Pretty much," agreed the monitor. "There's not usually much excitement from this kind of meeting, but all of the broadcasters are clearing their normal programming to run this encounter. Norin's had it in for Chal for years, and he seems to have finally decided he's got the First Citizen where he wants him. This is going to be a rough session, whatever happens."

"What's involved in this impeachment thingy?" asked Barclay, puzzled.

"It is a political process for removing a First Citizen from office," explained Saren carefully. "If the First Citizen has committed some egregious misuse of power or a crime while in power, it provides for his removal and arrest."

"Then I wonder what Norin has in mind?" mused Deanna.

"He hasn't revealed that yet," the observer said. "Just made a few wild accusations that he's got plenty of proof to get Chal impeached. The reporters are having a field day with speculation, of course—everything from bribery to infidelity."

Riker motioned toward the screen with his hand. "It looks like the fun's about to start." They all bent low over the monitor's screen, watching what was about to happen.

Like all politicians everywhere, Norin clearly enjoyed the spotlight. As soon as the presiding officer made a small speech, he turned over the floor—and all attention—to the flamboyant speaker.

Riker studied the man carefully, comparing him to Chal. The First Citizen was a tall, dignified man with slate gray hair and a pleasant, relaxed face. His flamboyant clothes were, if anything, slightly more conservative than the planetary norm, the colors being almost pastel. Norin, however, was a very different sort of person. He was running to fat, and his clothes were almost electric in intensity. He wore rings on every finger and a chain of gold and gems about his neck. He looked every inch the showman, and he soon proved that Riker's estimation was correct.

"I'm sure that we all appreciate what the First Citizen has done for this planet," Norin said, bowing mockingly in Chal's direction. "His policies have been controversial—to say the least—and frequently divisive. But I had never imagined that he had ever worked for any purpose other than the greater good of our country and our planet. Until today." He paused, his eyes scanning the audience he couldn't see and the colleagues he could, waiting awhile for the impact of what he was saying to settle in. "Though I've disagreed publicly—and loudly, as I'm sure you'll all recall—with most of his misguided efforts, I've always been willing to give him the benefit of the doubt. I had always thought that his half-baked schemes and puerile policies were the inventions of his own warped mind." He paused again. "It turns out that I was wrong."

Chal scowled at this accusation and glanced toward the visitors' gallery. The camera showed an attractive, though not so young, woman seated there, her lips tight. "That's Madame Chal," the monitor commented. "She always watches her husband in the Citizen's House. They're very close."

"It seems that someone else has been placing ideas into the First Citizen's head," Norin continued, warming to his subject. "I have incontrovertible proof that the First Citizen has been conspiring with others to allow the subversion and takeover of our country—and possibly our entire world. Farra Chal has been conspiring with alien creatures for several years."

In the silence that followed this stunning announcement, Riker could hear his heart pounding. This *had* to have something to do with today's raid on the observation post. But what was it all about?

The silence was broken by Chal rising to his feet, a bemused smile on his lips. "It sounds to me as if my . . . learned colleague has been orating too hard. I think he must have burst a blood vessel in his brain. *Alien creatures?* Really! That's the sort of nonsense I'd expect to see in the gutter press, and not on the lips of a supposedly responsible representative. Alien creatures, indeed!"

There was a ripple of laughter throughout the room, which Norin allowed to continue for a moment before smiling and shaking his head. "I can assure the First Citizen that I am in complete control of my faculties, and his fears about my health are unfounded. I can also assure him that I have absolute proof of all of my allegations. I would not waste your time with them otherwise." He turned to gesture to an aide who moved forward through the assembly with a monitor screen. "For reasons of security that I am sure you will understand in a few moments, I cannot reveal to you where the image you are about to see is coming from. But I can assure you that it is perfectly genuine."

The aide set the monitor up between the rostrum and the assembly and then turned on the screen. It flickered to life and showed what looked like a mortuary. A worker, clothed from head to foot in a contamination suit, nodded at the camera, which he then focused on the slab.

Riker felt his blood chill at what he saw there.

It was Dr. Starn, obviously dead. And very obviously alien. The Vulcan's skin was green-tinted, his ears obviously pointed.

Barclay gave a strangled cry and dived for an unused monitor station. His fingers flew over the keys, and he frowned in concentration as he worked. Riker had an idea what he was doing but didn't speak to interrupt him.

The effect of the picture on the Citizen's House was no less electric. There was a stunned silence until Chal finally spoke up. His voice was no longer as confident, but he was obviously still fighting back.

"An impressive picture," he agreed. *"If* it is genuine. Such things can be faked."

"They can be," agreed Norin with equanimity. "But this one isn't. I aim to prove that this creature you see on the screen is indeed an alien being. It was captured this morning and unfortunately died before it could be made to speak."

Deanna growled, "They *tortured* him to death. . . ."

"As we speak, I am having a team of experts assembled and rushed to the hidden location of the alien's corpse. There they will conduct an autopsy, which will be filmed in detail. This film will be made available to all interested parties. Its detail should prove its genuine nature."

"It might just work . . . if they *do* manage to film it, it'll really blow the observation post wide open and drive a hole through the Prime Directive large enough for a Romulan warbird to navigate."

On the screen, Chal spoke again. "If what you say is true—and, I repeat, *if*—then you will certainly have answered a question that has been plaguing the scientific community for millennia: Is there life on other worlds? I'm sure that they will be very grateful to you. But . . ." He paused, dramatically. "I still do not understand why you show this picture when you are screaming for my impeachment. I have nothing to do with that alien creature at all."

"So you say," Norin answered coldly. "But you lie." He scowled at the First Citizen. "One of this creature's agents revealed its location to a colleague of mine. That is how we were able to capture the creature in the first place. That agent is an associate of yours."

"He's talking about Maria Wallace," Riker muttered. "Is there any truth in what he's saying?"

"Very little," Saren responded. "Maria Wallace did pose as a native of this world, and in the course of her activities had met someone well placed within Chal's political group. That was the extent of their collaboration, however. She was certainly not an agent of Chal's."

"But Norin's claiming she was," Deanna replied softly.

On the screen, Norin was claiming precisely that. "This agent of yours is currently in the custody of a colleague of mine," he stated. "She is being prepared so that she will be able to testify against you in person, before this assembly."

Chal scowled. "These accusations are indeed serious," he agreed. "Of course, you will not be able to prove them, because they are untrue. However, by law I have to agree that you must be given time to aim these . . . *proofs* of yours. Will two days be sufficient for you to be ready?"

"More than sufficient," Norin agreed, smiling maliciously and bowing slightly.

"Then I have only one further question." Chal glared back at his opponent. "Why is this so-called agent of mine in the custody of this unnamed colleague of yours and not in the hands of the police, where she surely belongs?"

"Because the police are answerable to *you*," Norin answered. "This conspiracy against our world may run far and deep, and until we discover exactly who is involved in it with you, we cannot afford to trust any part of the power structure that you can control."

"That," growled Deanna, "and the fact that they're likely priming her with the answers she's supposed to give to lead to Chal's impeachment."

Riker straightened up from the screen. "I think the fun's over for now," he said wearily. He ran his hand through his hair. "Well, I'd say we're in *very* serious trouble now." He glanced at Barclay. "Give me some good news, Reg."

Barclay glanced up from his monitor as maps and figures scrolled across its screen. "Um . . . I know where they're holding Starn's body," he offered. "Will that do, Commander?"

"That will do very nicely," Riker agreed, feeling a weight lifting from his shoulders.

"I managed to track the video feed they were using for that monitor screen in the assembly," Barclay explained. "It was shielded, of course, but not well enough to hide from this equipment. It was transmitted from a small medical facility on the outskirts of the capital. I'm processing a map of the area now so that we can get there."

"Excellent work," Riker said approvingly. "Then that helps us with stage one of what we must do. Let's go and talk this over in Dr. Starn's office with Kessler and Vanderbeek. I think we know enough now to proceed with a retrieval mission."

Barclay gulped nervously. Then he managed a wan smile. "The away team is coming!" he murmured, sounding less than enthralled with the idea of imminent action.

Chapter Thirteen

PICARD WAS GLAD that Beverly had tidied up following her autopsy investigations. He wasn't squeamish, but seeing dissected corpses definitely ranked low on his pleasure scale. As it was, three of the bodies were covered discreetly, and the others were apparently in storage for the moment. Beverly greeted him grimly.

"I've run full autopsies on three of the crew, Jean-Luc," she reported. "In all cases, death was caused by the administration of a toxin."

Picard nodded. "Do you have any idea of which toxin, and how it was administered?"

"Yes." Beverly led him to one of her laboratory screens and called up a molecular diagram. "This is the culprit. It's a nasty little thing that attacks the nerve sheaths—oddly enough, a little like the plague.

If whoever did this was trying to make it look like the plague at work, a cursory examination *might* have led a doctor to suspect the plague, but there are absolutely no other similar symptoms. The toxin is very lethal and it's manufactured, not natural."

"Intriguing." The diagram meant very little to Picard. "Can you narrow it down further?"

"Oh, yes." Beverly pulled up another file showing the same molecule. "This is the culprit—it's called *feorin*. And you'll never guess where it's from."

Picard studied the new picture, identical in all respects to the first. "At a wild guess," he said slowly, "Buran?"

"A very good wild guess." She gestured at the right-hand side of the split screen. "I found that sample in the blood of one of the Burani I scanned in the hospital today. A very sick female named M'Riri."

"Ah." Picard rubbed his chin thoughtfully. "She was also poisoned, then?"

"Yes. I spoke with her before I called you. She'd been poisoned several months ago. There is a cure, apparently, if the poison is caught in time. She was diagnosed and cured in time. Then she contracted the plague."

"You think the two may be related?" asked Picard.

"I think the two *events* are related," Beverly replied. "But not the poison and the plague. I asked M'Riri how she'd come to have this trace residual in her blood and she told me about the poisoning. But she wouldn't explain it and suggested that you talk to J'Kara."

Picard scowled. "Privacy again." He nodded. "All

right, Doctor. Anything else I should know before I speak with him?"

"Well, the poison obviously came from Buran, Jean-Luc," she said. "And it's very lethal—usually it kills within two hours if the antidote isn't administered."

"Interesting," Picard said slowly. "And just when did the Andorians die of it?"

"About eight hours after they left Buran." Beverly sighed. "That means one of two things. Either one of the crew of the ship itself poisoned everyone aboard, or else the poison was administered on Buran at the feast that they all attended, with some sort of time delay."

"Is that possible?"

"Oh, yes. A sheathing about the feorin would be enough. If it was administered in the food, it would probably be undetectable to the palate. Especially if you were eating alien cuisine—the Andorians wouldn't have suspected anything."

Picard considered this. "That's the most likely scenario," he decided. "After all, the Andorians must have all died at the same time, or they'd have attempted to send a distress call, I'm sure. That meant that they must have all ingested the poison at the same time. I doubt they'd have attended a feast and then all decided they needed a midnight snack on their way out."

"That's the way I see it, too," Beverly agreed. "So, someone at the feast is the guilty party. I just don't see why anyone would want the Andorians dead—and certainly not *before* the plague manifested itself."

"I can think of only one reason," Picard informed her. "To prevent them from denying that they caused the plague. If they can't defend themselves, they can be found guilty by default."

Beverly frowned. "But surely whoever did it would know we were bound to find out the truth?" she objected.

"I suspect we've been a little faster than the plotters anticipated," Picard replied grimly. "I think they hoped to have us discredited and off the planet before we found the Andorians. If we'd tried to come back later with the news, we'd have been suspected of manufacturing the evidence ourselves as a cover-up."

Beverly nodded. "I've scanned the other bodies and confirmed that they all have feorin in their systems. Unless you want me to, I won't bother with further autopsies."

"I see no need, either," Picard concurred. "And now I'm going to talk to J'Kara and try to get some answers. Perhaps you had better sit in on this, too." He crossed to the nearest communications panel. "Put through a call to Prince J'Kara and tell him that it's of the highest priority," he instructed the technician. She acknowledged and set to work. Picard rubbed his chin and gave Beverly a reassuring smile. "I'm sure we're getting somewhere," he said. "If we can find out who killed the Andorians, we may discover the source of the plague at the same time. In fact—" He broke off as the communications panel lit up, showing a sleepy looking J'Kara. "Ah, J'Kara," Picard said. "My apologies if I've roused your from your rest."

"My sleep can always be deferred, Jean-Luc, especially if this is as important as you claim."

"It is." Picard outlined for the prince what Beverly had discovered. "So, according to this M'Riri, you're the one to ask about feorin. What can you tell us?"

"Shameful news," J'Kara answered, his face grim. "If you recall, Jean-Luc, I mentioned that there were protesters when we joined the Federation, and that not all of them were peaceful. There is a splinter group who call themselves the Brood. They committed many antisocial acts to try and prevent our membership in the Federation. Some included destruction of public property. One of their attacks was on the personnel involved in negotiating the treaty with the Federation. M'Riri was one of these contacts. The Brood poisoned her water with feorin. Fortunately one of their members who disagreed with the plan informed us in time, and we were able to counter the feorin with the antidote and save M'Riri's life."

"And no one else uses this poison?" Picard asked.

"Jean-Luc, we are a peaceful people for the most part," J'Kara answered. "It is not the way of the Burani to commit antisocial actions. I can imagine no other parties who would even be interested in having such a terrible weapon."

"I see." Picard considered the matter for a moment. "So you believe that this group called the Brood is behind the deaths of the Andorians?"

J'Kara inclined his head. "It seems to me to be the logical explanation."

"And to me, too . . . except for one thing. How did they manage it?" He leaned forward. "After all, I doubt you employ any of the Brood in the palace. So how did they gain access to the Andorians' food? And *only* the Andorians? Unless others were also affected?"

"No Burani were poisoned at the feast," J'Kara replied firmly. "The feorin *must* have been administered in the Andorians' repast then." He scowled. "I will begin investigating everyone who could have handled the dishes, Jean-Luc. One of them *must* have been in league with the Brood."

"Good luck with the search," Picard offered. "Meanwhile, I've got another possible way to find these terrorists of yours. I'll contact you again as soon as I have any news."

"Of course," J'Kara replied. "Anytime at all. Good night."

As soon as the screen blanked out, Picard tapped in again for Data. The android's face promptly stared back at him. "Data," Picard asked, "is it possible for you to reconfigure the sensors in order to scan Buran for a single artificial compound?" He gestured to Beverly, who called up her molecular diagram of the feorin. "This, to be precise?"

Data's golden eyes scanned the screen. "It is possible," he finally allowed. "It will require a great deal of fine-tuning, however. I assume we are not looking for large quantities of this substance?"

"Most likely not," Picard conceded. "However, I suspect you can cut down the search time a little. The feorin is likely to be in the vicinity of the palace or the capital city. Begin with this area and spread out the search from there. The poisoners are unlikely to hide their weapon at too great a distance from where it would be utilized."

"I estimate that this realignment and scanning will take twelve-point-three hours, Captain, if I begin immediately."

"Understood, Data," Picard acknowledged. "Make it a priority." As the android signed off, Picard stared thoughtfully at Beverly. "Well, Doctor?"

"It looks as if we have a suspect at last, Jean-Luc," she replied. "And if this Brood is behind the poisoning, then they're probably behind the plague as well. They may have deliberately started it as revenge on those who wanted to join the Federation."

"I'm not so certain," Picard confessed. "Poison, I can see. It's very specific. You can pick your victims individually. But . . . spreading a plague? It's very indiscriminate, killing both the guilty and the innocent."

"They're fanatics, Jean-Luc," Beverly pointed out. "That's what J'Kara said. They may be willing to kill the innocent just to get to the guilty."

"Perhaps." Picard sighed and shook his head. "I don't know. Maybe I've been reading too many Dixon Hill mysteries. I can't help feeling, though, that this solution is too pat. Still," he said, standing up, "we can't afford to pass up the lead. I'm sure Data will come up with some results for us soon. Meanwhile, I think a good night's rest wouldn't hurt either of us right now."

"All right," Riker said, glancing around the small meeting room he had commandeered to hold his away team. "It's high time for action. We have two objectives. First, we have to destroy Starn's body completely before it can be autopsied. Second, we have to find and retrieve Maria Wallace. This means we're going to have to split up into two teams." He glanced at Deanna. "Counselor Troi will, of course, lead one of these groups. Since nursing is one of the few professions females are allowed in on this planet, logically you'd be best suited for the raid on the morgue."

"Thanks," Deanna replied drily. "Why do I get all the fun assignments?"

"Because I like you," Riker replied with a smile. "You and Kessler will have to handle that phase of the mission. Meanwhile, Barclay, Vanderbeek, and I have a difficult task: getting to Maria Wallace. Any suggestions?"

Barclay cleared his throat nervously and then leaned forward in his seat. "She's obviously being held by Grell," he said. "I've checked the records here, and he has a private estate on a small lake just outside the capital. It's surrounded by high-tech security devices, armed guards, and so on. I'd bet that's where he's keeping her."

"Sounds reasonable to me," Riker agreed. "Can we break in?"

"Ah, I don't think there'll be too much trouble," Barclay answered. "What they consider high-tech I'd call junk."

"Yes, but it's not enough just to get us in there," Riker pointed out. "We've still got to watch the Prime Directive. That means not using Starfleet technology if we can avoid it. We don't want to give them evidence of an alien invasion to use against Chal."

"No problem," Barclay assured him. "I can scavenge enough stuff from their current technology to do the trick. Of course, I'm going to need access to the stuff, but if we use Maria Wallace's cover, along with some of the other covers of the observers here, we'll have plenty of currency to get what I'll need." He looked very happy. "The computer systems here are primitive, but they'll be okay for what I'll need them to do to get us into Grell's hideaway. Once we're in there, of course, we'll still have to find Wallace."

"Understood." Riker nodded. "That's my part of the job. Any other thoughts before we get to work?"

"I've had an idea," Deanna offered. "We still have the clothing and the weapons that the two dead raiders were using, don't we?"

"Yes."

"Well, why don't we use them in our raids? And accidentally on purpose leave a few clues behind us." She grinned wickedly. "That way, it'll look like Grell's behind this whole rescue mission."

"I like it," agreed Riker. "The security force will think he's simply trying to cover up his lack of evidence against the First Citizen. If we destroy Starn's body and recover Wallace, he'll be without proof for his charges, and everyone's likely to think he was just pulling a hoax to embarrass the First Citizen. And if his stuff turns up in the raids . . ." He grinned. "Talk about killing two birds with one stone. Deanna, you're a sly genius."

"It's so nice to be appreciated," she said smugly.

"Right, people," Riker announced, getting to his feet. "It's time to get busy. Dr. Saren will provide us with papers, money, and any background details we need. Let's get to it."

They all moved. Deanna and Kessler set off together to plan what they would require for their phase of the mission. Barclay and Vanderbeek fell in step behind Riker.

Barclay gave Vanderbeek a hesitant grin. "I love it when a plan comes together," he murmured.

Chapter Fourteen

J'KARA COULD NOT RETURN to sleep immediately after Picard's call. Too many troubling thoughts were passing through his mind. Besides, it was his duty to report what he had been informed of to his father. J'Kara moved wearily along the passageway of the palace that separated his quarters from those of his father. He passed several retainers, who studiously concentrated on their tasks so as not to interrupt him.

At his father's room there was one retainer on duty. There was no guard, naturally, since the Burani in general did not commit acts of violence, and an attempt on the life of a king was unthinkable, even for the Brood. "Does my father sleep?" J'Kara asked.

"I do not believe so," the aide replied. "I have heard sounds of movement recently." He turned and

145

rapped on the door. "Your Majesty, your son wishes to see you."

A moment later the door opened. T'Fara, looking tired but definitely not freshly wakened, glared out. "You'd better come in," he said brusquely. He retreated, leaving the door open. J'Kara followed, closing the door behind him.

T'Fara's chamber was small and the door to his bedroom beyond was ajar. The king's desk was littered with papers that he had obviously been studying. He turned and glowered at his son. "What is it now?" he asked. "I am very tired. Each party has its own agenda, and they all want me to take their side. I wish that the Federation would just leave us alone. That would solve a lot of my problems."

"It would not solve that of the plague," J'Kara insisted. "They are not guilty of causing or spreading it."

"My son," T'Fara answered, "I fear you have let your idealism take your intellect hostage. There is strong evidence suggesting their complicity. I'm trying to keep an open mind, but I cannot ignore the fact that the plague began when the Andorians left us, and that it began with those who attended their farewell feast."

"That's foolish!" J'Kara exclaimed. "The Federation has no reason to wish us ill!"

"I may be your father, but I am also your king," T'Fara said carefully. "And I do not appreciate being called foolish. You may be my chosen heir but I do have other hatchlings."

"I meant no disrespect, Father," J'Kara replied humbly. "And I am aware that you could name another of your sons to the monarchy after me. But we both know that none of the others would make a good king."

"That's true," agreed T'Fara with a scowl. "None of them can match you. But I wish you would consider the possibility that these Federation humans are not necessarily as innocent as you believe. Like me, you owe it to your people to keep an open mind in all things. If I did not, I would still be fighting every decision our people makes."

"The Federation will be exonerated fully," J'Kara answered stubbornly. "In fact, probably sooner than you think. The reason I came to disturb your rest is to inform you that they appear to be on the track of the *real* culprits who are behind the plague. The missing Andorian ship has been located."

The king's eyes narrowed. "Let me guess. The Andorians are either dead or claiming their innocence in this matter."

Frowning, J'Kara admitted, "They are dead. Why was that the first thought that occurred to you?"

The king sighed. "You are still so naive, my son. Consider this: if the Andorians *are* guilty of starting the plague, they would hardly wish to be questioned about the matter. And if the Federation is behind this, they would not want them to be interrogated."

"There is still no proof of their guilt," the prince insisted.

"And now none yet of their innocence, either."

J'Kara shook his head. "Father, the Andorians were murdered—but by a Burani. They ingested feorin."

"And the Federation does not possess such poisons?" growled T'Fara in frustration. "You think they are *incapable* of murder? You would rather believe that one of us—your own people—killed these aliens sooner than think that another alien might have done it?"

"From where would Captain Picard or his people have learned about feorin?" demanded J'Kara. "Our people wouldn't even send them details about the plague until I ordered it. They certainly were never told about feorin. The poison *must* have come from a Burani, and we both know who is most likely to have used it."

The king shrugged his wings dismissively. "But we have no idea where the Brood are hiding. It will be a long time before they can be accused and be interrogated about their possible complicity. By the time that happens, our entire race might well be wiped out."

"It will not take as long as you seem to think," J'Kara answered. "The *Enterprise* has tremendous capabilities, far more than you realize. I think they will find the Brood faster than you imagined."

"Perhaps they will," conceded his father. "But then what? Who is going to arrest them? I'd be very surprised if Picard didn't want to do it. And if he does, what are his motives? Consider that. Perhaps he wants to aid us, but perhaps he wants to conceal the truth. I know you wish to believe the best of your friends, but a king cannot allow sentimentality to interfere with his judgment." He considered for a moment. "If Picard wants to help us to find the Brood, we shall, of course, accept his help. But I cannot allow his men alone to go after them. What if the Brood are all accidentally shot while resisting arrest? If this Picard is framing them for the actions of the Andorians and the rest of the Federation, they will never be taken alive, you mark my words."

J'Kara shook his head in frustration. "All right, let us compromise," he suggested. "I shall send along ten of our own police officers with any team that Picard wants to take after the Brood. They will be eyewitnesses to whatever occurs. Let them say whether the humans will try to kill the Brood or not. Will that satisfy you?"

The king considered for a moment and then nodded. "Very well," he agreed. "And I can only pray that your *friends* don't murder ten good men during the raid."

"Thank you, Father," J'Kara said wearily. "Captain Picard and his people can be trusted. They will expose the guilty and help to cure this plague. I know this."

T'Fara sighed loudly. "I admire your faith, my son. I only wish you would cultivate a little more caution in your outlook. It would serve you better." He waved dismissal. "You and I had better get some rest now. If you are correct, the morning may bring further developments, and we'd best be fresh to greet them."

Nodding, J'Kara withdrew from his father's room. He bowed slightly to the retainer outside and then hurried back to his own quarters. Despite his father's pessimism, J'Kara was convinced that the morning would indeed bring some form of resolution to this disaster facing his people.

Why, then, did he have such a feeling of dread?

* * *

Picard hurried onto the bridge early the following morning. With the *Enterprise* in continuing orbit of Buran, there was only a skeleton staff on the bridge monitoring the ship's status. Both Data and Chief Engineer Geordi La Forge were bent over one of the science stations together, working intently on Data's planned scan. Picard considered asking for a report but knew he'd be disturbing them. If there was progress to report, they'd tell him. Instead, he relieved Lieutenant Van Popering, who had the command chair.

"Anything to report?" he asked, taking his seat.

"Nothing much, sir. Commander Riker sent a short update message about his own mission." Van Popering shrugged. "Everything else has been perfectly routine."

"Thank you, Lieutenant. I assume command now, and you may stand down."

Van Popering smiled. "Thank you, sir." He turned on his heels and left the bridge.

Picard checked his messages, and found a nonurgent one waiting from Beverly. The report from Will Riker could wait for a short while, at least. It was frustrating to have to read those kind of reports, since there was absolutely nothing he could do about it right now anyway. Instead, he murmured to his chair: "Computer, locate Dr. Crusher." He didn't want to page her if she was sleeping.

"Dr. Crusher is in sickbay," the computer replied emotionlessly.

Picard tapped his communicator. "Picard to Crusher."

"Good morning, Captain," she responded. "I hope you slept well."

"As well as can be expected." Picard had no intentions of telling her about the nightmares he'd suffered through. "You wished to speak with me?"

"Yes, Captain. Dr. Margolin and I have been working on the plague again, without any luck." He could hear the frustration in her voice. "Nothing we have tried so far seems to halt it, let alone cure it. We've worked our way through almost the entire pharmacopoeia of Buran."

"That's bad news," Picard murmured.

"It's peculiar news," Beverly responded. *"Something* should have had an effect on this disease. At least, it should if it is natural."

Picard's skin began to tingle. "Yes, you mentioned that you had some doubts about that," he said.

"Well, those doubts are growing. In fact, I can say with confidence that this is not a natural disease." Her voice was hard and grim now.

"A genetic construct?" Picard asked.

"Precisely. Someone created this disease out of nothing with the sole purpose of murdering Burani."

"Any idea *who?"* he demanded, his mind racing.

"Two possibilities, I'd say," she offered. "First of all, the Romulans."

"I don't know," he answered slowly. "It's hardly their style, is it? They prefer direct assault over biological weapons."

"True," agreed Beverly. "But that very reason might be an argument as to why they *would* do it: Nobody would expect it of them. Anyway," she added, "I doubt it for a more fundamental reason. Where would they get the medical data they'd need to construct this disease? The Burani are very tightfisted with their personal information."

"I know what you mean," Picard agreed. "Still, if the Romulans *are* behind this, they might well have raided the planet on the sly and kidnapped a few unwilling participants for their experiments."

"They might have," agreed Beverly. "But we're multiplying *maybes* like crazy here. I think that the second possibility is far more likely: A Burani or group of Buranis caused this disease."

Picard nodded, forgetting for a moment that she couldn't see him. "It does seem more logical," he commented.

"What about those terrorists you're after?" she countered. "They're already murderers. Wouldn't this fit their style?"

"It's possible, I suppose," Picard agreed. "I'll have to speak with J'Kara to discover if there are any of the Brood who have the skill to manufacture an artificial disease. Still," he mused, "if they *are* the perpetrators, then they presumably have also created an antidote for the plague, so that they can survive it. I don't get the impression that they'd want to wipe out their entire species just to make a point."

"That's something we can hope and pray for," Beverly agreed. "Now all we have to do for the moment is to try and figure out how the disease is being spread."

Picard frowned, puzzled. "But, surely, you've already told me that it's highly infectious. Those dreadful lesions on the victims' bodies . . ."

"Yes," agreed Beverly. "That *would* be sufficient. Except, as I told you before, Captain, the Burani doctors are quite efficient. They confine all patients in their hospital wards as soon as the symptoms start to become evident—*before* the lesions occur. That way, they should have been able to contain the disease. It isn't working—the disease is still spreading. That means that there's some other factor involved here."

"Our unknown plotters seem to be very thorough," Picard commented.

"Extremely," agreed Beverly. "But at the same time, when you know what to look for it becomes rather obvious. They've been trying to make the plague look entirely natural. If that fails, they're trying to make it look like *we're* the ones behind it. But if it's springing up all over the planet in places we can't possibly be reaching, then we're very obviously innocent."

"True," Picard mused. "Well, there must be some common factor involved in the plague incidents. All we have to do is to discover what it is."

"That's what I'm working on right now, Captain," she answered. "I was getting nowhere with a hunt for a cure, so I thought a hunt for the source might be easier to find. I'll notify you if I find anything at all. Crusher out."

Picard leaned his chin on his hand and his elbow on his knee, musing. Beverly's findings had given him plenty of food for thought. It might be as well to notify J'Kara of these latest findings. He had Worf patch him through to the palace.

"Jean-Luc," came J'Kara's polite response. "You have fresh news for me?"

"I'm afraid I do," Picard replied. He told his friend of Beverly's findings and their suspicions. "I hate to be the source of bad news," he apologized, "but it looks as though we are going to be hunting for a Burani who is behind this plague of yours." He expected a rebuttal or protest, but for several moments J'Kara didn't speak.

"Forgive my rudeness," he finally said, and coughed. "Your theory is not too surprising, Jean-Luc. I had begun myself to suspect something along those same lines. Perhaps the Brood is behind this after all. At any rate, we should be able to tell when we find them. Have you had any progress in that matter yet?"

Picard glanced at where Data and La Forge were still hard at work. "Our search is progressing," he answered. "It shouldn't be too much longer before we have a location, I think."

"Good. Then I have a favor to ask of you, Jean-Luc." J'Kara sounded very apologetic. "My father still insists that the Federation is behind this disease. I am sure he will manage to come up with an explanation that satisfies him as to how you could have done it. He believes that you do not aim to capture the Brood alive, but dead, so that they can be blamed posthumously for your evil deeds. Naturally I do not believe that his suspicions are correct, but it might be best to assuage them."

"Agreed," said Picard, frustrated at the continuing lack of trust the king was showing. "Did you have something specific in mind?"

"Allow ten of my own men to accompany any

raiding group you may send after the Brood," J'Kara responded promptly. "I will have them standing by to join you at any moment you request them. They will be able to aid you and to confirm that you are acting completely honestly."

"That sounds like an excellent idea, J'Kara," Picard agreed. "Very well. As soon as we locate the base of the Brood, I will notify you. When my security forces beam in to arrest them, we shall transport your men along, too."

"I knew you would agree, Jean-Luc," said J'Kara, audibly relieved. "Thank you, my friend, for all that you have done." He sneezed. "Excuse me. A head cold, I fear."

"I hope so," Picard said, with concern. "Perhaps you should have it checked, just to be certain."

"I shall," J'Kara promised. "I will speak to you again shortly."

Picard signed off, and then glanced over at where La Forge and Data were still hard at work. Despite his best intentions, the suspense was becoming unbearable. Jumping to his feet, he crossed to the science station. "Anything to report?" he asked briskly.

Data glanced up. "Not yet, Captain," he replied. "Geordi and I have reconfigured the sensors to scan for feorin. We started outside the palace grounds and have so far found only a single trace."

"Surely that's worth reporting?" Picard commented.

"Not really; it's in the local hospital," Geordi answered. "That would be a logical place to have some of the poison. They'd need it, I gather, to

155

generate the antidote. We did contact Dr. L'Tele, who informed us that it is in the poisons cabinet, and under lock and key. He physically checked this to confirm it for us."

"Nothing else, then?"

Data shook his head slightly. "Scanning for such a small quantity of a single molecular structure is bound to be time-consuming, Captain," he responded. "As I informed you, I estimated a minimum of twelve hours. It has only been ten hours, forty-seven minutes, and—"

"Yes, yes, all right, Data," Picard said hurriedly. "I'm sorry that I've disturbed you. Continue with your scans."

Data bent back to the panel. As he did so, there came a pulsing beep, and a sector of the map on his screen lit up. "It appears that I overestimated, Captain," he commented. "We have just detected a second trace of feorin."

"Excellent work, gentlemen," Picard said warmly. "Where is it?"

Data examined the chart. "In the mountains close to the capital," he announced. "It seems to be an underground cave system. There is a large amount of feorin registering."

"Then I suspect you just discovered the Brood's hideout," Picard said, pleased. "You had better continue scanning just in case, but we'll definitely investigate this finding." He stood up straight and turned to the security station. "Mr. Worf, report to transporter room three with a dozen of your men immediately. Heavy armament. You are to lead the raid on this underground base."

Worf's eyes lit up eagerly. "Aye, sir!" he snapped, and set off at a run.

Picard moved to the communications panel. All that was left to do now was to notify J'Kara and the joint raid could commence. In a short while, they should have some answers—and, he hoped, a number of suspects. With any luck, they would also have the antidote they so desperately needed.

Chapter Fifteen

"HOW'S IT GOING?"

Barclay glanced up from the ground vehicle they
had bought an hour earlier, using some of Saren's line
of credit. Removing the screwdriver from his mouth,
he grinned. "Fine, Commander," he replied. "It's not
a bad little machine, and with just a bit of tweaking
I've managed to increase its efficiency and speed by
about twenty percent. Uh, nothing that an Iomidian
couldn't do, of course . . . *if* they thought about it."

"Good," Riker replied. "Anyway, Vanderbeek and
I have the rest of the equipment that you asked for."
He gestured to the pile of boxes that the security
officer was unloading from their rental gev. "Except
for one of the electronics components." He studied
the list that Barclay had drawn up. "He didn't have
any hoop inducers in size four, but he claimed that

158

two size threes would do the trick. Since I haven't the vaguest idea what he's talking about, I hope he wasn't just trying to con me."

Barclay shrugged. "We'll have to wait and see, sir," he answered. "I'll know when I start installing the stuff. Meanwhile, do you think that you and Paul could start work on reinforcing the front of the gev, while I begin with the electronics? We're going to have to crash the gate, probably, and it would be nice to have a little padding."

"You got it," Riker promised. "How long do you think this is going to take us?"

Barclay shrugged. "Hard to say exactly," he answered. "Another hour, if we don't run into any problems. I *think* I've got the local science down pat, but it's kind of hard constantly having to think down to their level."

Riker patted him on the shoulder. "Don't worry, Reg. I have faith in you. I'm sure you can sink to any level necessary."

"Thank you, Commander," Barclay replied uncertainly. "I think . . ."

"We're just going to walk in there?" asked Deanna, concern in her voice. "Lorie, there are armed guards on duty."

Kessler surveyed the hospital entrance. There were indeed two armed men standing there. "We've got the right clothing and forged ID passes. And we're just a couple of dumb women. They'll let us through."

"A couple of dumb women with automatic weapons and plastique in our bags," Deanna pointed out, worried. "What if they want to search us?"

159

"They won't, as long as we don't look worried," Kessler promised. "Trust me, Counselor. Eighty percent of this is to look as though you know precisely what you're doing and don't expect to be stopped."

"And what's the other twenty percent?"

"Pure luck." Kessler flashed her a smile.

Deanna couldn't help smiling at her companion's self-confidence.

She fell in step beside Kessler as she started for the hospital entrance. "Anyway," she continued, slipping into her assigned role, "I had this really hot date last night with Darin Thal."

"Thal?" squealed Kessler. "That hunk from purchasing?"

"The same."

"So," Kessler asked, breathlessly, "do I get to hear the details?" They had reached the bored-looking guards, and Kessler held out her ID but had her entire attention focused on Deanna—at least to all appearances she did.

"Well, he took me to this intimate little ethnic restaurant down in the Poornal district," Deanna said, lowering her voice conspiratorially and flashing her own ID. "We had such a lovely meal."

"I don't want to know about the *meal,*" Kessler said, impatiently. "Get to the good stuff. Did he . . . you know?"

The two guards were grinning as they waved Deanna and Kessler by. One of them eyed Deanna appreciatively, which she pretended not to see.

"Did he *what?*" Deanna asked, pretending to be coy and shocked at the same time.

"You know . . ."

The door slid shut behind them. Deanna risked a quick glimpse over her shoulder. The two guards were exchanging low comments—comments Deanna was just as glad to have missed. "Well, we're in," she said with a sigh of relief.

"So far, so good," Kessler answered. She shifted the large shoulder bag she was wearing slightly. "Now for the morgue."

Deanna pulled the hospital map Barclay had procured for them from her bag. "The next corridor on the left leads to the elevator bank," she commented. "The morgue's in the basement."

"Logical place to keep it," Kessler replied. "Let's go."

They threaded their way through the maze of corridors, still chatting mindlessly about Deanna's supposed date the previous night. None of the other workers or visitors paid them much attention, aside from a couple of glances from young males. Nurses' uniforms seemed to be form-enhancing on all worlds, Deanna decided.

The only other person who got into the elevator with them for the trip down got off at the floor before theirs, thankfully. Deanna had been afraid of complications otherwise. As soon as the elevator doors closed behind the man, she turned to Kessler.

"There's no way we can pull the same trick there as we did upstairs," she said.

"This time we have to get rough." Kessler nodded in agreement.

When they left the elevator, Kessler jammed a

small perfume holder in the door to prevent it from closing behind them and stranding them. They needed a prompt getaway when they were done. Deanna studied her map.

"The next left," she said. "Then a right, and the morgue is straight ahead of us." She glanced around the deserted corridors. "At least it's quiet for the moment."

"The morgue's not the most popular room in the house," Kessler observed. "Which simplifies our job, at any rate."

The two women walked cautiously down the corridor, and as they approached the right hand turn, Deanna said, "It's down *here,* I tell you. Honestly, your sense of direction is appalling."

They rounded the corner to see the morgue door ahead of them. In front of it stood an armed guard, who was scowling in their direction. "What do you think you're doing?" he demanded, his firearm pointed at them.

"Oh," said Deanna, as if surprised. "Maybe you *weren't* wrong, then." She gave the man an apologetic smile. "We're new here, and we were sent to storeroom seven to pick up supplies. I was *sure* it was down this corridor, but . . ."

The guard sighed. "Women," he grumbled. "Let me have a look at your map and I'll show you where you went wrong."

Deanna smiled gratefully and held the map out as she advanced on the man. "These things are *so* hard to read," she said breathlessly.

"Right," the man agreed, raising his eyes to heaven.

"Look, it's dead simple. We're here, at the morgue, and—"

And he collapsed forward, Kessler easing him to the ground. Grinning, she showed Deanna the knockout patch held in her fingers. "Isn't it convenient that they underestimate women?" she commented. "It gives us a great element of surprise." She let the patch fall to the floor. "He's going to be out of it for at least an hour, according to the analysis of those drugs that Saren ran. That should be plenty of time for us." She straightened up and opened the door to the morgue.

A second guard stood ready, his gun raised.

Before Deanna even had time to blink, Kessler exploded into action. One long leg whipped up, kicking the guard's gun aside. She whirled around and delivered a blow to the man's neck that felled him instantly.

"Don't threaten," Kessler muttered, patting her hair back into place. "It's not polite. Or wise." She glanced back at Deanna. "I think that's the lot."

"I hope so," Deanna observed. "Nice work."

"It's my job." Kessler pushed the unconscious guard aside and then slapped another of her knockout patches on his neck. "For security," she commented, as Deanna dragged the first guard into the room and then closed the door behind them. "We've got about an hour. Let's get busy."

The morgue was chilled, naturally, and aside from the two sleeping guards, deserted. There were cabinets about the room that were obviously designed to hold the bodies of the deceased, and a door at the far end of the small room.

"I'll bet Starn's body's through there," Kessler commented, gesturing. "It would be kept separate."

"Let's take a look," Deanna suggested as she opened the door.

As it was, nothing happened. The room beyond was small but held only a small table and video equipment.

On the slab was Starn's stiff body, naked and awaiting the arrival of the autopsy team. Deanna felt a pang of sorrow for the unfortunate Vulcan, a feeling that intensified as they closed the door behind them and approached the body. There were cuts and bruises all over it, and green blood had clotted on the skin.

"I'll bet he told them nothing," Kessler said softly. "Vulcans are too tough to be made to talk."

"So they aim to make him serve their purposes in here," Deanna said, unable to keep the anger from her voice. "This Grell is one sick person."

"Well, we'll just have to derail his plans," Kessler said simply. She set her bag down on the floor and started to rummage inside it. Knowing what she was after, Deanna removed the incendiary devices from her own bag as well. Kessler lay them carefully about Starn's body and then inserted a fuse. "This is all Grell's stuff," she said, "taken from those two terrorists of his. I'm sure there will be enough residue left over for the police to analyze."

"Just in case," Deanna murmured. She took a handgun from her bag and slid it under the TV camera. "Oops. I lost my gun in the excitement."

Kessler grinned back at her. "Okay, this stuff should atomize his body," she said. Glancing around the room, she added, "And probably a lot of this room in the bargain. I've set the fuse for ten minutes, which should be plenty for us to get out of here. Let's beat it."

In the outer room, Deanna paused beside the unconscious guards. "We'd better get them closer to the elevator shafts. We don't want any accidental deaths, after all." She opened the door, and grabbed one of the unconscious men in a firefighter's lift.

Kessler hoisted the other and they dumped the two men beside the still-open elevator. Kessler, with another grin, took a small piece of cloth from her bag and placed it in one guard's hand, closing his fist about it. "I got that from one of Grell's raiders," she explained. "That should be plenty of evidence for the police, don't you think?" Removing the makeup holder from the elevator door, she stepped inside. "Going up."

Deanna joined her and the doors slid closed. "Five minutes," she said as the elevator rose slowly. "As long as nothing goes wrong." There was a knot of worry in her stomach. It seemed to take forever for the elevator to reach the ground floor, but eventually the doors opened and they stepped out. Visitors and attendants took their place inside.

"Just a moment or two," Kessler said checking her timepiece. "We don't want to be the first out, after all."

They dawdled about in the corridor close to the main entrance, pretending to chat. Deanna's tension was growing with each passing second. There was so much that could go wrong still. All that was necessary was for someone to go into the subbasement and find the two sleeping guards. Then all hell would break loose. If the incendiaries were discovered and defused, it would make a second raid almost impossible.

It was hard for her to concentrate. How much longer did they have left?

Everything *seemed* to be okay, but how much could she rely on appearances?

Then all hell *did* break loose.

The floor shook slightly, and there was the muffled sound of an explosion. Several people yelled, and everyone stopped what they were doing. Nobody knew what was happening for a second or two, so Deanna helped them to make up their mind.

"Fire!" she yelled loudly, slapping the alarm button. An ululating drone filled the building. "Don't panic!" she screamed, apparently panicking. "Clear the building immediately."

As the alarm howled, nobody needed a second warning. Visitors whirled and dashed for the exit, followed almost as swiftly by the staff members. Deanna gestured to a patient in a chair, with what appeared to be a broken limb.

"Get him out," she told Kessler. "And meet me outside."

Kessler nodded and grabbed the poor man's wheelchair. "Let's get you to safety," she said, and he burbled gratefully at her. She knew that the devices they'd used weren't really likely to start an uncontrollable fire, but all the panic they could generate would help them now. She pushed through the exit doors as the two guards on duty outside shoved inside, yelling into communication devices they held for help.

Perfect. They didn't even glance at Deanna as she

heroically carried two children, whom she immediately dumped by the far wall.

Kessler went to join her, and they watched a trickle of smoke coming up from the basement doors with satisfaction. "Not bad for two dumb women," Deanna murmured.

"Let's hope the three big strong men do as well with their part of the mission," Kessler answered. She nodded at the main gate. "Time to beat a retreat, I think."

"Indubitably," agreed Deanna. She glanced back as they hurried out of the hospital grounds and toward where they'd stashed their rented gev. Smoke was pouring out of the basement. The unfortunate Starn was definitely spared his revealing autopsy now.

Phase one completed. She wondered how Will, Reg, and Paul were doing with phase two. . . .

Chapter Sixteen

WITH A GROAN that was half ache, half pleasure, Farra Chal eased himself into his favorite seat. "Thank the gods that's over with for now," he grunted. "I don't want to see another reporter for a month."

"You may have very little choice in the matter, my love." Rona Chal slipped in behind her husband and began to massage his shoulders. Chal could feel her strong fingers going directly to his knotted muscles and forcing them to relax. She always knew what to do to help him the most. "I would think they'll be clamoring at the door again as soon as Norin's had his little sideshow in a few hours."

"No doubt," agreed Chal, trying hard not to imagine all the cameras pointed in his direction again. "Brak, tell me—what do you think the chances are that he really *has* uncovered an alien?"

Tral Brak moved into view. He was a tall Iomidian, almost half a meter taller than the man he served. He was dark-haired, and had a pleasant open face that smiled easily. At the moment, though, the smile was gone, replaced by a look of concern. "I don't know, Citizen," he replied. "I mean . . . it doesn't make a lot of sense, I know. But would he have dared to make such a ludicrous assertion if he didn't have *some* kind of proof to back it up with?"

"A good point," agreed Chal, wriggling uncomfortably. "But—an *alien?* Where would he get such a thing from?"

"Presumably," his wife murmured, "from another world. But that's not what concerns me. What really bothers me is this business of claiming that you're in league with these supposed aliens, and plotting against our planet."

"Yes," her husband responded drily. "That worries me, too. Since we all know it's not true, what does he expect to gain by claiming it? I assume he must have *some* kind of evidence that he'll drag out to try and prove the claim with."

"I would think so," Brak agreed. "After all, Norin may be an opportunist, but he's a clever opportunist. He's obviously seized on something that he feels will be able to drag you down; otherwise he'd never have exposed himself so obviously to potential ridicule."

Impatiently Chal pushed his wife's hands away. "Apparently. But *what?*" He turned to Brak. "And why did we know nothing at all about this in advance?"

"Sir," Brak said apologetically, "it is not our policy to spy on your political foes. You know that."

"Of course he knows that," Madame Chal answered for her husband. "He's just tired and frustrated, that's all. This has been, to say the least, a great shock." She patted her husband affectionately on the shoulder. "I'll go to see to dinner, dear, while you talk."

"Sounds wonderful," Chal agreed. "We'll be in shortly, I promise." He watched as his wife left the room, and then returned his gaze to Brak. "Well?" he asked grouchily.

Brak started. "I'm sorry, Citizen?"

"I can tell by that look in your eyes, Brak, that something's upsetting you," Chal informed him. "So—out with it. What's on your mind?"

Brak licked his lips for a moment before replying. He appeared to be gathering up his nerve. Finally he blurted out, "It's your wife, sir."

"What about her?" Chal growled. "Don't tell me you're thinking of having an affair with her?"

Brak flushed deeply at the thought. "Sir!" he protested.

"A poor joke," Chal apologized, waving his hand. "It's been a rough day. Well, what's your problem with my wife?"

"Well, I simply think you listen to her too much," Brak replied, calming down a little. "She's only a woman, after all."

Chal snorted good humoredly. "I can tell you're not a married man, Brak. No married man would think he could listen to his wife too much."

"I don't mean on a personal level, sir," Brak explained. "Your personal life has nothing to do with me."

"No," the First Citizen agreed. "It hasn't."

"I mean in matters of policy," Brak continued. "You allow her to advise you far too much."

"Ah." Chal rose to his feet. "So that's it, is it? Not merely that I listen to her, but that I often take her advice over yours."

"I *am* supposed to be your advisor," Brak said stiffly.

"Yes, you are." Chal patted his arm affectionately. "And you do a very good job of it, too. But . . ." He wandered over to his desk and poured himself a glass of *tarn*. "Want one?" he offered. Brak shook his head. "I probably should wait, I know," Chal commented, as he sipped at the drink. The warmth felt good as it passed down his throat. "The thing is, Brak, that Rona knows what she's talking about. I listen to her not because she's my wife, but because she makes sense. I know her ideas aren't usually in accord with yours, but she's generally right. I owe her for a great deal of sage advice."

"And a great deal of foolishness," protested Brak. "You *know* how unpopular some of your decisions and policies have made you."

"Not with the people, Brak," Chal answered, finishing his drink. He considered having another, but decided against it. If he had to face the reporters again later, it wouldn't do to be roaring drunk. Unfortunately. "Only with certain politicians and marketeers. What I do, I do for my planet—not for my pocket or that of anyone else. Brak, *think* about it!" he urged his assistant. "In ten years we could have a single government running this world. Then all of the waste, all of the loss of life, all of the resources tied up in fighting or preparing to fight one another could be over. Instead of working against one another, we could be working *with* one another! It will be a glorious time."

"If you live to see it," Brak snapped. "You *know* you have enemies. Maybe we should be monitoring them, after all."

"Every successful man has enemies," Chal observed. "And I know I've been more than successful. But I can't be looking over my shoulder every second of the day. Besides, you know full well that no First Citizen has ever been assassinated."

"It's not through want of trying," protested Brak. "Your bodyguards might not be able to stop the next attempt on your life. The two they have prevented—"

"Were just lone fanatics," Chal broke in. "Fanatics invent their own reasons for their crimes, Brak. And their excuses simply to cover up their own incompetence. And their very incompetence means that they'll inevitably get caught."

Brak shook his head. "I knew you wouldn't listen to me."

"On the contrary, I *always* listen to you," Chal said, slapping him on the arm. "I just don't always agree with you. Especially when it comes to my wife."

"So I notice," Brak replied drily. "But she worries me. She's too ambitious. She likes the power you wield, and I sometimes think she covets it. I think she's jealous of you."

Chal snorted at the thought. "Rona's happy to be First Wife," he said. "And she's too intelligent ever to think that she could be more than that."

"She *is* more than that, if you keep taking her

advice and ignoring mine," Brak objected. "She's virtually in office as it is."

"Then she's doing a very good job of it," Chal replied, refusing to rise to the bait. "Now, let's go and see if she's managed an equally good job of getting our dinner ready, shall we?"

Worf and his security team materialized within the Burani palace grounds. Waiting for them was a small squad of Burani troops. Each carried what appeared to be nerve disruptors and wore light body armor. The tall dark-plumed avian in charge came forward to meet with Worf.

"I assume your men are ready to be transported to the Brood base?" Worf asked curtly, eyeing the Burani carefully. They did not appear to be physically intimidating, but perhaps they looked more efficient to other Burani.

"Almost," the officer replied. "You are Worf?"

"I am. And you are D'Nara?"

"I am." D'Nara glowered at Worf's phaser. "Is your weapon meant to kill?"

"No," Worf replied. "A dead target does not readily answer questions, and we have many that need to be asked. Our phasers are set to stun."

"I'd like to believe that," the Burani answered. "I do not trust you Federations."

Worf bristled at the insult. "I would be more than happy to demonstrate it on you," he offered.

D'Nara smiled. "Thank you, but no." He stared at Worf in amusement. "Perhaps a more effective demonstration would be if you allowed me to use it on you."

Worf felt like growling but settled for a grunt of annoyance instead.

"Still," D'Nara commented, "that might delay the mission, and enough of my people have died already." He paused. "I shall be watching your back, Federation."

Again, Worf forebore replying. He simply glowered at the security man.

D'Nara smiled again. "I'm starting to like you, Worf. I hope that you really are on our side. I should hate to kill you."

Worf glared at him. "Please have your men assemble with mine, with their weapons at the ready. We do not know what we shall find when we arrive at our target."

"A wise precaution," agreed D'Nara. He removed his own weapon, signaling his troops to do the same. Then they fell in with Worf's security team. Together, they were twenty strong. The sensor scans of the hidden base had shown only forty life-signs, though there was a margin of uncertainty, since the *Enterprise* had been scanning through layers of rock.

Tapping his comm badge, Worf announced, "We are ready for transport. Energize."

The web of the transporter field caught them up. There was a momentary dazzle, and then they were all standing inside a large cavern. It was lit by small, portable lamps set up at irregular intervals on convenient rocks or shattered stalagmite bases. The main cavern was about forty meters across and thirty high. Several smaller caves or passages led off from this first one.

There were about twenty Burani in the cavern, most

of whom jumped when Worf's voice thundered out: "You are surrounded! Surrender immediately!" Some stayed on their feet, pale and shaken. The rest drew or dived for weapons.

"Fire at will," Worf called. "Do not kill!" He responded to his own command by phasering a Brood member who had jumped toward a heavy-duty disruptor.

Phaser and disruptor fire erupted about the cave. Most of the Brood were felled before they could return fire, but three of the quicker ones managed to get their weapons up and blazing. One of Worf's team yelled and fell writhing to the cavern floor. A Burani took out the assailant with alacrity.

Worf scanned the cavern quickly as the firefight continued. This was obviously the main room, as several bedrolls and cooking fires proved. Crates of materials were being used for chairs, and pots of food were steaming away. It was clearly the main retreat for the Brood, but they were not all in this one cavern. Worf estimated that twelve of them were already stunned and four more were surrendering peacefully. That left more than twenty others, and the idea of having twenty terrorists at loose in these caves did not appeal to him.

"Brogan and Deest," he called. "Go to the left and search for more Brood members."

"Acknowledged." The two officers peeled off, staying low to avoid disruptor fire. Worf turned to see D'Nara behind him, as the Burani had promised. "We should check to the right. There are at least twenty other members of the group unaccounted for."

"Agreed," D'Nara said, falling in beside him now. "You suspect an ambush?"

"It is always better to suspect the worst," Worf answered. Crouched over, he ran toward the passages he had noted. One of the Brood was lodged behind a rock and fired as they approached. Worf and D'Nara dodged in opposite directions. "I will draw his fire," Worf offered, and started forward again. A disruptor blast shattered a stalactite beside him, and Worf fired back. As the Brood member rose for a second shot, a bolt from D'Nara sent him spinning unconscious to the cavern floor.

"A good shot," Worf acknowledged.

"As I said, I'm starting to like you," D'Nara replied. "Maybe I *am* watching your back, after all."

Worf grunted and led the way warily past the unconscious rebel. This tunnel was short and led only to a supply room. Worf ran a quick scan with his tricorder. "This must be their munitions room," he stated. "The feorin is in here, as are many explosives."

D'Nara grinned. "Maybe we should dispose of it all, to prevent it being used against us?"

"A reasonable notion," Worf agreed, "except for the fact that we might need the feorin for their trials."

The Burani's eyes widened slightly. "They are clearly guilty. What need do we have of a trial?"

"They are not necessarily guilty," Worf argued. "Appearances can be deceptive. We should get someone from each of our teams to guard this room, and move on."

"As you wish." D'Nara called one of his officers, as

did Worf, and had the two stay together to ensure the Brood didn't get to further weapons.

It was probably an unnecessary precaution. The sounds of firing were dying down. The Brood had clearly not anticipated a raid, and they were not doing a very good job of recovering from their shock. Between Worf's security team and D'Nara's men, the roundup was progressing well. Still, Worf had no intention of being overly optimistic. He and D'Nara cautiously approached the next cave off the main tunnel, staying out of sight of the entrance. When they were ready, Worf nodded at D'Nara and then dived across the entrance, his phaser ready to fire at the first sign of resistance.

There was none. Worf rose to his feet and D'Nara moved out to his side. Together they moved carefully into the body of the cave and then stopped dead in their tracks.

This was where the rest of the Brood members were, but they were in absolutely no shape to attack. Worf and D'Nara exchanged worried glances, and then Worf tapped his communicator. "Worf to *Enterprise.*"

"Picard here," came the instant reply. "What is it, Mr. Worf?"

"The raid has been a success, Captain," Worf answered. "We will have some twenty prisoners for interrogation when they recover. However, I do not believe that the Brood is behind this plague."

"What makes you say that, Mr. Worf?"

The Klingon's eyes scanned the cave he was standing in. Sickbeds lay everywhere with infected Burani on them. Many were unconscious and all of them were bleeding from open sores. D'Nara had gasped and retreated from the room as fast as he could.

"Because the Brood is also suffering from the plague. If they had caused it, they would have an antidote. There is nothing like that to be found here." All that Worf could see was disease and suffering. There were none of the answers that the captain so badly needed.

Chapter Seventeen

"WHY DO YOU PERSIST in putting your trust in these . . . aliens?" demanded S'Hiri, glaring at her fiancé.

J'Kara studied her carefully before replying. "Because they mean to help us," he finally replied.

"They are *outsiders,*" S'Hiri spat.

Smiling, the prince shook his head. "My sweet, until two generations ago we would have been outsiders to one another. We are from differing nests, after all. If it had not been for my grandfather's and father's work, you would not be betrothed to me right now. We would not even be speaking to one another. Is *that* the past you would have us return to?"

"Of course not," she snapped, her feathers bristling at the thought. "You know that I would not have that.

Unity among ourselves is definitely the best course of action. A strong people, united under a single rule."

"Ah." J'Kara gave her an understanding glance. "So that's what this is really about, is it? Not the Federation so much as my not being sole ruler."

"So what if it is!" she exclaimed, her frustration evident. "You were born to rule, and yet you persist in this foolishness of democracy. What our people need, now more than ever, is a strong ruler who knows what is best for them and pursues this goal with single-minded devotion. And does that not describe you, my dearest?"

"Yes," he admitted, refusing to give in to false modesty. "It does. I do believe that I know what is best for my people. And that is both democracy and union with the Federation. Neither my father nor you can change my mind on this issue, much as I love you both." *You have to understand me—you, above all, S'Hiri! We can no longer remain isolated from the rest of the galaxy. True, we could ask the Federation to leave, and they would go. They are honorable people and would not force themselves upon us. But there are other races in the galaxy who are not as compassionate or understanding. The Romulans, for example, who covet our world. They would not let us remain in isolation simply because we asked for it. No, for our own greater good we must ally ourselves wholeheartedly with the peoples we are kin to. And, whether you wish to admit it or not, we are kin to these people from the Federation."

S'Hiri moved closer to him, concern on her face. She stroked his neck feathers. "I am starting to worry about you, my sweet. Thinking that these aliens are kin to us! That is not sane."

"True, they don't *look* like us," J'Kara replied. "But they have souls like ours, and aims like ours. They long for the good of all, not just the individual, and they strive for what is right. This Captain Picard, for example, is a good person."

"He looks as if he's been plucked," S'Hiri observed. This brought a smile to his face.

"We should not judge them by their appearances, S'Hiri, but by their hearts and deeds. They are our friends, though I know you are suspicious of them. For *my* sake, could you not accept this?"

"For your sake I could accept anything," S'Hiri assured him. "If I thought you were right. But in this matter I *know* you are wrong. Perhaps these Federation people *are* good and kind, and everything else that you claim they are. It doesn't matter. What matters to me is that you should understand your birthright. You were born to be king, J'Kara, and you should live up to that heritage. Don't throw it all away because of some foolish ideals you've adopted. The best thing for our people will be for you to rule, and rule firmly. Especially at this time of grave crisis, our people need a strong leader."

J'Kara sighed. "It is you who do not understand," he replied. "Power cannot be given; it must be earned."

"And who has earned it more than you?" S'Hiri cried in frustration. "You have labored unceasingly for our people. If your birthright doesn't give you the power to rule, then the compassion of your heart surely does!"

"No," he replied, gently. "I am set in my course and so are my people. That is not a decision I can or will change."

"You are so stubborn!" S'Hiri exclaimed. "There are days when I wonder why I love you so much. I will not give up in my efforts to make you see reason."

"And I will listen. But I know I shall not be persuaded." He smiled fondly at her. "It may take a long while," he cautioned her.

She smiled back. "I hope to have a long while with you, my stubborn, foolish love." Then, shaking her head, she left his room.

J'Kara coughed and shook his own. She simply could not see the point in his logic. But she would, he was certain. Sooner or later, she would understand.

Riker smiled as he looked at the finished ground-effect vehicle. To the casual eye there was nothing to distinguish it from any of the other similar models that hovered along the city's streets. But appearances were very deceptive, as he knew well from his two hours of hard work. The front end of the small craft was now fortified with a triple layer of steel and alloys, and the interior of the vehicle had been changed to allow room for all of Barclay's electronic improvements.

"I guess we're all ready," he decided. "Reg, is your equipment up and running?"

"Yes, sir," Barclay answered. "Ah, I'll be able to get us in through the compounds force shields without alerting them. And my computers should be able to crack the access codes for the main bridge to the island."

"Excellent." Riker turned to Vanderbeek. "And after we get there?" he asked.

The security officer offered him a hefty pistol. "I've adapted the local police's tranquilizer guns," he explained. "One each." He handed another to Barclay. "I've souped up the tranquilizer stew they use a bit—not too much, but just enough to give us an edge. One touch, anywhere, from these darts will be enough, so you don't need to aim too carefully. On the other hand, the drug takes about two seconds to kick in, so don't wait to see if your victim is shooting back."

"That should be enough of an edge," Riker decided. "And we don't want to be forced to kill any of the locals." He slid the pistol into his waistband. "Well, I guess that's everything we can prepare for. Let's move out." He clambered into the gev's driving seat and pulled the door shut behind him. Barclay climbed in the back, where he sat with his computers. Vanderbeek took the passenger seat, a slight grin on his face.

Riker powered up the vehicle, and felt it rising on its cushion of air. He tapped on the throttle slightly and the gev surged forward. A small map on the panel before him lit to show where they were. Barclay had coded in the path they were to take to Grell's island, so it should be simple to get there. "We're on our way."

Picard turned from the science station to greet his latest visitor. This was D'Nara, the head of the Burani security team that had worked with Worf to raid the Brood's den. The Burani did not look at all happy. "Is everything all right, D'Nara?" asked Picard.

"No, everything is not all right," the officer snapped. "Although your Dr. Crusher insists that I have not been infected by this plague virus, I still can't help feeling terribly unclean. I want to scratch myself clean down to my bones."

"I would be happy to help with that," growled Worf.

D'Nara smiled at this. "I'm sure you would."

Picard raised an eyebrow. Obviously the pair of security officers had bonded in some way. This was evidently their idea of witty conversation. "Well, let's get on with things," he said firmly. "I've spoken to Dr. Crusher, and she assures me that the same plague that is killing your people has affected the Brood. This suggests that they are innocent of complicity in the spread of the disease."

"It is possible, sir," Worf pointed out, "that they have allowed themselves to be infected as a suicide bid to infect the rest of the planet."

"It's possible," agreed Picard, "but not too likely. The Brood wants their policies implemented, and if they kill everyone off they're hardly likely to get what they desire, are they?"

"I agree with your judgment, Captain," D'Nara stated. "The Brood is fanatical, but not suicidal. I do not believe that they are the guilty parties either. The few members of the Brood I have spoken with expressed their belief that *we* had infected them in an effort to eradicate them."

"A logical suspicion," Worf commented. "If somewhat extreme. Would your government risk its own people in order to wipe out a minor trouble spot?"

"Of course not." D'Nara looked shocked at the very thought. "We do not take life so lightly, Worf."

Picard sighed. "Well, if neither the Brood nor the government started this plague, then we're right back at square one. So, about the feorin: Was that the same batch of poison used to kill the Andorians?"

Worf scowled. "Dr. Crusher is running an analysis on a sample right now, sir," he replied. "However, I doubt it."

"So do I," agreed D'Nara. "If the Brood is innocent of the one crime, they are likely to be innocent of the other also. Especially since I was in charge of security for the celebration that the Andorians attended. I *know* that no unauthorized persons attended that feast."

"Which leaves only the authorized ones who could have done the poisoning, then," Picard pointed out.

D'Nara growled. "Yes, I realize that. I am having my men reevaluate the records of everyone who attended the feast in the hope that something will show up."

"Let's hope something does," Picard replied. He turned back to the science station where Data was still absorbed in his search. "How is it going, Mr. Data?"

The android glanced up briefly. "I have found no further caches of feorin," he reported. "I have scanned out to a distance of three hundred kilometers from the palace."

"It's not likely to be any further out than that," D'Nara commented. "Maybe you'd better try again?"

Picard nodded. "An excellent suggestion, D'Nara. Mr. Data, have you tried setting your sweep to look for smaller amounts of feorin?"

Data inclined his head. "Not yet, sir," he replied. Any smaller amount than I have been scanning for would take a lot longer to detect, and the possibility of error would also increase." Nevertheless he bent to reset his equipment.

"Understood," Picard commented. "I shall not expect swift results." His communicator beeped and he slapped it. "Picard here."

"Crusher, Captain," came Beverly's voice. "I've just finished my analysis of the feorin sample that Worf just brought me. There are trace amounts of iridium in it that definitely do not occur in the sample that killed the Andorians. I would definitely say that the Brood did not kill them."

"Thank you, Doctor." Picard frowned as he looked from Worf to D'Nara. "So, it looks as though the Brood is completely innocent in this matter."

"So it would seem," agreed D'Nara.

Picard sighed. "I only wish that we had found something that would help us with this plague, though. We're back to square one."

D'Nara studied him uncomfortably. "Like many of my people, Captain, I was highly suspicious of the Federation's motives at the start of this investigation. Now, however, having worked alongside Worf and having met you and seen what you are doing to help us, I realize that I have sadly misjudged you. I do believe that you are doing your best to aid us."

"That is what we have been trying to tell you all along," Worf growled.

Picard smiled slightly. "Well, it's good to know that you realize we're all working on the same team. Let's just hope that we can be productive together."

There was a sudden beeping from the science station, and Picard whirled to stare at it and Data. "Another trace?" he asked, eagerly.

The android officer looked puzzled. "It is indeed, Captain," he agreed. "But I am not currently scanning for feorin."

Picard frowned and stared at the screen. "What do you mean?"

"I mean that I have simply reset the scanning device," Data answered, his fingers flying across the board. "It is not in search mode."

"A malfunction?" suggested D'Nara.

Data shook his head. "Serendipity," he replied, raising an eyebrow. "The default setting for the scanner is the palace itself, from which I was ordered to begin the scan."

A terrible realization started to dawn on Picard. "Are you saying what I think you are, Data?" he asked.

"Yes, Captain," the android answered. "There *is* another cache of feorin—and it is within the palace itself. Someone in the palace is the poisoner we are seeking."

Chapter Eighteen

RIKER SURVEYED THE BRIDGE ahead of them that led to Grell's private island. It was about a kilometer long and the near end was protected by an electronic gate. Ornate rampant beasts flanked a small computer terminal. The island at the end of the bridge was all but invisible behind thick trees.

"So," he asked Barclay, "do you think you'll have any problems getting us in?"

"Um, I don't think so," Barclay replied. He was working on his portable computer, accessing the guard unit's database. "There aren't any live guards, which helps a lot."

"Why are we bothering with this?" asked Vanderbeek, gesturing toward the bridge. "This is a ground-effect vehicle, after all. Why don't we just buzz across over the water?"

"All the vehicles on this world are gevs," Barclay answered absentmindedly. "As a result, privacy fields tend to compensate for them. There's a particular wave disruptor in the waters. If we tried going across, we'd lose our air cushion and sink."

"Sneaky," Vanderbeek said approvingly, and settled back to watch Barclay at work.

It took him less than two minutes. "Got it," he grinned and tapped the transmit code. There was the slightest of pauses, and then a light winked orange on the stand. "Okay, we're all clear—at this end, at least. I've given the proper access codes, so it won't alert anyone monitoring in the house that we're coming."

"What about cameras?" Vanderbeek asked. "They'll probably have surveillance at work. *I* would."

"Covered," Barclay replied. "I've tapped into their circuits from here, and I'm ordering the system to play a continuous five-minute loop of footage while we cross. Nobody'll see us coming, unless there are live eyes at the other end of the bridge."

"There's bound to be a real person somewhere in all of this," Riker pointed out. "We can fool the security devices for only so long." He started the gev and moved forward onto the bridge.

"That's true," agreed Barclay. "But this should buy us at least the element of surprise. We'll have to deal with any further measures as we come across them." He swallowed. "I—ah—don't anticipate too many problems."

Riker nodded, guiding the gev along the narrow bridge. It barely fit. There wasn't much traffic, obviously, since it was so narrow. Skimming along, he glanced on either side. The waters were choppy and there was no sign of traffic on it, or even birds. The exclusion field was obviously very effective.

As they approached the end of the bridge, Riker slowed slightly. The island was about ten kilometers across, he guessed. Barclay had produced a map, which Vanderbeek now taped over the gev's map screen. According to this, the road from the bridge led straight to the main house. To the south of this was a smaller house by a large in-ground pool. To the west was a separate building for Grell's staff.

"My best guess," Vanderbeek commented, "is that they'd be keeping Wallace in the pool house. The pool's not in use right now, and that's probably not in use either."

"Wouldn't they keep her in the main house?" Barclay objected. "Close at hand?"

"It would be very risky," the security officer answered. "Grell's a prominent businessman and has lots of people constantly visiting him. Keeping a kidnaped alien around is likely to cause trouble. I'll lay odds she's in the pool house."

"We'll try it first," Riker decided. "If she isn't there, then we raid the main house. Okay, on the alert—here's our exit."

They had reached the far end of the bridge and he slowed to a halt beside the next security device. There was a shimmering barrier ahead of them, and another of the stone animal pairs flanking a computer terminal.

Barclay worked over his equipment again and then grinned. "Hmm. There's a different code for this end, and a different sequence, too. Luckily, it's not a problem." His hands flew over the keyboard. "Open sesame!" he chuckled. His smile faded quickly as he noticed his companions' serious expressions.

The barrier dissolved and Riker eased the gev forward and onto the island proper. Behind them the shimmer reappeared. The road forward led through a wide tree-lined way, and there was a road on either side. Riker took the one to the south into a thickly wooded section of the gardens.

"Time to ditch the transport," he said reluctantly. "Someone's bound to spot it if we take it much further." He slid it into a patch of trees, parked facing the road out, ready for a quick getaway should it be needed. "Grab whatever you'll need, and let's head on out." He picked up his own pack and checked the pistol that Vanderbeek had given him. He left the power on in the gev and the door open—just in case. Barclay and Vanderbeek fell in beside him, both with their pistols and packs. "All right," Riker told them, gesturing. "The pool house is this way. Stick close to the trees, and watch out for guards. And dogs. Or whatever the local equivalent is. There are bound to be further security measures. This is one paranoid individual we're dealing with."

The gardens were well tended but they were clearly at the end of the growing season. There was a slight chill in the air. As Vanderbeek had said, the pool wasn't likely to be in use then. That helped them, too, because it meant that the pool room would be empty. As the three men slipped through the neatly trimmed bushes and plants, Riker scanned about constantly.

They had to pause only once when they saw three gardeners at work a distance away. They were not a real problem, however, and Riker led his team across a short exposed stretch of ground while the workers were busy.

It took them ten minutes to reach the pool area, which was nestled among trees and ornamental gardens. In the height of summer it undoubtedly looked extravagantly delightful. At the moment, though, it looked empty. The pool had been drained and the first leaves of fall were drifting across the ground.

The house was a smallish building to one side. The front portion was obviously changing rooms for guests, with lightweight doors. Riker shook his head and led the group around the back where the building was far more solid.

There they encountered their first live guard. Riker gestured for the others to stay back and then moved out into the pathway, falling to one knee, his pistol raised. He fired and heard someone move and then tumble to the ground.

"All clear," Riker murmured, leading the way. The other two men hurried after him. There was a stunned guard sleeping on the ground. A slight cut in his head trickled blood, but otherwise he seemed unharmed. "Inside," said Riker. "I'll check."

He opened the heavy door and glanced swiftly around it. Then he took a longer look. "All clear." He covered them with his pistol while Vanderbeek and Barclay each took an arm of the fallen guard and dragged him inside the door. Then Vanderbeek closed the door behind them.

He wished they could have chanced bringing along a tricorder. It would have been very nice to know if there was anyone else in the building—especially Wallace. The presence of a guard, though, indicated that *something* was being hidden here.

The pool house wasn't large, which made their job a lot easier. There was only a T junction directly ahead of them, leading to a short corridor. Riker chanced a look beyond the corner, and saw no further guards. There were four doors off either side of the corridor.

"Stay here," he told Barclay at the corner. "Watch for anyone else coming." Then he and Vanderbeek started checking the doors. Since it was simply a fifty-fifty chance, Riker chose the left-hand corridor first. The first two doors were the heating unit and a storeroom.

The third was paydirt.

It was locked, and refused to budge when Riker tried it.

Vanderbeek gestured him aside. "There's no need for subtlety, I guess?"

"Not at this stage."

"Good." The security officer braced himself, raised a foot, and then kicked in the door. It whipped open, crashing against the wall, and swung half-shut again.

There was a rough cot in the windowless room beyond, with someone in it who wasn't moving. There was no light in the room, but a foul stench greeted Riker's nostrils as he moved forward.

He could see, even at this distance, that Maria Wallace had not been cooperating with Grell on a voluntary basis. Her skin was broken by bruises and cuts, all left untreated. She was breathing with a rasp that suggested internal injuries, and there were welts on her arms from injections.

He felt cold fury and anger. "That's how they got the access codes to the observation post out of her."

Vanderbeek nodded and bent to examine her. "She's in pretty bad shape," he commented. Riker could hear the pain and anger in his voice, mirroring his own feelings. "Her right hand is broken."

"Can we risk moving her?" Riker asked softly. He bent over her shattered form, wincing in sympathy as he saw her wounds. "God, look at her."

As they spoke, her eyelids fluttered and she gasped. Her eyes opened and she stared up at them dully at first.

"Maria," Riker said, urgently. "Can you go with us?"

She struggled to focus and he could see the pain that this simple action was causing her. What she must have been through . . . then there was a faint look of surprise on her face. "Will?" she asked, her voice feather light. "Is it really you?"

"Yes," he told her, wishing he dared press her hand in reassurance, but knowing it would hurt her if he did. "It's really me. We're here to rescue you."

"Too late for that," she murmured. "I'm dying— thank God. It's been so hard, but it's almost over. They went too far and I'm not going to recover."

"We can get you to help," Riker assured her, hoping that he was telling the truth. "Our shuttle's in orbit, and we can transport you up there pretty soon. They'll be able to patch you up again, never fear."

She didn't bother arguing with him. "I've been such a fool, Will," she gasped. "I should have listened to Starn, but I was so sure I was right."

"That's not important now," Riker replied. He eased a hand under her shoulder and saw her wince with pain. He could feel the roughness of her skin and dried blood wherever he touched her. "Can you walk?"

"No," she answered. "I've lost two toes on my left foot." She gestured downward and Riker saw a flimsy, blood-soaked bandage over that foot. She was right: She'd never be able to walk on that.

"Then I'll have to carry you," he said simply.

"Don't be a fool, Will. One of us in this room is enough. I made such a mistake trying to ignore the Prime Directive."

Vanderbeek met Riker's eye across her shattered body and shook his head slightly. So she was telling the truth: She wouldn't make it out of here. Still he couldn't abandon her. He *had* to try. "Well, you'll know better next time," Riker said lightly.

"I wanted to warn Chal," she continued, ignoring him completely. "That's what I went to do, but there's a traitor. . . . I spoke to the wrong man, the one who worked for Grell. Instead of taking me to warn Chal, he brought me here at gunpoint. They wanted . . . information. I tried not to give it to them, Will, but I couldn't help myself."

"Save your strength," he said gently.

"For what?" she asked, and gasped for breath. "I won't be needing it for much longer. I know they got the security codes from me. Is everything all right?"

"Everything's fine," Riker lied. "We changed the codes. Then we came after you. Now we're going to get you out of here." He slipped the pistol in the front of his tunic so his hands would be free. "I'm going to lift you up," he said. "It's likely to hurt, so steel yourself." She nodded and then he slid his left hand under her shoulders and his right under her knees. The bare tatters of clothing she had left barely concealed her modesty but they couldn't hide her wounds. She winced with pain and gave a sharp intake of breath that made her cough as Riker picked her up, cradling her in his arms. She was terribly light.

Vanderbeek moved on ahead to make sure the door was open. Riker followed, carrying Wallace as gently as he could. She was still breathing harshly and her eyes were screwed shut again. In the corridor they rejoined Barclay. He went white and then red as he saw what had been done to the woman. He swallowed and was about to speak. Riker shook his head. He didn't want her answering any further questions.

The security officer took the lead and stepped over the still-sleeping guard to reach the outer door. Cautiously Vanderbeek opened the door and looked around. Then he nodded back at Riker and led the way outside. Barclay brought up the rear and silently closed the door behind them.

They had walked about five meters before they heard the sound of handguns being cocked.

The other guards were on the roof of the pool house, seven of them. Riker found himself staring into the muzzles of their weapons. From the corner of his eye Riker could see that Vanderbeek looked annoyed and embarrassed, but he wisely made no move with his own pistol.

"Well," said a female voice from behind Riker, "I think you've gone quite far enough for now with that poor girl. Why don't you just put her down?"

Riker turned slowly to scan the woman who was approaching them from around the corner of the house. She was tall and dressed totally in white. Considering the garish tastes the locals usually evinced, that was remarkable in itself. She had long, straight, dark hair, and darker eyes that showed very little of the humor that was in her voice. She gestured to the guards and one of them leaped down from the roof of the pool house. He dragged a lounge chair from a stack and pushed it toward Riker. Realizing he had very little choice in the matter, Riker gently laid Wallace down on it, trying not to wince as she gasped from the pain of her wounds on the cold chair. He straightened up carefully, keeping his hands in view at all times.

"That's better," the woman said. She moved closer, carelessly holding a handgun of her own. "Now, if you'll all just let your weapons and packs down to the ground—*very* slowly, or my men will be forced to shoot you."

Again they had no option but to obey. Riker discarded his pistol with reluctance and stood there watching his opponent through hooded eyes.

"Good," she said happily. "Now we can have a little chat." She glanced at where Wallace lay gasping. "I knew that you'd eventually have to come for your little friend here. Frankly you took a lot longer than I expected to arrive. Trouble with your chemistry set?"

"We weren't sure exactly where she was," Riker answered.

"Oh, dear. Were my little clues too subtle for you, then?" The woman shook her head. "I may have overestimated you aliens. Perhaps you're not quite as bright as Tok seems to think. Still, it's nice having more of you to . . . play with." She nodded towards Wallace's broken body. "I've finished with that one."

"You did that?" Riker asked, feeling his temper and stomach rise.

"Oh, yes," the woman answered. "I do *all* of the real work around here. Tok doesn't have the stomach for it, but he understands the necessity of it."

"I don't." Riker glowered at her.

"You will," the woman promised. "We're going to have several interesting little chats, you and I. There's so much I want to know. Where your spaceship is, for one thing."

"You'll get nothing out of us," Riker informed her coldly.

"Oh, yes, I will," she whispered back. She gestured at Wallace. "She wasn't going to tell me anything at first, either. But she did." She shook her head. "Now what shall I do with her?"

"Let her go," Riker answered. "She's no further use to you."

The woman's eye lit up at this response. "You're

quite right: She isn't." Her eyes went cold, and she pulled the pistol up and fired once.

Riker paled, shock and anger fighting for dominance. "You didn't have to do that," he said coldly.

"On the contrary, I did." The woman stared back at him unblinkingly. "Now you know that I will carry out any threats that I make, without hesitation."

Chapter Nineteen

PICARD STRODE DOWN THE CORRIDOR to the transporter room with Beverly, Worf, Data, and D'Nara accompanying him. The Burani security chief looked alternately stunned, angry, and determined. Picard could imagine what must be going through his mind, knowing that his loyalties had to be in question right now. In fact, his own possible complicity had to be faced.

As they entered the transporter room Picard gestured for Data and Beverly to proceed to the pad, and took Worf and D'Nara aside. This was going to be difficult enough without embarrassing the Burani with further witnesses.

"I am sorry to have to raise the issue," Picard said softly. "But I have no option. Data's information proves that someone within the palace has a cache of feorin. This suggests it is someone with power and authority."

"And you wonder if it might be me?" suggested D'Nara, his eyes hooded.

"The thought had occurred to me," Picard answered.

"And to me," Worf rumbled. He stared at his Burani equivalent. "You, after all, had access to the Andorians, and unquestioned authority. You also came along with me on the raid, ostensibly to keep an eye on me—but perhaps in reality to check that I found nothing useful."

D'Nara sighed and brushed idly at his feathers with one claw. "I expected suspicion on your parts sooner or later," he admitted. "But I can only assure you that I am not the guilty party. I was assigned to watch you, Worf, by Prince J'Kara."

Worf nodded solemnly. "I believe you," he said simply. Turning to Picard, he added, "During the raid, D'Nara stayed with me all of the time. He had the opportunity to plant evidence to frame the Brood, had that ever been his intention."

Nodding, Picard faced the Burani again. "Then that leads me, unfortunately, to a second question I must ask of you. If the guilty person turns out to be someone highly placed in your affairs, what will your response be?"

D'Nara bowed his head a moment and then looked Picard in the eyes. "I would be very ashamed," he confessed. "But I would have to arrest that person, whoever it might be. I may have been appointed to my post, but I take its responsibilities no less lightly for that. I will not be bought off from doing my duty."

Picard nodded. "This may prove to be very difficult for you," he said with sympathy.

"It is already difficult for me," D'Nara confessed. "It is not likely to get any easier. However, I will do whatever is required of me. You may count on that."

"I believe him, Captain," Worf offered. "He is a good officer."

"So do I." Picard gave D'Nara a grim smile. "Well, gentlemen, I think it's time that we went down to the palace for the next phase of the investigation. Prince J'Kara will meet us when we arrive." He led the way to the transporter pad, and as soon as they were ready, gave the order to energize.

They appeared inside the throne room of the Burani palace. This time, it was virtually empty. Only J'Kara and two of D'Nara's men were waiting for them. The room seemed vast and lonely without the courtiers crowding it.

"Jean-Luc," J'Kara said in greeting. "What is happening? D'Nara only said that you have discovered where the feorin is, and to tell no one."

"That is because, painful as it is, the guilty party must be one of the people in the palace." Picard gestured at Data, who stepped forward. "Mr. Data?"

The android showed the instrument to J'Kara. "I have configured this tricorder to scan solely for feorin," he explained. "From orbit, I could determine no more than that the poison is present somewhere within the palace. Once this device is activated we shall be able to determine in which room it is located."

"Within the palace?" J'Kara sounded shocked and

confused. "But . . . who would do such a thing? One of our staff, perhaps?"

D'Nara stepped forward. "That is what these people will help us to determine," he said gently. "And I *must* arrest whoever has possession of the poison, my prince. I am sorry, but that is my duty."

Pulling himself together, J'Kara nodded. "Of course you must." He turned to Data. "Very well—begin your work." He gave a small cough and nodded.

The android officer tapped in the command to his tricorder, which immediately began registering. "Three hundred meters," he announced. "If I may lead the way?" He started off, the rest of the party falling in behind him. Picard noticed that D'Nara and his men had their disruptors drawn. They were indeed taking their jobs seriously.

Beverly fell in beside Picard. "I have something to tell you, too," she murmured. "Once this is over. I think Dr. Margolin and I have tracked down the origin of the plague."

"Excellent work," Picard said warmly. "It looks as though we may be making serious progress at last. But let's see this through first."

Data led them down a corridor and then into a side turning. As with the rest of the palace, the corridors were wide and highly decorated. Vases, paintings, and statues were littered about, but Picard had no time to examine them. He focused on the double doors at the end of the short corridor. Behind him he heard J'Kara give a strangled gasp.

Data halted beside the doors. "The feorin is in the room beyond," he stated.

D'Nara stepped forward, his face strained and his eyes flickering toward the prince. Picard could feel the tension in the air. D'Nara said briefly, "Open it."

His two men moved forward and rapped on the door. Without waiting for a reply they threw open the double doors.

S'Hiri leaped to her feet, shock and fury on her face. "What is the meaning of this?" she exclaimed, glaring at the party. "How *dare* you?"

Ignoring her, D'Nara turned to Data. "Can you specify precisely where it is in this room?" he asked.

Examining the tricorder, Data announced, "Inside that closet." He pointed at a side door. "I cannot be more accurate, I am afraid."

"That will do." D'Nara pushed past S'Hiri and strode toward the closet.

"You have no right to go in there!" she yelled. "That's my personal property." She turned to her fiancé. "J'Kara, stop this immediately!"

"No," he said softly, his voice catching in his throat. "We will see this through to the end."

S'Hiri looked shocked. "What are you doing to me?"

"We shall have to see," J'Kara answered, shame and anger on his face. "D'Nara?"

The security officer had thrown open the closet door. Pushing aside the clothing, he scanned the room. Then he pounced forward and emerged with a makeup tray. On it were several jars presumably containing perfumes or powders. He brought the tray over to S'Hiri's table by the door. Data scanned it with the tricorder.

"That one," he said firmly, pointing to a small jar.

S'Hiri was shaking. It was impossible for her to look pale, of course, since she was feathered, but her shock and fear were apparent. "What are you doing?" she asked, her voice shaking.

D'Nara examined the container. "Feorin," he spat, giving her a disgusted look. "This hardly qualifies as a makeup item."

"I . . . I don't know how that got there," S'Hiri protested. "I've never seen it before."

D'Nara handed the jar to one of his men. "Take that immediately to the laboratory for examination. I have absolutely no doubt that it is the same poison that killed the Andorians, however." The Burani nodded and left at a trot. D'Nara turned back to the shaken woman. "And you are under arrest, my lady, on the charge of murder."

"What?" S'Hiri stared at him, appalled. "You can't be serious."

"I am extremely serious," D'Nara replied. "You have the poison in your possession and you had the best opportunity to use it. At the feast, you were seated with the Andorian guests and had easy access to their meals."

S'Hiri turned to J'Kara. "You can't allow him to *arrest* me!" she cried. "This is a horrible travesty of justice!"

J'Kara looked back at her with pain in his eyes. "I cannot and will not interfere with the course of justice," he said slowly, his voice almost breaking. "Not even for your sake, my dear one. D'Nara has his job to perform for the good of our people. And," he admitted, "I find the evidence against you to be very strong."

She glared at him furiously. "You *believe* this?" Then she pointed at Picard. "It must be all his doing, don't you see? The humans placed the feorin there to be found. They're trying to create a rift between us, for their own ends. They're trying to set us at each other's throats!"

"Why should they do that?" demanded J'Kara. But Picard could see in his face that he desperately wanted to believe that his fiancée was somehow innocent of the crime of which she had been accused. He couldn't blame the prince for that, but he couldn't allow any doubts to remain about the Federation's involvement.

"Perhaps we can help with something else," Picard suggested. He turned to Beverly. "Doctor, you mentioned that you and Dr. Margolin had tracked down the origin of the plague. Would you care to elaborate?"

Beverly nodded, all eyes now on her. "Not exactly the origin of the plague," she admitted, "but we have worked out how it is being spread. With the aid of Dr. L'Tele, we made a computer analysis of the spread of the disease and checked it against other factors, including shipping. It turns out that the plague area is the same as that covered by the shipment of a native grain called tubisin. L'Tele then checked a sample of the grain that was on sale in his local market and discovered that the infection was indeed present inside the grain, where it would lie dormant until ingested."

"Tubisin?" J'Kara's eyes widened and then narrowed as he faced S'Hiri once again. "Your father is one of the largest distributors of tubisin on the planet," he stated flatly. "Is this, too, something that you know nothing about?"

S'Hiri looked bewildered and trapped, but she still shook her head. "It is nothing I know about," she insisted. "It's another of their tricks. It *has* to be. J'Kara, if you love me you must believe me!"

"I wish I could," the prince said with a sigh, and then coughed. "I am desperate to believe you, but I cannot deny the evidence that is mounting up." He slumped a little as he stood before her. "You will have your chance in a court to proclaim your innocence. Until then, I think it will be best if you are locked away."

"Wait," Beverly begged, and stepped forward. "S'Hiri, if you *are* the one who is spreading this plague, then surely you must have an antidote for it! Please, stop this madness and save your own people. Let us have the antidote."

S'Hiri stared at her with steely eyes. "I have nothing to say to you."

"Then say it to me," begged J'Kara. "Do you know of an antidote?"

"I know nothing about any of this," S'Hiri insisted. "If, as they claim, the plague is carried in the tubisin grain, all you have to do is to stop the sale of it." She glared at him coldly. "That will probably ruin my father, of course, but you might as well victimize my entire family while you're at it."

Beverly nodded. "L'Tele is already arranging for the infected grain to be withdrawn," she stated. "That will stop further outbreaks. But the thousands of infected and dying Burani will not be helped by this. They need a cure, not prevention."

"If you're so brilliant," S'Hiri growled, "then *you* come up with a cure."

"We're trying," Beverly told her. "But this plague is a very lethal disease. We can't get to all of the places it infects without a specific treatment, which we haven't found yet."

"How convenient." S'Hiri turned back to J'Kara. "So now you feel even more indebted to the Federation than before?" she asked. "Can't you see how they must be planning all of this to win your trust and affection? They have *found* that the disease is being spread by my father's grain, and thus stopped any more plague cases. Do you feel grateful to them, as they wish?"

"Of course I'm grateful," J'Kara snapped. "They are helping my people, and that is the only thing that is important to me."

"I thought that *I* was important to you," S'Hiri said. "And yet you listen to their word rather than mine."

"I *must,*" he told her. He stared at her, his face riven with pain and shame. "I, too, have the plague." He coughed again.

"What?" S'Hiri stared at him in shock and horror. "No, you can't have!"

Beverly whipped out her medical tricorder and quickly scanned the prince. Her eyes widened. "It's true," she said. "He's in the first stages of the disease."

"No!" S'Hiri cried. "You *can't* be infected. It isn't possible! T'Fara promised me—" And then she broke off, realizing what she had said.

J'Kara grabbed at her shoulders. "T'Fara!" he hissed. "What has my father to do with this?"

Trapped by her own words S'Hiri stared at him, then D'Nara, and finally the *Enterprise* crew. Anger, frustration, and fear showed on her face. Finally she bowed her head, realizing that she had been outmaneuvered. "Your father," she said slowly, "was the one who came up with this plan. He is the one who approached me with it. I did what I did at his behest. Perhaps you had better speak with him now."

J'Kara threw back his head and howled in betrayal and agony.

Chapter Twenty

RIKER GLARED AT THE KILLER before him and then at Barclay, who was licking his lips nervously following her threat. "All right," he said tightly. "What do you want from us?" He gestured at Wallace's dead body. "She was a trap, wasn't she?"

"Yes." The woman smiled cheerily. "But I'm forgetting my manners, aren't I? Let's go on inside, and we can continue this discussion in pleasanter surroundings." She gestured to the guards, who jumped down off the low roof, handguns constantly trained on the away team. Then she led the way past the pool and up toward the main house.

Riker nodded tightly to Barclay and Vanderbeek, who fell in behind him. They had no choice but to do whatever this woman wanted right now, and look for an opportunity to turn the tables on her. The walk was short, through more of the well-tended gardens. The main house was large and very impressive as befitted an industrial tycoon of Grell's stature. It was only two stories tall but sprawled on both wings. There had to be at least sixty rooms in a building that size, Riker estimated. As they drew closer he saw that steps led down into a basement area, and revised his estimate up to about a hundred. The woman led them through the front doors, which were opened by uniformed flunkies who didn't bat an eyelid at the sight of so many weapons, or the three prisoners. Riker had to wonder how many times they had seen a scene like this before.

The hallway they entered showed garishly bad taste. Statues, furniture, paintings, and light fixtures appeared to have been chosen for their value, not their style, and much of the decor clashed horribly. The woman led them into a side room, and her men closed the doors behind them. Less than subtly, they moved to cover every exit from the room, their handguns constantly held ready for use.

There were several comfortable-looking lounges in the room, as well as three high-backed chairs. The woman took one of the latter and gestured for Riker, Barclay, and Vanderbeek to take three of the former.

"I'd rather stand," Riker said.

The woman's eyes narrowed. "And I'd prefer for you to sit," she said gently. "And I *always* get my way."

Riker sat, and the others hastily followed his lead.

"That's better." The woman smiled again. "Isn't this much nicer?" she asked. "Could I get you a drink, perhaps? You've had a busy morning, after all."

"I'd sooner you get to the point of all this," Riker snapped.

"My." Her eyes opened slightly wider. "Aren't you the impatient one? Well, so be it. As you so cleverly surmised just a little too late, this was indeed a trap. Maria Wallace was quite cooperative—after we pumped her full of drugs, of course. I was quite intrigued with what she told me. When Tok first . . . obtained her, we thought she was merely some busybody who had happened to stumble on our plans for the First Citizen, but it soon became apparent that she was much, much more than that." Her eyes sparkled. "Oh, but there I go again, forgetting my manners. We haven't been properly introduced, have we? My name is Toma Sar, and I'm Tok Grell's personal assistant. But I didn't catch your name."

"I didn't give it."

Toma sighed theatrically. "Do we *have* to start getting unpleasant after such a short acquaintance? Either tell me your names—your *real* ones, of course—or else I shall be forced to do something unpleasant." Her eyes lit on Barclay.

Barclay paled and looked to Riker. "I'm completely impervious to pain," he said unconvincingly.

"Really?"

"Well, not my own, of course," Barclay admitted.

This amused Toma, and she laughed briefly. Then she looked at Riker once again. "Well?"

"I'm William Riker," he replied, knowing that it wasn't worth fighting her yet. She already knew that they were aliens, so telling her their names couldn't hurt further. "This is Barclay and Vanderbeek."

"Charmed," Toma murmured. "See? Isn't this a

much nicer way to do business, Riker? Now, where was I? Oh, yes. Wallace was a trifle reluctant to open up at first, but she finally decided to be quite chatty. She told us all about herself and her mission on this world. You are from an organization known as the Federation of Planets. That's a kind of banding together of worlds for mutual protection and profit, am I right?"

"Roughly."

"Good. One of the things that you do is to evaluate interesting worlds, to see if they are ready to join your little cartel. Then you set up observation posts to evaluate the lucky planets and make a decision. Again correct?"

"Yes," Riker admitted.

"And it's the turn of our small planet." Toma looked thoughtful. "Wallace thought we might be ready for membership shortly, but one of the requirements for membership is a unified planetary government—one of our First Citizen's idealistic dreams. Wallace discovered Grell's plan to assassinate Chal and then decided that she had to stop it from happening." She frowned slightly. "The next part is the thing I don't quite understand. She seemed to think she would be in trouble for this rather altruistic gesture. Perhaps you could explain this to me?"

Riker considered the point. If she knew this much, a little more wouldn't hurt. It would at least buy them some time. "We have a very strict policy that we call our Prime Directive," he told her. "This forbids us from interfering with the normal running of any planetary societies, and especially those who don't know of our existence. Wallace should not have tried to stop the assassination."

"Ah!" Toma looked pleased. "Let the filthy little primitives do whatever they like to one another, is that it?"

"No. It's simply that if we interfere in any society without knowing all of the factors and all of the risks involved, good intentions aren't enough. Inconceivable damage might be the result of such a rash action." He gestured at the armed guards. "This is a case in point. Wallace's intentions were good, but the result of her interference is to create a rather unpleasant problem for me."

"I shouldn't let that worry you, Riker," Toma murmured. "I'm sure I'll be able to help you out."

Riker's eyes narrowed. "In what way?"

"Patience, my dear fellow, patience." She smiled again. "So, once I had these snippets of information from Wallace, I saw that our plans could be substantially altered by this new intelligence. Tok's ambition is, of course, to make lots of money and to hold as much power as he can. He doesn't have the presence or the ability to speak in public, so he has no chance of becoming a politician. He's not subtle enough, I'm afraid."

"So he buys the politicians he wants?" Riker supplied. "Like Brak Norin?"

"My, aren't you well informed?" purred Toma. "Yes, indeed. But Norin doesn't have a chance of becoming First Citizen while Farra Chal is alive. Chal is *very* charismatic. He also has some dangerous ideas, like planetary unity, which would cut into poor Tok's profits."

"No wars, no weapons, no cash flow," Riker said.

"You *do* grasp things very quickly," Toma said appreciatively. "That's exactly right. Since Chal refuses to listen to reason and change his policies, I'm afraid the only way to stop him is to kill him. We were simply going to have him assassinated, as Wallace discovered, but her inadvertent aid has made the game much more interesting."

"The charge of conspiring with aliens."

"Precisely." Toma waved her hand again. "Tok had his heart set on killing Chal, so I evolved the plan to do this. The trouble was that it really wasn't very elegant. Simply having him murdered would leave him a martyr, and who knows who might be able to take up his mantle? But if we can discredit him first and then murder him before he can reply to the charges, he'll not be a martyr but a disgrace that even his former supporters would want to forget. That is a so much better solution to the problem, don't you think?"

"I can see that it would have its appeal for you," Riker agreed. "So you come up with this silly charge that he's working with aliens against his own planet."

"Exactly. Not only does that discredit him, but it also gives us a vast new market to exploit." She smiled dreamily. "I can envisage our being able to convince the Citizen's House that we need to protect our world against alien invaders. That will mean defensive satellites, missiles, laser emplacements, even, on a few of our moons. Lots and lots of lovely profits."

Riker glared at her. "You know full well we're of no threat to you."

"Well, yes," Toma drawled. "*I* know that, and *you*

215

know that, but nobody else on our planet does. When we reveal all that we know, there will be such delightful panic that anything we want will be granted us. Especially if Norin is in power by then."

"And the raid on the observation post?" asked Riker coldly. "What was the reason for that carnage?"

"There were several, actually." Toma didn't appear at all bothered by talk about the death and suffering of which she'd been the architect. "First of all, to obtain that . . . Vulcan, isn't it? Wallace had made it clear that he was in charge of your base on this planet, so he was the logical one to interrogate. Second, Wallace was by that time in no real position to use as a witness against Chal. She was already far too damaged to be credible. And third, she wasn't alien enough for my purposes. Oh, there was the missing rib, of course, and a few other internal differences, but she was too close to normal for what I wanted. A green-blooded, pointy-eared alien is *much* better."

And one you'll hopefully never get the chance to use, thought Riker, hoping that Deanna had managed her part of the mission better than he was doing right now. "Then why did you kill him?" he demanded.

"It was an accident," Toma said simply. "He had an amazing tolerance for pain."

"Vulcans tend to be like that," Riker informed her coldly. "They have a greater control over their pain centers than other people do."

"Ah. I shall have to remember that next time."

Riker glared at her, amazed at her viciousness.

"You're sick," he informed her.

She shrugged. "By your standards, I probably am," she agreed lightly.

There was a slight noise and then the door opened. Riker glanced around, and saw a tall flashily dressed Iomidian male walk in. He looked inordinately pleased with himself and raised an eyebrow when he saw the gathering.

"My dear," he murmured, "I had no idea that you were entertaining." He moved to look down at Riker. "And who are these charming people?"

"They're Wallace's friends, Tok, dear," Toma replied.

Grell scowled at the news. *"More* aliens?" he growled. "What do you want more of them for? It will only cause trouble."

"Don't be so worried, Tok," Toma said. "I'm going to look after these three very well."

The financier glowered at her. "Toma, I know full well what *that* means. You've already killed far too many of these aliens. They're obviously very advanced. What will we do if they decide to punish us for what you've done?"

"Ever the worrier," purred Toma. "Well, don't fret. They have this delightful moral rule which forbids them to interfere with alien civilizations. And, unless I miss my guess, that means that they can't punish us for what we've done. That would be interfering. So the worst they can do is to simply pack up and go home again. Isn't that right, Riker?"

Riker didn't reply. If Grell was worried, the best thing to do was to make him worry further. If he and Toma could be set at each other's throats, that would be a great help. It might provide an opportunity to escape and turn the tables on her.

"If their own people consider them all expendable,

then I don't see that we have a problem with that. Do you?"

"Perhaps not," Grell agreed. "But we need only one of them alive to discredit Chal." He glanced at Riker. "Can we get him to say what we want?"

Toma shrugged. "I'm sure we can. He seems to be in charge here, and he is concerned for these two men. He will have to talk to save them."

"If I did that," Riker said slowly, "it would be interfering with your planetary development. Our Prime Directive expressly forbids it."

"I'm sure it must," Toma agreed. "Then we shall have to test your dedication to this Prime Directive." She turned back to Grell. "Is there anything else you'd like from them, my dear?"

Grell considered and then said slowly, "I don't recall Wallace mentioning a Riker as a member of her observation team."

Laughing, Toma clapped her hands. "Tok, you're *so* perceptive. You're right—she didn't. Nor did she mention a . . . Barclay, wasn't it? And whatever your friend's name was. You three aren't a part of her team, are you? You're *fresh* aliens!" She snapped her fingers. "Specialists. Troubleshooters." She laughed again. "And not very good at it, either. Certainly not as good as I am."

Something came to Riker then. "Which of you is in charge here?" he asked carefully. "I'd heard that it was supposed to be Grell, and you even told me that you were just his personal assistant."

"She is," Grell growled firmly.

Riker could see the anger in Toma's eyes, and now knew he had hit a raw nerve—one that might bear a little working over. "Women and men are equal where I come from."

"Really?" Grell shook his head. "Yet I notice that all three of you are male—or, at least, you look to be. If women are your equals, why are there no women in your party?" That was one question Riker dared not answer. If they found out about Deanna and Kessler, there might still be time for Grell to stop them. The industrialist took Riker's silence for acquiescence. "See, Toma, my dear? Even on alien worlds, men are in charge."

"They shouldn't be," she snapped. "You know full well that without my brains you'd never be more than half the man you are today. This whole scheme was *mine.*"

Grell abruptly backhanded her, sending Toma spinning against a chair. Her eyes were flames, but Grell didn't seem to care. "I am in charge here," he said coldly. "Which is as it should and will always be. If you don't like that, you're welcome to leave." He gave her a cold smile. *"Permanently."*

This was what Riker had been hoping for—dissension in the ranks of their enemies. With a little good fortune, this flame of anger could be fanned into a blaze. "That's right Grell, keep her in her place," he suggested.

Grell whirled around to face him. "Don't get any bright ideas, alien," he warned. "Or I promise you I'll let her loose on you." Then his false smile returned. "It must almost be time," he announced. He pulled a small device from his pocket and clicked it at a blank spot on one wall.

The whitewashed wall dissolved and a picture

formed upon it. Riker realized that there had to be some sort of built-in video monitor there, some two meters across. The large picture was silent for the moment, but it showed the Citizen's House surrounded by a crowd of people.

"You're very fortunate to be here right now, aliens," Grell informed them. Behind him Toma rose to her feet again. She seemed unusually subdued for the moment.

"And why is that?" asked Riker.

Grell gestured at the screen. "Because you're about to witness my rise to ultimate power on this planet," he replied. "You have ringside seats to watch the assassination of Farra Chal. In about . . ." He examined a timepiece from his pocket. ". . . ten units of time." He smiled. "I hope you'll find it as interesting as I shall."

Chapter Twenty-one

TORMAK MOVED TO THE EDGE of the roof and glanced down. The side exit from the Citizen's House was a welcome sight to him. He'd been assured that it would be, but he had survived this long as a soldier only by trusting no one but himself. He hadn't dared come up here before, though; he didn't want anyone remembering his face. As it was, nobody was likely to recall a vidscreen repairman on a day like this . . .

It hadn't been difficult to cause a problem in the vidscreen receptors in this apartment building, and no one was likely to find the body of the real repairman until much later in the week. Tormak had hidden it well. He set down the box of tools he'd obtained with the repair gev on the flat roof, and hummed softly to himself as he went to work. He was wearing gloves so that even when the tool kit was found, the police would get nothing from it. There were still eight units left until Chal was due to emerge from this supposedly secure side door.

Removing the top layer of tools from the kit, Tormak uncovered the bundle he'd slipped inside. It was in oilskin cloth, and he laid it gently on a nearby vent before unwrapping it.

Within lay the parts of his high-powered rifle. He snapped on the stock first and then checked that the firing mechanism was clear and working perfectly each time. It wouldn't do to have it jam on him at the crucial moment. When he was satisfied, he fitted the telescopic sight and then laid the rifle aside for a moment. He assembled the small wide-based tripod and placed it in position. Then he attached the rifle to the tripod and checked that it could still move unimpeded. He should need only a single shot, but he had to be prepared for several. Things didn't always run as smoothly as planned.

Finally he took the small case of bullets from the tool kit. He removed six of the crosscut bullets and fed them into the rifle one at a time. They would mushroom on impact and then splinter, so that even a shot that would normally just graze its victim would become very serious indeed. Tormak was determined that Chal not survive.

Then, happy that everything was in order, he glanced at his chrono again.

Four units left . . .

He lay on his side beside the rifle and propped it firmly against his shoulder. He moved about a little until he felt comfortable, and then smiled in anticipation. Everything he could do was accomplished. Now if only Chal would come walking out of that door. . . . He aimed through the sights and had a perfect view.

After the job was done, it would be a while before the security force investigated this roof, and by then he'd be a long way away. The rifle would tell them very little except that it wasn't from one of Grell's factories. Tormak had carefully bought one of Grell's rival's pieces for this job. No trail for any suspicious investigators to follow there.

Three more units, and then a slight squeeze on the trigger . . .

"Come on, *move it!*" Haron yelled. Why was it that security details always seemed to be running behind. It seemed that no matter how much he planned, something always got screwed up.

Like Madame Chal suddenly realizing she'd left her makeup pouch in the ladies' room.

Haron had ordered one of his men to go and get it before he realized what he'd said. Then he'd had to call the man back and send one of the woman staffers after it. Madame Chal had wanted to go, but Haron didn't want to risk any further problems and had insisted that she stay with her husband who was heading for the side door.

He didn't like using that door, but it had been Brak's suggestion to avoid the media interviewers, and First Citizen Chal had liked that part. Haron knew how sick the First Citizen was of having cameras and tapers shoved in his face, so he supposed it made some sense.

The problem was that Haron hadn't had a chance to check the route out for any hazards, and that disturbed him. He'd tried to convince Chal to go the usual route, through the main entrance, but Chal had refused to do this.

"No more damned interviewers," he growled. "I've had more than enough of them, and I'm going to be stuck with even more before the day is through. I just want to get out of here without something flashing in my eyes, Haron."

"The side door," agreed Haron with a sigh. He'd managed to send one team out ahead, though, to check the route to the transport. So far, they had no problems to report, but Haron wasn't willing to believe that there wouldn't be any.

The corridor leading to the door was crowded. His men were still surrounding the First Citizen, keeping the representatives away from Chal. Everyone wanted to ask him about this damned stupid alien invasion scare that Norin had thrown out. Couldn't they all see that it was no more than a rather foolish political ploy? Admittedly Haron couldn't see any reason behind such a dumb accusation, but he wasn't a politician, just a security officer doing his duty. You could never tell what was going on in a politician's mind. He strongly suspected that the answer was "very little."

The woman he'd sent for the makeup pouch pushed her way through the crowd, aided by the burly officer Haron had designated to accompany her. She handed the pouch to a grateful Madame Chal, and the group started to move again.

Just a few more units of this nerve-wracking corridor, and then they'd be outside heading for the armor-plated transport. Until Chal was safely inside it, Haron wouldn't be happy.

Just a few more units . . .

"Just a few more units," breathed Grell, staring raptly at the wall screen. "It's just a shame that the cameras won't catch this live."

Toma licked her lips in anticipation. "A pity."

"I'm sure it will be rerun, my dear," Grell assured her. "All hell is going to break loose there in just a couple of units. This is going to be the happiest day of my life."

Riker stared at them both with revulsion. There was nothing that he could do to stop this, even if the Prime Directive didn't forbid him to interfere. While they were occupied with the screen might be his best chance to do something to win their freedom. Carefully he started to edge toward Toma. If he could jump her and get the gun she held, then maybe . . .

He felt something cold and hard at the side of his neck.

"Going somewhere?" asked one of the guards. They were on the alert, obviously.

"Just stretching my legs," Riker murmured. "I'm getting a little cramp."

"Endure it," the guard answered unsympathetically. "Or you'll get a little dead. Understand me?"

"Yes," Riker replied. "I understand you."

"Good." The metal was removed.

"Watch the show, Riker," Toma said without turning. "You don't want to miss the good part, do you?"

Disgusted, Riker returned his eyes to the screen

showing the main entrance to the Citizen's House. It wasn't going to be very much longer. . . .

Deanna shook her hair free and smiled at the security guard who'd carefully allowed them back into the observation post. As the main entrance closed behind her and Kessler, Saren strode into the room.

"Did all go well?" he asked.

"Perfectly," Deanna replied. "We destroyed Starn's body. There won't be any autopsy."

Saren nodded solemnly.

"Any word from Commander Riker yet?" she asked as they followed him into the corridor.

"No." Saren bowed his head slightly. "But I am not surprised. He did have a difficult mission. The First Citizen is leaving the House for a short rest break. The autopsy is due to start shortly, and he will have to be prepared to face his accusers this evening."

"Oh. It's still pretty quiet, then." Deanna didn't give the screen a second glance. Nothing important was happening. "Time for a quick snack while we wait for Will, then." She frowned slightly. "I hope nothing's happened to slow him down."

Kessler gave her a reassuring smile. "The commander's pretty fast on his feet," she said. "I wouldn't start worrying about him yet."

"All right," agreed Deanna, heading for the replicator. "Let me know when I should start worrying, okay?" She frowned. "I wonder if this thing's programmed for chocolate ice cream with hot fudge?"

* * *

On the roof Tormak watched the scene below through his sights. The First Citizen's transport was in position close to the door. He smiled in approval. The head of security was doing a nice job under the circumstances. Chal would be exposed for only about five seconds as he moved from the door to the transport. There were bodyguards scanning the area down there, but Tormak knew they'd never spot him before he fired. Nothing could go wrong now—as long as the First Citizen came out of that door, as was the arrangement.

He felt a thrill of anticipation as he held his finger lightly on the trigger. This was the part of the job he loved—the single act that fulfilled his task. It wasn't the killing that he enjoyed so much; the thrill was in the sense of accomplishment. Finishing the job and knowing that no one else alive could have done what he had done. Grell had entrusted *him* with the raid on the alien base, not Toma. She would have wasted time butchering innocent bystanders instead of getting the alien chief and retreating. But Tormak would kill Chal swiftly and efficiently with his first shot. The job would be done, neatly, tidily, and swiftly.

The door opened.

Steadying himself, Tormak increased the pressure of his finger on the trigger slightly, ready for his victim. He wouldn't be the first one out, of course. As Tormak expected, one of the bodyguards emerged, glancing around and then confirming with the others by the transport that everything was fine. The man turned back and called something through the door.

Two more guards emerged, handguns at the ready, eyes scanning around.

And then . . .

Chal stepped through the door, partially shielded by Haron, the head of security. Haron was willing to take any shot that might be aimed at Chal. It showed wonderful devotion, either to his job or to his boss.

But it wasn't enough to guard against Tormak. As the two men moved together, Tormak had a momentarily clear view of the First Citizen's heart.

His finger pulsed and the rifle spat.

In the sights, Tormak saw Chal's chest explode as the bullet ripped into it. The First Citizen was dead already, before he could even start to fall, but Tormak fired a second shot that blew out his brains as well, just to be absolutely certain.

Then he abandoned the rifle, slid backward from the edge of the roof, and then sprinted for the doorway down. Without a backward glance he hurried down the steps toward freedom and anonymity on the streets. Behind him, he heard the wail of sirens and screams of shock and anguish.

A job well done.

Chapter Twenty-two

WHAT WAS NEEDED NOW was a firm hand. Picard stepped forward and said gently but clearly, "Enough, J'Kara." The even control in his voice reached through the prince's numbing grief, and he clamped his beak shut. "We all sympathize with you," Picard continued, "but this is not the time."

J'Kara struggled with his raw emotions and finally managed to shake his head. "No," he said hard and gasping. "I must be strong. You are quite correct, Jean-Luc." He took a deep breath and then glared at his fiancée. "We must confront my father. You will come with us and repeat what you have accused him of doing." S'Hiri was obviously going to refuse, but subsided when she saw the cold gleam in J'Kara's eyes. The prince then turned to D'Nara. "This is likely to become problematic. You are theoretically bound to serve my father. Will this impede you?"

The security officer shook his head slightly. "I serve the *people,*" he stressed. "Though your father selected me for this job, I cannot allow that to influence my duty." There was a rumble of approval from Worf at this comment.

"Good." J'Kara turned back to Picard. "Jean-Luc, this is a very painful and embarrassing time for me. That my fiancée should have killed your colleagues is abominable to me. That my father may have killed my people is beyond my expressing."

"Do you wish to confront him alone?" asked Picard gently.

"No." J'Kara took a deep breath and steeled himself. "You and your people have been blamed for this plague—and by no one more vociferously than my father. You have a right to be there to clear your good name. Besides which, without the help of you and your staff, this may never have come to light."

"Thank you," Picard replied. "I confess I would like to hear some explanations for all of these terrible actions."

"So should I," J'Kara said grimly. "So should I." He turned to S'Hiri again. "First of all, from you. How *could* you have done these things? I thought I knew you better than anyone, and yet you have betrayed everything I have ever believed in."

"Everything *you* believed in, yes!" she cried furiously. "But not what *I* believed in. J'Kara, I believed in you, and I did this for you. It is your birthright to rule Iomides, and I aim to see that this is what you do. You never could see this. You wanted to give away your power—first to the rest of the planet with this ridiculous democratic ideal of yours. And then when you accepted these Federation aliens and wanted to allow them to rule over us, too—that was the final straw. You had to be protected from yourself. The only way out for me was to ensure that the Federation was discredited and removed from Iomides. *That* is why I murdered those Andorians—for *you.*"

While J'Kara was floundering for words, Picard stepped forward. "The Federation does not and will not rule your world, S'Hiri," he informed her. "We do not interfere with internal matters on any planet, unless it affects the rest. We are here to help, not to conquer."

"So you say," she spat. "But I see you here, and your officers, accusing us of these deeds."

"Which you have confessed you have in fact performed," Data observed. "We have accused you only of what you have done."

S'Hiri glared at him. "I have done what I have done for the greater good of my people, and for the sake of the person I love. If that is a crime then I will pay for it."

"*If* it is a crime?" echoed J'Kara. He shook his head. "S'Hiri, you have killed a shipful of Andorians, and you have helped to murder thousands of your own people, and you say that *if* it is a crime, you will pay?" He gave a strangled cry. "I was wrong: I do not know you at all. These are not the actions of the woman I thought I loved. These are the works of a degenerate mind." He turned to D'Nara. "That is enough here. She will accompany us to confront my father. You may need to call further guards for what

231

must follow." D'Nara bowed and hurried off to speak with one of his men. The prince turned to the others in the room. "Come. We shall speak with my father now, and finish this affair."

He swept from the room, the others falling in behind him. Beverly hurried to catch up with him.

"J'Kara," she asked, "how *did* you contract the plague? I assume that the palace has a separate food supply, and the contaminated grain isn't eaten here. That is why no one in the palace has come down with the disease."

"You are correct, Doctor," he agreed, not pausing in his grim strides. "The palace has its own farmland, and all the food for the palace is raised there. However, I have been deliberately eating the contaminated grain."

Beverly narrowed her eyes. "You *knew* it was infected?" she asked, shocked.

"Not knew, suspected. And only very recently," he confessed. "Now my belief has been confirmed."

"But *why?*"

He stared at her. "Because the tubisin grain is produced by S'Hiri's father. I thought *he* was the one behind the plague, for whatever reasons he may have had. I suspect he is definitely involved in the plot. The grain could not have been infected without his knowledge. I, too, had realized that the grain and the plague areas seemed to overlap."

"But why deliberately infect yourself just to test the theory?" persisted Beverly.

"I have my reasons," J'Kara answered. "You will learn them in a while, I promise you. One, though, was to keep the accusations I intended to make against S'Hiri's father as private as possible. I did not want his shame to reflect badly on her." He made a sour face. "And now, it would appear that it was the other way around. She has the far greater shame. I was a fool for not seeing this earlier."

"You love her," Beverly replied. "It's always hard to imagine someone whom you love could be guilty of anything at all—let alone murder on such a scale."

"You try to excuse my blindness," the prince murmured. "But I have been a fool many times over. Now I must make up for my failure."

"Listen to her, J'Kara," Picard urged him. "This is not your fault."

"My father and my fiancée have conspired together, and I have not seen this. How can it be anything *but* my fault? They played me for a fool," J'Kara said bitterly. "And I played that role well, didn't I? Well, no more." They had reached the door to the king's quarters. The lone retainer on duty stared at them in bewilderment. "Stand aside," J'Kara ordered.

"But . . ." the official spluttered. "What is the meaning of this? I can't simply . . ."

"You will step aside now," J'Kara informed him. "Or I shall have you arrested for interfering with police business. Make up your mind, because we are going inside whether you stand aside or not." The retainer bleated and dashed for cover. "A wise decision." J'Kara stepped forward, thundered a fist on the door, and then threw the door open.

The party moved into the small anteroom, crowding it seriously. The door at the far end leading to the king's bedroom opened, and T'Fara stepped out. His eyes narrowed as he saw the size of the group awaiting him.

"What's this all about, my son?" he asked innocently. "I would prefer it if you didn't bring those aliens into my private quarters. I know that you trust them, but I cannot afford to as yet."

"You have more important things to concern yourself with, Father," the prince replied coldly. "You have been accused of spreading the plague that is slaughtering our people."

T'Fara stood straighter and glared back at him. "And who accuses me of this?" he demanded.

J'Kara gestured to his fiancée. "She does—before witnesses."

"These aliens?" T'Fara snorted. "They are not witnesses under our law."

"No," agreed J'Kara. "But I am, and so is D'Nara. And your response is all I needed to tell me that her accusation is true. You *have* been murdering our people for your own selfish ends."

The king stared at him a moment and then looked at S'Hiri. She didn't meet his gaze, but stared at the richly patterned carpet. "So," he said slowly. "You *did* accuse me."

"They tricked it out of me," she replied in an almost inaudible voice.

The king turned away from S'Hiri in disgust. "J'Kara, you must understand that I have done this for your sake," he said in a measured voice.

"My sake?" J'Kara repeated. He shook his head. "That is her claim, too. Do both of you think me so feebleminded that you have to arrange my life for me?"

"Yes," T'Fara snarled. "That is precisely what I think. I think you have temporarily lost your mind over these alien interlopers. With them gone I was certain you would once again become the son I know and love. The one who will succeed me as the next king."

"And that is why you spread this disease?" J'Kara asked, anguish in every syllable. "You murdered your own people who trusted and loved you, simply to get rid of the Federation?"

"They didn't love me or trust me," T'Fara snapped back. "They went against my wishes when they voted for union with the Federation. I warned them that the gods would be angry, and that they would pay for rejecting my advice. But they ignored me and went ahead with joining this Federation."

"So you decided that you would be the instrument of your gods and make certain that they paid for their crimes against you," suggested Data.

"Yes," agreed the king. "And they *have* paid. And they will continue to pay until they throw the Federation off Buran and restore the power to where it belongs—my son!"

"Intriguing," Data murmured. "Revenge under the guise of restoration. It is quite unique—and extremely aberrant."

"It's disgusting!" J'Kara yelled. "I am so sickened and dishonored by what you have done, my father."

"I have done all of this for you," T'Fara insisted. "Our people need a strong hand to guide them."

"*Your* strong hand has *poisoned* them!" J'Kara exclaimed. "When you became their king you vowed to protect them and their nestlings. Instead you have deliberately murdered them."

"I *am* protecting them," insisted the king. "They made a foolish decision to join the Federation. If I had allowed that decision to stand, it would have ruined many more lives than the plague has. Can you not see how vital it is that we force the people to rethink their decision?"

"No," answered J'Kara. "I am more convinced than ever that they made the right decision. The Federation is doing nothing but helping them. You are the one who has poisoned them. The people are far better off without a king like you. I am ashamed to be your son."

D'Nara stepped forward. "Dr. L'Tele has already given instructions for the contaminated grain shipments to be halted. There will be no further spread of the disease, at least. S'Hiri's father is being sought and will be placed under arrest." He glared at his king. "My next, distasteful duty is to arrest you."

"*Me?*" T'Fara stared back at him in shock. "On whose authority? I *made* you what you are!"

"No," D'Nara said firmly. "You appointed me, but the power of my office is invested in the trust of the people and no longer in your whim. That is one advantage of the power of democracy. No one—not even the king—is above the power of the law. You are under arrest for the crime of murder. Several thousand individual charges will be brought against you, and against S'Hiri and her father also."

T'Fara stared at his officer in astonishment and then rounded on his son. "Are you going to simply stand there and let him do this?" he demanded.

"No," replied J'Kara. "I am going to stand here and *insist* that he do it. Father—and you cannot understand how ashamed I am that you *are* my father—you have committed the worst and most vile crimes I have ever heard. You will be punished for them, of that I swear. I shall not go to my grave before you are punished for your despicable actions."

"No!" exclaimed S'Hiri. "You will not die, my love."

"Die?" T'Fara stared at her in confusion. "What are you talking about now?"

She turned to the king. "J'Kara has deliberately infected himself with the plague. That is why they were able to trick me into implicating you. You promised me before we began that J'Kara would not be harmed."

For the first time, a genuine emotion other than anger seemed to possess T'Fara. He stared from S'Hiri to his stricken son in concern. J'Kara simply nodded, confirming the news. There was a long pause while T'Fara obviously struggled to accept what he had been told. Then his eyes hardened. "It's hardly my fault that the idiot deliberately infected himself, is it? What are you blaming me for?"

"Well," muttered Beverly to nobody in particular. "That shows just how much he really loves his son, doesn't it?"

"I don't care how or why it happened," S'Hiri snapped back at the king. "I love him."

"He doesn't love you," T'Fara said bitterly. "Not anymore. Nor me, either, I'll wager. Why should you care what happens to him?"

"Because I still love him, come what may," she replied. "All that I have done I have done for his sake. I will not see him die. Give him the antidote."

Beverly gasped. "You have an *antidote* for this plague?"

"Of course I do, you fool," the King snapped. "I was aiming on producing it after the Federation had been thrown off of Buran. I had no intention of killing all of my people—just enough to free our world from your influence. And to punish them for what they have done. Then I would have cured them."

"Then, for the sake of your people, hand it over!" Picard urged him. "We have to start replicating it and distributing it immediately."

"No," T'Fara said firmly. "I am the only one who knows what the cure is. The scientist who accidentally created the plague came to me in guilt and horror at what he had done. He wished to destroy it, but I saw a use for it. He also created the cure. He told no one about this creation and I told only S'Hiri. The inventor then killed himself from remorse."

Beverly stared at him in disgust. "You'd allow your people to continue to die, even though you could save them?" she asked, shocked. "You're insane."

"No," T'Fara replied thoughtfully. "I am in a position of power here. I have the cure; you need it." He smiled at his son. "I think it is time to negotiate, don't you?"

"No," J'Kara replied.

"What is it you want?" asked Picard quickly.

"A pardon, first of all," T'Fara said, eyeing D'Nara with contempt. "I will not be placed under arrest like some common criminal."

"There is nothing common about your crime," growled Worf menacingly. He stepped forward slightly. "Allow me to converse with him," he suggested to J'Kara. "I guarantee that I will make him tell us where the cure is." He raised one huge fist. "I can be very . . . persuasive."

"No," J'Kara said, smiling slightly at Worf's intensity. "There is no need for that." He turned to his father again. "The cure must be in your rooms somewhere. You would not allow it out of your sight—or grasp. We will simply take your rooms apart. We will rip the artwork to shreds if we must, and reduce the rooms to dust, but we will find the cure." He turned to Beverly. "I am sure that you will be able to recognize it when we find it, won't you, Doctor?"

"Yes," Beverly agreed. "I know a rough form it would have to take."

"We would not need to destroy anything," Data offered. "I could simply run a tricorder scan of the rooms and search out anything that is medicinal in nature."

J'Kara turned back to his father. "So, you see, Father," he said, with some measure of satisfaction, "the Federation that you so despise will reveal your secrets eventually. Why not simply tell us now where the cure is?"

"No," T'Fara said stubbornly. "I will not aid you in any way. Find the cure if you can. I shall have nothing more to do with it. And nothing more to say to you.

As far as I am concerned, you are no longer my son. You do not exist."

"I wish that I were not your son," J'Kara replied. "However, that is a luxury denied to me. Very well, D'Nara. Take my father and S'Hiri into confinement to await trial." He deliberately turned his back on the two people he had loved more than any others. To Picard he said, "You have my leave to begin the search of these rooms, Captain. I pray you will be successful—and swift." There were tears in his eyes as he turned away and slumped, lost in his own wretched thoughts and emotions.

"Very well," Picard barked. "Data, Doctor, Worf: Begin your scan immediately. We need quick results." But he knew that the results could never be quick enough to satisfy the heartbroken prince.

Nothing was likely to satisfy him again after this terrible day.

Chapter Twenty-three

THERE WAS NO SOUND of a shot. Haron was just ahead of Chal, with a hand on the First Citizen's arm, when the bullet tore into its victim, exploding his chest in a shower of blood and bone. The second shot followed almost instantly, taking off the top of Chal's head. Haron knew instinctively that there was no point in attempting to do anything for the First Citizen. Instead he pushed the door behind them closed to prevent further potential targets from emerging, and dived for cover behind the armored transport.

He didn't have the luxury of time to react to Chal's death. The First Citizen's body lay where it had fallen, and Haron was splattered with his blood. Handgun at the alert, he scanned the area, calculating where the shots must have come from. Across the way, that tower of apartments. It had to be. Into his microphone he snapped, "Apartments, cover all exits. Arrest *anyone* leaving, even the children. Backup, out now, and reinforce them." His forerunning guards hadn't prevented the assassination, but he was determined that the killer would not escape.

There were no further shots, and Haron finally allowed his mind to begin processing other information. The screaming and howls of the bystanders he simply ignored for the moment. He attempted to do the same with the shock, dismay, and guilt he felt when he saw Chal's shattered body. Reaching into the open transport, he jerked out a blanket and threw it haphazardly over the fallen corpse to shield it from sight. Then he warily stood up. The killer wouldn't stay where he had fired from, that much was certain, and there was probably no risk of further bullets, but there was always that twinge of uncertainty.

He had failed to protect the First Citizen, and he expected to pay for his dreadful mistakes later. But right now he was the only one who could act. He rapped on the closed door behind him. "It's Haron. All clear for the moment."

The door opened and he was greeted by the sight of a muzzle. Behind it were the eyes of one of his men. The gun lowered slightly, allowing him back inside the packed corridor. Again he had to ignore the yells of fear and panic, and he glanced at Madame Chal. She was ashen and shaking, which was hardly surprising.

"My husband—" she gasped.

There was no point in lying. "He's dead, ma'am," he replied gently. To one of his men he ordered, "Get a medical team here, now, and go outside to guard the body until they arrive." The man nodded and vanished promptly. "I'm so sorry," he apologized horribly inadequately to Madame Chal. To another of his men, "Get her back inside the House and guard her." He grabbed her shaking arm and shoved it into the man's grasp. Then he forgot about her, turning to another agent. "Get hold of the moderator," he snapped. "Tell him nothing, just bring him here. This news is going to break on the vidscreens, and we'd better be ready with a statement fast." Trying to ignore his own emotions, he concentrated on the task at hand.

Then he saw Brak, the First Citizen's personal assistant and advisor. The man was shaking and pale, but there was something . . .

It had been his idea to use the side door. And the assassin had known that. . . .

With utter certainty Haron now knew what had happened. Grunting in fury, he pushed through the hangers-on and attendants toward Brak. The man must have seen the look of rage and vengeance in Haron's eyes because he paled even more and tried to flee.

In this crowd that was pointless. Haron shoved aside two people and gripped hold of Brak's arm. He jerked the panic-stricken man to a halt, and whirled him around. His handgun leveled with Brak's terrified eyes. "Give me an excuse," Haron said in a menacing tone.

Brak simply whimpered. With disgust Haron thrust the wretch into the arms of one of his men. "Take him inside," he ordered crisply. "Lock him up and charge him with being an accessory to assassination."

"I didn't—" Brak started to wail.

"Save it for the courts," Haron snapped. "I *know.*" He turned around, fiddling with his earpiece. "Where's that damned medic transport?" he demanded. A voice in his ear told him it was on its way.

There was nothing more to do inside the House now. It was time to move outside again. Not caring who he might be shoving or bruising, he pushed back through the crowd to the door. "Let no one out until I tell you otherwise," he ordered his two men on guard there. He didn't wait for their acknowledgment but went out of the door, slamming it shut behind him.

The blanket over Chal's corpse made him wince with guilt and pain again, but he tried to ignore it and the small cordon of his agents guarding it. Instead he headed across the street and sprinted to the entrance to the apartment complex.

His men there had already rounded up six people. Two were women, one with a small, screaming child. He could probably forget about them. But only probably. Maybe the assassin was a woman, who would be least suspicious. But his eyes went to the three men. One was a shirtless man, his eyes wide and panicky. Someone who'd seen the mess from his room, probably, and rushed down to gape at the blood. Haron dismissed him for the moment. The second man was in business attire, a bolero tie a trifle askew about his throat, a pouch on his back. Someone returning home from work? He was licking his lips, his eyes wide and scared.

The third man was a workman, a vidscreen repairman by the look of him. He seemed puzzled and intimidated.

Haron paused, something nagging at the back of his mind. He turned to the agent in charge of the team. "Are these the only ones who've tried to leave?"

"So far," the man answered. "Others are bound to be out soon, though. You want us to keep holding them?"

"Yes. And get someone up to the roof. That's where the shots came from. The weapon's probably still up there." He turned to the repairman. "Where were you?"

The man jumped slightly at being addressed. "Uh . . . in one of the apartments, fixing a feeder lead," he said.

"Then why are you out here?" Haron demanded.

"Uh, I needed a part from my gev." The man gestured. Haron glanced around and saw a vidscreen repair gev parked off the street. "To finish the job."

Haron's eyes narrowed. "You weren't on the roof?"

"No."

There was something about the man that simply didn't ring true. Then he realized what it was. Every vidscreen worker he'd ever seen wore a belt of tools. This one didn't. "Which apartment were you in?" he asked, his eyes narrowing.

"Uh, in—" The man half-turned to gesture back over his shoulder. Then he threw himself forward, trying to grab for Haron's gun.

Haron had been prepared for this, however, and brought the weapon down in a chopping gesture, slamming it into the side of the man's neck. The repairman grunted and fell forward, stunned by the blow. Haron glared down at the man. "I think we can call off the hunt for now," he told his agent as the man grabbed and locked the suspect in restraints. "This is the killer." With some satisfaction he scanned the onlookers, who were too stunned by the sudden nature of what had happened to be able to react yet. "Take him away. And you can let the others go."

Maybe he hadn't prevented the First Citizen's death, but Haron was resolved that whoever was responsible would not escape him. Two down . . . how many more to go?

He would find out.

Riker watched the wall screen with a mixture of revulsion and fascination. The off-picture narrator had been burbling on about Chal leaving the Citizen's House for a short break, with a general picture of the impressive House on the screen. Then, abruptly, that had changed.

"Dear gods," the narrator suddenly said, and then, as the picture suddenly leaned over and started to move, "We've just heard reports that the First Citizen has been shot. We're heading to the side exit from the House now, to see if we can get a look for you of what is happening there." The cameraman had to be jogging with him. The picture rose and fell. Riker was getting almost seasick watching the ebb and flow of buildings on the screen. He became even more nauseated when he heard Grell chuckling softly in triumph.

The picture suddenly steadied, and they were looking down a cordoned-off street. Over the heads and shoulders of the police, the picture focused in on a heavy-looking dark gev, with a rear door open. On the ground beside it was a bright orange blanket, clearly covering a body. Two growing red patches showed against the electric orange color.

"The body on the ground is supposedly that of First Citizen Chal!" the reporter was yelling, to be heard over the howls and screams of the horrified onlookers and the wail of approaching official vehicles. "We've had no confirmation of this as of yet, so I stress this is not official."

Grell tapped his hand control and the picture went silent. Looking very pleased with himself, he poured himself a glass from the table. "Well," he murmured. "I do think congratulations are in order."

"Indeed," purred Toma as she hugged and then kissed him. "My plan seems to have gone off without a problem."

Scowling, Grell pushed her away. *"Your* plan?" he demanded. "Don't you forget that it was my power and connections that made this possible."

"But it was my scheme," Toma snapped, glaring at him.

Riker could hardly believe this. With the First Citizen lying dead, these two maniacs wanted to claim responsibility and what they considered to be glory for having engineered the scheme. "Don't worry," he said brightly. "I'm sure that the police will be happy to give you both credit when they catch you."

That got their attention. Grell scowled at him now. "They won't catch me," he said with certainty. "Oh, I'm sure they'll find someone to pin the blame on. Perhaps even that expendable idiot Tormak. But they can never trace it back to me." He smiled. "Perhaps I'd better compose some sort of condemnation of this killing to be released to the media," he mused. "It would look rather good, don't you think?"

"Don't hurry to do it," Toma cautioned him. "You don't want to make it look like you're evolving an alibi for yourself."

"Of course not, my sweet. I'll wait until I'm asked for it. But it would be best to prepare one, I think." He smiled again. "Inspiration strikes me. I think I'll leave you to entertain our guests while I compose." Swirling his drink, he left the room.

Riker studied the anger on Toma's face. "It didn't look to me as if Grell appreciates your contributions at all."

She turned her cold eyes on him. "Don't try and create friction between us," she said. "I know precisely how little Grell values me, Riker. And that is immaterial. He has his uses and I aim to keep on using him."

"Don't you have ambitions?" asked Riker, watching her carefully.

"Of course I have ambitions!" she exploded. "But you cannot understand how difficult it is to be a woman in this society, can you?"

"No," admitted Riker. "It's not something I've had much experience with." She was clearly working up to something that was festering within her, and Riker wanted to see it brought out. The more worked up she became, the greater the chance was that she'd make a slip he could seize upon.

"To be powerless," she told him. "Despite your better mind, your stronger resolve, and your higher ambitions. As a woman I can't hold more than a token public office. I have to defer to men at all turns—men who are slower, stupider, and less capable than I am. You have no idea how galling that can be. To watch festering incompetents like Grell get to the top of the heap simply because of the fact they were born male! I know I can do anything better than any man, but I am forced to work through people like Grell to achieve my ambitions." Abruptly she smiled. "At least, I *was.*"

Riker's eyes narrowed. "What do you mean?" he asked warily.

"I mean that *you* are the answer that I've been seeking, Riker." She moved to stand in front of him again. "I was willing to settle for ruling this world hidden behind Tok Grell. With Chal out of the way now, Norin will become First Citizen, I'm certain. Grell is the power behind Norin, and I am the power behind Grell. A few days ago, that would have been enough for me. But now . . ." She studied him with a hunger and greed that scared Riker. "You have changed all of that."

"In what way?" asked Riker uneasily.

"Why should I settle for being the power behind the power behind the scenes on this one small, backward, little planet?" she asked. "Wallace told me that there are thousands of planets out there, many of them far more advanced than Iomides. Why settle for this world when there are worlds to conquer out there that are far more appealing. Worlds where, so you claim, women are valued as much as men. Worlds where I can rule openly!"

Riker shook his head. "There are worlds where men and women are equals and partners," he agreed. "And you'd be despised on them all for what you've done here. Torture and murder are valued on none of those worlds."

"Your foolish moral judgments don't interest me," Toma replied imperiously. "I have a destiny to fulfill, and you will help me to achieve it."

Riker shook his head. "The only thing I'll ever help you to do is to get inside a jail cell. Preferably for the rest of your unnatural life."

She snorted in contempt. "Really, Riker, you are so slow. Like most men you don't have vision." She stared at him thoughtfully. "You arrived on this planet recently. That means you have a ship somewhere around here. And I want that ship. You will give it to me."

Riker laughed incredulously. "Give it to you? You must be joking."

"No." She smiled sweetly at him. "I am deadly serious. You will hand your ship over to me and explain how I can use it."

"No chance." Riker folded his arms.

She didn't get angry. Instead she laughed, a bubbling, cheerful noise. "Well, Riker, if you want to see how I really *do* joke around, you will get your chance."

Chapter Twenty-four

THE SEARCH DIDN'T TAKE VERY LONG. After just five minutes Data emerged from a closet the size of a small house holding a thick insulated flask. "This would appear to be what we are seeking," he announced.

Beverly hurried over and scanned the container. "Yes," she announced happily. "From these readings, I'd say this is most likely the cure." She turned to Picard. "Of course, I'll have to test it out on the infectors first, to be absolutely certain."

"Naturally." Picard felt a huge sense of relief. "How long will that take?"

"An hour or so, I'd guess," she replied, clutching the flask to her chest protectively. "Then we can begin replicating the serum."

"Excellent," Picard said approvingly. "I'll have the

replicators taken off-line and dedicated to the task for as long as you need them. I'm sure the crew won't mind skipping their privileges for a while to help out here."

Beverly nodded and then tapped her badge. "Crusher to *Enterprise*—one to beam up, directly to sickbay."

As the sparkling effect took hold of her, Picard turned to J'Kara, who had witnessed the search in mute blankness.

"It's over now," he said gently. "I'm sure that's the cure your people need. With the *Enterprise*'s replicators working at full capacity, we should be able to turn out all the serum you'll need in a matter of hours."

J'Kara turned haunted eyes on him. "That's wonderful," he said dully. "Only a few hundred more people will die before then."

"I wish we could save them," Picard answered, feeling the anguish of the tortured Burani. "But we *have* to be certain that's a cure and not a false lead before we use it."

"I'm not blaming you, Jean-Luc," the prince replied. "I know that you and your people have done extraordinary things in order to help my people. Believe me, we are all truly grateful. It's simply that . . ." He faltered and coughed. "It's simply that there will be several hundred more deaths on my conscience."

"It's not your fault," Picard assured him. "You've done everything that you could to alleviate the suffering and deaths of your people. You bear no guilt in this matter."

"My father and my fiancée planned and executed

this nightmarish scheme. I am contaminated by their guilt and sins."

"No one has been stronger or braver in their search for truth than you, J'Kara," Picard assured him. "You have more than made up for the evil that your father has done. His shame belongs to him, stains him. It does not and cannot touch you."

J'Kara managed a weak smile. "Jean-Luc, you have been good to my people, and you are good to me. I respect you and your judgment. But in this you are wrong. My father's sins stain me also." He sighed. "There is at least one good thing to come of this. My proposals to dismantle the monarchy have met with stiff resistance in the past. I have had some popularity with the people, and they have not wanted me to disavow the throne, even though it would be best for my people to elect their own leaders. When the truth about this matter comes out, I am certain there will no longer be resistance to my desires."

"I'm sure you're right about that," Picard agreed. "You are a rare individual, J'Kara. For the sake of your people, you have willingly laid aside the throne many people would strive to seek. *Did* strive after, like S'Hiri and your father. Yet the idea of power seems to appeal to you not at all."

J'Kara snorted. "Of course it appeals to me, Jean-Luc. How could it not? Don't we all dream of having such authority? In fact, you and I both possess it to a large degree. If either of us gives an order, there will be someone who will snap to attention and run to obey us, to earn our pleasure. Would you willingly give up your command?"

"No," Picard answered thoughtfully. "Not unless I

was certain that I was no longer able to perform my job to the best of my ability."

"A sentiment I echo heartily, Jean-Luc," the prince replied. "Believe me, it is not easy for me to say that I should not take on the throne of Buran. I, too, desire it—though not as desperately as my father or S'Hiri would wish me to. But I am committed to one thing greater than my own wishes, and that is the good of my people."

"I repeat," Picard said smiling, "that you are a very rare individual, J'Kara. I feel honored to be called your friend."

"And I am privileged to be called yours," J'Kara replied. "Remember me in your travels, Jean-Luc, and pray for my people."

"You have my word on it," Picard promised.

"Then I am satisfied." The prince coughed again, harsher this time. "I am afraid I am feeling fatigued. I think I had better rest."

"A good idea." Picard glanced around the room. "My crew and I will return to the *Enterprise* now. I'll notify you as soon as we can begin dissemination of the serum. Bear up," he added, touching the prince's shoulder. "You will have your cure within hours. We'll have you well again in no time."

J'Kara shook his head sadly. "I shall never be well again," he replied, and then walked slowly away.

Watching him, Picard felt sorrowful and impotent to aid the Burani. The weight of guilt J'Kara felt because of his father's actions had battered down his soul. The disease that was fighting to control his body would be curable in a short while. The disease that held sway in his heart and soul would be a much harder thing to cure.

Deanna watched the video broadcast, shocked and dismayed. Despite everything, she had hoped that Grell's planned assassination of the First Citizen would somehow never happen. And yet it had. Chal was dead and the continent was in a panic and uproar. She felt sick and could empathize with Wallace in her desperate desire to stop the murder. Now that it had happened, the turmoil had begun. Infighting among the political groups was just beginning, as they vied to see who would succeed Chal.

"Still no word from Commander Riker?" she asked the technician on duty. He shook his head. Deanna turned to Kessler. "It's been too long. I think something's happened to them. I think it's time for plan B."

Kessler nodded, coming alertly to her feet. "I didn't know we had a plan B."

"We don't," Deanna admitted. "I'm improvising." She turned back to the technician. "Barclay was supposed to put a homing device inside their gev. Can you raise it?"

The man worked the controls for a few moments. "Yes," he replied. "It's parked just within the perimeter of Grell's island."

"Maybe they simply couldn't reach it and had to leave a different way?" suggested Kessler.

"Maybe," agreed Deanna doubtfully. "But I don't think so. It appears to me that they've run into some kind of trouble. They may need our help."

Kessler considered this. "If they've run into trouble, then this may be a trap to get hold of us as well."

"That's possible," agreed Deanna. "So I think we'd better go in there prepared." She tapped her communicator. "Troi to Porter."

"Porter here, Lieutenant," came back the shuttle pilot's voice.

"Two to beam up," Deanna replied. "Energize when you're ready."

A moment later she felt the transporter beam lock on to her, and then in a shower of light she reappeared on the shuttle's pads. Porter glanced at her from the controls. "Is everything okay?" she asked.

"Possibly not," Deanna answered. She passed over a data chip. "Program in these coordinates, and prepare to beam us to them." She turned to Kessler. "I think we'd better risk taking full equipment this time," she decided. "Phasers and tricorders. I've set the materialization point close to the main house, but we should be able to arrive unmonitored." She turned back to Porter. "I'll keep the communicator open so you can monitor us," she added. "At the first sign of trouble yank us out of there. If anything happens to us, be absolutely certain to get the phasers and tricorders back. We can't afford to let any of our technology fall into the hands of the locals."

"Understood." Porter finished her work. "Everything's ready," she reported. "We can transport you down when you're ready."

"Good. It'll just be a few moments." She took the phaser and tricorder that Kessler handed to her and flashed the security woman a grin. "It looks like it's up to us to save their butts."

Grell sauntered back into the room, a wad of paper in one hand and a pen in the other. "This is going well," he murmured happily. "How is it with you, my dear?"

Toma smiled back at him. "I'm going to have to . . . persuade Riker to speak."

"Ah." He nodded his comprehension. "They're not cooperating, I gather. How foolish."

It was hard for Riker to keep his temper, faced with these two sick individuals. "I can't do what you're asking of me," he snapped. "I can't turn over any of our technology to you—let alone a shuttlecraft. And even if I wanted to, my pilot would never land here. It's against her instructions."

Toma's eyes narrowed. "I'm sorry to hear that, Riker, but I don't believe you. Even if it were true, it won't save you."

She broke off as a faint beeping sound filled the room. Frowning, Grell went to a small speaker mounted by the door and snapped it to life.

"What is it?" he demanded, lifting the receiver of what was evidently the local form of communications. He listened for a moment and then paled. Finally he slammed the receiver down in fury and whirled around to face Toma and Riker. "The hospital has had a fire," he snapped, his fingers tightening on his pen. He threw his papers aside. "The alien's body was completely incinerated—before it could be autopsied."

Toma scowled. "That will weaken Norin's case against Chal," she said. "This could cause a problem."

"It may be a serious setback," Grell agreed. He turned to Riker. "This is your doing, isn't it?"

"Yes," he admitted cheerfully. "You wondered where the women of my party were, didn't you? Well, *that's* where they are. They've done this."

Grell rushed across the room and backhanded Riker with all his force. "You're trying to destroy my plans!" he screamed.

Reeling from the blow and the stinging pain in his cheek, Riker managed to shake his head. "It's nothing personal," he answered. "But we have to prevent your planet from contamination. Stopping your nasty little scheme is just a bonus."

"It's not stopped," Toma insisted, moving forward. "We still have three aliens, Tok. One of these can be used for the autopsy instead."

"They're not as much use," Grell complained. "They look too human. We *needed* that Vulcan!"

"We'll make do," Toma insisted. "Pull yourself together, Grell! Don't go to pieces just because of a minor setback. The rest of my plan is still working perfectly."

With a howl of rage, Grell backhanded her again. *"My* plan!" he yelled. "Never forget that. It's *my* plan."

"Uh, speaking of plans," Barclay called out, "maybe you should be watching this broadcast?" He gestured at the silent screen. "I'm not very good at lipreading, especially in an alien language, but I think there's something there you might want to see."

Grell whirled around and then fumbled in his pocket for the screen's control. His hand was shaking as he reset the sound.

There was an official-looking figure on the screen, being questioned by reporters. Riker didn't recognize him, but a scroll appeared at the top corner proclaiming him to be Dral Haron, head of security.

". . . can sadly confirm that the First Citizen was indeed shot and killed a short while ago," he was saying. "This is a black day for our world."

"And do you have any idea who's behind the killing?" the unseen reporter asked.

Haron stared out of the screen. "The assassin is in our custody. He's been tentatively identified as one Pol Tormak. According to our records, he's a onetime soldier who was discharged and went into private service."

"With whom?"

Haron smiled grimly. "At this moment in time, I'd rather not say. We are pursuing several leads actively, and expect Tormak to talk."

"He'll *never* talk," hissed Toma, her face redder than ever with anger.

"He'd better not," Grell snarled. "If he does he could lead them straight here!"

"Keep it down," Barclay complained. "Some of us are trying to listen."

Riker grinned. Barclay was doing a fine job of pushing their buttons. "The best laid plans," he murmured in mock sympathy. "I think it's all coming unraveled, Grell."

Despite themselves Grell and Toma stared at the screen. Haron was still talking and gesturing to a manacled man being led to a police vehicle. "Chal's personal assistant, Tral Brak, was also involved in the plot," he was explaining. "He has been placed under arrest and will be cooperating with us shortly."

"Brak as well!" Grell howled, scared and angry. "The man's a fool! He's going to break, I just know it!" He whirled on Toma again. "Your plan is coming apart at the seams!"

"Oh, so it's *my* plan now there's trouble, is it?" she yelled back. "Well, it's not over yet. You have agents on the police force. All we have to do is to have them kill Brak and Tormak and we'll be covered. They can't talk if they're dead."

Riker turned to the closest guard. "I hope you're paying attention," he murmured. "You're hearing how your bosses treat retirees." He saw the worry and uncertainty on the man's face and knew that it had to be reflected in the minds of the other six guards, too. "A generous pension plan you have," he remarked to Grell. "Is that what these boys have to look forward to as well? Being murdered if they become inconvenient?"

Grell glowered at him furiously. "Shut up!" he screamed. "Shut up! I need time to think!"

"Think?" howled Toma. "I'm the one who does all the thinking for you. I can still salvage this, despite you."

Now . . . Riker caught Vanderbeek's eyes and then Barclay's and nodded slightly. Then he jumped to his feet and delivered a right to the jaw of the closest guard. The man grunted and started to fall forward. Riker grabbed the man's handgun and twisted it free of his loosened grip.

Barclay and Vanderbeek had followed his lead, taking out two further distracted guards. Before the others could respond decisively, Riker had his captured gun against Grell's neck.

"Drop the weapons," he ordered. "Or else your paycheck here dies." Slowly they laid down their weapons and backed off, their hands raised.

"Against the wall," Vanderbeek ordered them, collecting the handguns. He herded them ahead of him, a slight smile on his face.

Riker thrust Grell away from him, into Toma. The pair of them grunted and straightened up, their eyes angry and worried. "Well," Riker murmured cheerfully, "it seems that the tables have turned, doesn't it?"

At that moment, the far door opened. Riker whirled around, his handgun at the ready. Then he relaxed slightly.

"Oh, Will," Deanna chided, moving into the room with Kessler, their phasers at the ready. "How could you hold a party without inviting us?"

Chapter Twenty-five

BEVERLY STEPPED CAREFULLY through the ranks of the suffering and dying. Doctor L'Tele walked beside her, a slight smile on his face for the first time since she'd begun working with him.

In her hand, Beverly clutched her hypospray kit.

It still hurt her heart to see so many beings in pain and torment, but at last there was hope. More than hope, if she was correct.

She halted beside the pallet on which M'Riri lay. The Burani woman was thinner than before and her feathers discolored by puss and blood. She looked wretched, but somehow she managed to scare up a smile from deep inside her when she saw her human visitor.

"It is good to see you again, Doctor," she murmured. "I did not expect to live this long." She coughed and her body spasmed.

"You'll live a lot longer," Beverly promised. Kneeling, she pressed the hypospray to M'Riri's upper wing and injected the serum. "We have a cure, and I wanted you to be the first recipient. Without your help, it would not have been possible."

"Truly?" M'Riri asked, her eyes widening and fastening on L'Tele.

"Truly," he replied happily. He took the hypospray as Beverly handed it to him. "Starting now, with this ward, the plague will end. Thanks to the Federation, and especially to Dr. Crusher."

"And thanks to you," Beverly informed the Burani woman. "The plague ends now."

"Aah!" M'Riri settled back with a sigh. "I wish I could speak longer, but I am so tired. . . ."

"Rest," Beverly insisted. "We'll speak later, when you are better." She patted the woman gently on the arm where there were no sores, and then rose.

The first of the hyposprays were being distributed now to eager nurses and doctors. There was a flurry of activity that warmed her heart as medics bent to inject patient after patient in the ward. Shaking back her hair, she moved to join L'Tele, who beamed at her. "It looks like you've got this well in hand," she said. "Captain Picard is arranging for further supplies to be sent to every hospital. We should have every one of them covered by this evening. The plague is going to be over when night falls."

"Thank you," L'Tele said simply. Then, smiling, he added: "I owe you an apology, Doctor."

"It's not necessary," she began, but he waved a claw.

"It *is* necessary. Like so many of my fellows, I was deeply suspicious of your motives for being here. I was wrong. You came here out of compassion, and despite the mistrust you were faced with, you acted honestly and well." He coughed self-consciously. "I am very proud to have known you, Dr. Crusher. You have saved many thousands of my people from suffering and death. We can never repay you."

"There's no need," Beverly answered. "We're glad that we could help. And so terribly sorry for what happened to you."

L'Tele nodded sadly. "It is a terrible tragedy. That our own king should have been the one to loose this evil plague . . ." He shook his head. "But that is past. I do not think that any Burani will now argue that we should not be a part of the Federation. You have shown us that there is nothing to fear and so very much to be gained by our membership."

"Then I'm glad." Beverly smiled at her colleague. "Some good has come out of all this evil after all."

"Yes," agreed L'Tele. "We have discovered good friends."

"Hi, Deanna," said Riker, his grin spreading. "Nice of you to drop in." He gestured to their prisoners. "You might like to meet Tok Grell, and his psychotic conspirator, Toma Sar. She's responsible for the death of Maria Wallace. And that of First Citizen Chal." To Grell, he added, "This is Deanna Troi. She's responsible for the fire that destroyed Starn's body." To Toma he said, "And a very efficient woman, who's equal to any man I know."

Toma growled wordlessly at this and Grell simply scowled.

"Charmed, I'm sure," Deanna murmured. "Will, isn't it about time to say good-bye? Or are you enjoying being a bandit?"

"No," Riker replied. "I've had more than enough of this pair, believe you me."

"What . . . what are you going to do to us?" asked Grell, shaking. He evidently feared the worst.

"Nothing," Riker replied. "As I told you, we have a rule against interfering with other cultures. I'll leave it to your own people to punish you. After all, you must be implicated in Chal's death by now."

Deanna frowned slightly. "Don't they know an awful lot about us, though?" she asked. "Wouldn't that be a breach of the Prime Directive?"

"Perhaps," Riker conceded. "But we don't have time to wipe their minds. And I don't think it'll be necessary. With the disappearance of Starn's body, their proof is gone. We'll take Wallace's body with us, and Grell will have nothing to prove his story with." He grinned at the financier. "You might try telling them all about us, of course," he added. "That might just get you an insanity plea, don't you think?"

Once again Toma just growled angrily.

"Hold it a minute," Barclay said, staring at the wall screen again. "I think something significant is happening in their Citizen's House." He turned up the sound again.

Watching Grell and Toma with one eye, Riker tried to follow what was happening on the screen.

The reporter had switched to the interior of the assembly hall now, where the moderator was calling for order again. Both Norin and Madame Chal were visible near the speaker's platform, Norin looking flushed and furious.

"It's a travesty!" he was yelling. "She has not been elected to office, and to allow her to speak would be against all of our rules!"

"At this time of tragedy," the moderator said forcefully, "I do not think that this body would begrudge the Widow Chal the chance to address us all. Do we need to take a vote on this matter?"

There was a chorus of no that rose and swelled. Scowling, Norin stepped back, acknowledging the inevitable. He skulked back to his normal seat and flopped into it.

Madame Chal stepped forward. Her face was streaked with tears and her makeup was gone. Yet, with all of that she possessed a clear inner dignity. The moderator bowed to her and sat down, leaving her alone at the podium, watched by the political heads of Tornal and what had to be a huge video audience.

"Thank you all," she said, slowly and clearly. "You have shown great compassion and understanding on this dreadful day. Less than an hour ago, my husband was shot down and murdered as he left this assembly. I do not have to tell you how much this has affected me. Nor do I need to tell you how much it has affected our entire planet. Messages of sympathy and shock have already started to pour in from Mellim and the other cities. Offers of peace have accompanied them.

"My husband's entire life was devoted to the good

of all Iomides. Now, it would seem, his death has brought this dream of his to an end. Yet it need not end here." She surveyed the room. "You are, on the whole, good men. You, too, want the best for our world. So at this time of tragedy, I ask you—I *beg* you—do not allow my husband's dream to die. We can bring some good out of this evil if we want it badly enough. Let us take these overtures of genuine sorrow and friendship from those we sometimes believe to be our enemies, and let us instead work with them.

"Make my husband's death have meaning. Make his dream rise from the ashes. Make our planet whole."

There was a thunder of applause as she spoke; many of the members of the assembly rose to their feet to cheer her on. She held up her hands. "Please," she begged. "Hear me out." The noise died down and she shook her head sadly. "Now I must bring even sadder news. Security Officer Haron has spoken with my husband's aide, Tral Brak, who was involved in this plot to kill my husband. Brak has begun to make a confession that this scheme was the work of industrialist Tok Grell. Grell, it seems, did not want my husband's dream of peace to succeed. If it did, then his munitions plants would be out of business.

"My husband was murdered simply for the profit of one evil man." She stared at Norin. "A man who is the main backer for Brak Norin," she added. "It may be that Norin is innocent of any involvement in this plot, but he will have a lot to answer for."

Norin sprang to his feet, his face flushed. Before he could say anything, however, two security guards slid into place beside him, disconnecting his microphone. He started to argue with them, but they gripped him firmly and led him from the floor.

"I hope that Norin is innocent of any complicity in this matter," Madame Chal continued. "Otherwise, it would be a terrible stain on this Citizen's House. There remains still his accusations against my late husband of his conspiring with alien beings to the detriment of our world. These allegations must and will be investigated, but I have some news there, also. The hospital that was storing this so-called alien corpse suffered a fire. The only casualty, it appears, was this corpse, which has utterly vanished. Weapons belonging to Grell were discovered there, so he clearly is behind this disappearance. His bloodred hand shows through this whole conspiracy to discredit and destroy my husband.

"Again, I beg of you: Do not let this succeed. Rescue my husband's dreams and pursue his goals. Forget all this silly foolishness about alien invaders, and work together to unite our world. We have a great destiny ahead of us. It is time for us to seek it out together."

The applause began again, and this time it refused to be silenced. It swelled from the ranks of the assembly and carried Madame Chal along in its wake.

"Now *that's* some woman," murmured Deanna in appreciation. "I think she deserves every accolade she's getting, don't you?"

"Yes." Riker, smiling, turned back to face Grell and Toma. "Well," he said cheerfully, "it looks like the good guys have won through again. And a woman with real talent is getting recognition." There was a chime from the speaker on the wall. Riker gestured to Grell. "Maybe you'd better answer that?" he suggested.

Shaking and pallid, Grell complied. "Who . . . who is it?" he gasped.

"Police," came the reply. "We have your island surrounded, Tok Grell, and are here to arrest you for complicity in the assassination of First Citizen Chal. Lower your shields and allow us to enter."

Grell's numb finger fell from the controls, and he stared at the wall in shock.

Riker grinned again. "That sounds like our cue to leave," he murmured. "Have a nice life," he said to Grell and Toma.

Deanna tapped her communicator. "Troi to *Isaac Newton.* Five to beam up."

"Don't forget to tell them about this part," Barclay called, as the transporter effect took hold on them all. "I'm sure they'll love it."

As the room started to fade, Riker saw Toma throw herself toward Grell, screaming furiously. "You *idiot!* You *moron!* You *failure!* To think I had faith in you!"

Grell's face twisted in fury and despair and he whirled to meet her charge. Riker saw the flicker of a knife in his hands and then pain on Toma's face as the blade was buried deeply into her chest.

There was little chance she would have survived that blow, Riker thought. He did not feel sorry for her, but he couldn't help wondering what the police would make of yet another murder at the hands of Grell.

* * *

Haron turned to his assistant at the bridge to the island. "It looks like he's going to be difficult," he said with a sigh. "You'd better break it down." He gestured at the computer console. The man nodded, and started work on the panel.

He wasn't too surprised that Grell hadn't admitted them, but the man surely had to realize that he couldn't stay inside forever. At the very least they could starve him out. This was just a waste of time and effort.

"It'll be interesting to see him in court," murmured another of the officers to Haron. "I wonder what his plea will be?"

Before Haron could reply, there was a flash of light from the trees on the island, and then a huge, pulsing shock wave that threw them all to the floor as the force screen collapsed. A second later the vast roar of the explosion hit them. Bits of masonry and dust rained down from the darkening cloud that filled the sky.

Battered but essentially unharmed, Haron stared at the devastated landscape that had been Grell's island. The explosion had leveled it, tearing apart every tree and shrub and reducing the grand mansion at the island's heart to burning rubble. The water below the bridge bubbled and foamed, crashing against the shore.

As soon as the ringing in his ears died down and he could think and speak again, Haron turned to his companion. "I take it he wasn't planning on pleading not guilty," he commented.

Chapter Twenty-six

"It's GOOD TO HAVE YOU BACK aboard again, Number One," Picard said, as the crew of the *Isaac Newton* emerged. "I'm looking forward to reading your report. Did you have an interesting time?"

"Interesting?" Riker smiled. "Yes, I think you could call it that." The smile vanished. "Maria Wallace is dead, as are Dr. Starn and several other members of the observers. First Citizen Chal is dead, and the conspirators are in jail." He shook his head sadly. "Quite a death toll, I'm afraid."

"Indeed." Picard placed a hand on Riker's arm. "But you did a splendid job in recovering the situation."

"I couldn't have done it without Deanna," Riker

replied honestly. "Or Barclay, for that matter. They were invaluable."

"I know. They always are." Picard turned to Deanna. "Come along, Counselor." He led the way back to his ready room. "It seems that both of our missions have concluded successfully. And they were, in some respects, quite similar. I believe they both show us how difficult the transition can be from an isolated society to a community of many worlds."

Riker nodded. "That's a transition Iomides will be facing pretty soon," he predicted. "And one that Buran is still undergoing."

"And both worlds had rulers who tried to do their best for their people, even in the face of opposition, hatred, and murder," Deanna observed. "One of them has died for his beliefs, and the other has more than suffered."

Deanna broke off as the communications panel chimed. "Yes?" Picard said.

Worf's face appeared on the screen. "I am receiving a message from Buran," he replied grimly. "D'Nara wishes to speak with you."

"Their security chief," Picard informed Riker. To Worf he added, "Put him through. Perhaps you had better join us also, Mr. Worf."

The screen changed, showing the strained face of D'Nara. "Captain Picard."

"D'Nara," Picard murmured. The door hissed, and Worf entered the ready room, moving to stand beside Riker and Deanna. "What can I do for you? Is everything still proceeding well with the cure?"

"Better than we could have hoped," the Burani replied. "Almost all of the infected victims have now made complete recoveries." His eyes were hooded and almost unreadable. "In fact, there has been only one death due to the plague since the serum was administered."

"That's good news," Picard answered. Seeing the grim expression on D'Nara's face, he added, "Isn't it?"

The Burani shook his head slightly. "The one victim was Prince J'Kara."

A cold stab of pain went through Picard. *The prince . . . dead?* "I don't understand," he admitted, shaken. "Did the cure not work on him?"

"He did not take the cure."

"Not . . ." Picard shook his head, trying to make sense of all this. "But . . . why ever not? Surely, he knew that he would die without it?"

"Yes, Captain," D'Nara answered. "That is why he refused to take it. He was overcome by shame at the actions of his father and fiancée and could not bear to live with the dishonor. He felt that the only course of action open to redeem himself was to show unity with all of his father's other victims. Therefore, he refused the cure."

Picard bowed his head. "He will be sorely missed," he said frankly. "He was a good person and a wise leader. There are few born like him at any time."

"Indeed," agreed D'Nara. "A period of public mourning has been ordered. He will be given a state funeral. He deserves one."

"Yes," agreed Picard. "I will have the *Enterprise*

return to Buran for the funeral. I wish to pay my respects and those of the Federation at the ceremony."

D'Nara managed a slight smile at this. "It will be greatly appreciated, Captain. I look forward to seeing you again shortly. D'Nara out."

The screen went blank. With a heavy heart, Picard turned to face his officers. "It is a great loss," he observed. "J'Kara was a very enlightened person. Buran will not fare so well without him."

"It's such a terrible waste," Deanna commented.

"No!" said Worf, firmly. "He acted with great honor. Had he lived, his father's shame would have forever clouded his family name. By his heroic death, J'Kara has expunged his father's shame. In future generations, he will be remembered with respect and honor. It was a noble death." He inclined his head slightly. "He would have made a great Klingon."

"I don't know, Worf," Deanna said. "He had so much to offer in the service of his people, and he threw it all away because of misplaced feelings of guilt and shame. It smacks more of selfishness than bravery to me."

Picard sighed. "I think there are merits in both points of view," he commented. "The prince *was* suffering from shame and also depression at the betrayal of the two people who meant more to him than anyone else. That undoubtedly played a part in his action. But he also felt strongly that he had to atone for his father's deeds. In any case, whatever the moral underpinning of his decision, J'Kara will be sorely missed." He breathed in deeply. "I'd better tell Ro and Data to have us head back to Buran for the ceremony." He clapped a hand on Riker's shoulder. "You and the counselor will like this world, Will. They're good people."

"They seem to be," Riker agreed. He glanced at the Klingon. "If Mr. Worf likes them, they have to be something special."

"They are. In fact—" Picard broke off as the communicator chimed again. "Now what?" he grumbled.

Ro's face appeared on the screen. "Incoming message from the planet, Captain," she reported. "It's Dr. Saren, asking to speak with Commander Riker."

Picard raised an eyebrow and then stepped aside, gesturing for Riker to take his place.

"Put it through," Riker ordered.

The screen lit up again. The Vulcan's impassive face stared back at them. "Commander. Forgive my intrusion, but there have been some fresh developments on the planet that I thought might be of interest to you."

"They would indeed, Doctor," Riker answered. "What's happening?"

"First of all," Saren answered, "the police did not arrest Grell. He took his own life to avoid arrest."

Riker's eyebrows shot up. "Well, I can't say I'm too surprised," he replied. "He wasn't the kind of guy to sit around and rot for the rest of his life in a jail cell. And I can't say I'm sorry he did it. Iomides is better off without him."

"I concur," Saren said. "The other news is of some significance. The Citizen's House has decided that there will be an emergency election in two days to replace the late First Citizen Chal." He paused for a moment. "One of the candidates announced is Madame Chal. She would appear to be the favorite candidate for the post. Several other politicians have stepped down rather than oppose her."

Deanna's eyes met Riker's and both smiled broadly.

The Vulcan continued. "It appears highly likely that she will win the position. I suspect her influence will unify the planet even faster than her husband might have managed it. I believe that many of his plans and visions were, in fact, inspired by her in the first place. I thought that you would find this information of interest."

"You thought correctly," agreed Riker. "It's very encouraging news."

"Saren out." The screen went dead.

"Well," said Picard firmly, "I think it's time to head back to Buran now."

"Yes," Deanna answered with a smile. "But I suspect it won't be that long before we return to Iomides—to welcome another new world into the Federation."

Coming Next Month!

STAR TREK
DEEP SPACE NINE®

The
Tempest
By
Susan Wright

Dax believed that one of the best ways to get to know somebody was to go on a long shuttle trip with them. She had figured that out while she was a cadet at Starfleet Academy, where she had been introduced to the concept of the two-person team.

During the past few months, since she had resolved things with Curzon, she was better able to appreciate the fact that she had attended the Academy simply as Jadzia. After being kicked out of the Symbiont Institute on Trill, where the focus had been on generating competition among the Initiates, it was a joy learning how to cooperate with the others.

"Nearing the storm front at ten thousand kilometers," Dax announced. "How bad is that graviton interference?"

"It's holding steady now that the bleed has been boosted," Keiko confirmed.

Dax could already tell that Keiko was a competent technician—their first flurry of stabilizer adjustments had proved that. And her meticulous handling of Ops indicated that she was a perfectionist. But Keiko herself was still a mystery, not only to Dax but to a lot of people on DS9. Maybe even to Chief O'Brien.

"Leeta says you're going to be on the survey for another few months," Dax commented. "How is it going?"

"Oh, we're making progress." When Dax made it clear she was waiting for more, Keiko added, "Actually we're working so well together that Starfleet expanded the survey to include the archipelago of the southern continent. We're finding some rich calcium-complex vegetation that grows in the wet climate along the coast."

"So you like being on Bajor."

Keiko smiled at the nonquestion. "It's tough moving around with the survey team, never in the same place for more than a few weeks. But the work itself is fascinating." Then she sighed. "I guess you can't have everything. . . ."

"Why not?" Dax asked.

Keiko looked at her. "For one thing, it's physically impossible to be on the station and Bajor at the same time."

Dax concentrated on the helm, letting Keiko's

answer fall lightly into silence. She sympathized with Keiko's dilemma.

"Was Molly all right when you left her?" Dax asked.

"She'll be fine." Keiko acted as if leaving her was perfectly natural, though Dax knew that mother and daughter were seldom apart. "I activated the pony program, even though I swore I'd make her wait until tomorrow." She checked the chronometer. "It'll be over soon, and then the nanny program can deal with her. Miles doesn't know how lucky he is."

"He didn't look so happy standing on the service pad."

Keiko shrugged. "You have to admit it happened awfully fast. He was surprised, that's all."

Dax grinned. "I'd say it was fast! He was still trying to ask about radiation levels when you shut the hatch in his face."

Keiko looked uncomfortable, as if her mask had slipped. Dax remembered the way she had stared at the image of O'Brien on the viewscreen as the *Rubicon* rose to the launchpad. The chief kept waving until they were out of sight. Only then had Keiko taken a deep breath and returned to the launch sequence.

"I wonder how they're doing with that freighter," Keiko said.

Dax checked the station logs. "It's been secured. But Captain Sisko has issued an evacuation recommendation to all vessels below class two, due to the turbulence."

Keiko's eyes widened. "I thought there were no more quarters available on the station."

"There aren't." Dax frowned over the sensor data as the runabout shook from the emission waves. "If the shock waves are this bad out here, what about the turbulence within the storm?"

Keiko glanced at the viewscreen. The pure velvety black mass blocked out most of the starfield, but the leading edge was defined by veins of flashing energy discharge, marking the point where the plasma encountered normal space matter.

"Slowing to half-impulse," Dax said. "The shock waves are getting stronger."

"Sensors are calibrated," Keiko confirmed. "The link to the biometric program is engaged. We're getting additional data on a wide range of Doppler shifts."

Dax prepared a burst transmission to send the new data back to the station. Communications would probably be lost once they were inside the storm.

"This close," Dax said thoughtfully, "I thought we would encounter line and recombination radiation. Even with a reflection level as low as one percent we should be getting *something* on the interior of the storm."

"There's those energy discharges along the edge," Keiko indicated. "The filaments are being spectrally recorded, but we have no background comparison with the main body of the plasma mass."

"So we can't tell if particles are being excited or emitted."

"It's an ideal blackbody," Keiko agreed. "Rate of absorption and emission is the same. I wonder what's happening inside."

"My guess is that it's rotating on its own axis," Dax told her.

Keiko widened her eyes. "I didn't think plasma did that in a natural vacuum."

"Why else can't we get a fix on the wavelength angles?" Dax had finally thrown out Planck's law after wrestling with that impossible variable for most of the afternoon, trying to phase the momentum with value of energy release. "This isn't getting us anywhere. The spectroscopic analysis is giving us the same readings on the emissions that we got on the station—helium, carbon, nitrogen, oxygen, sulfur, calcium . . ."

"It's the bulk of the interior elements we need to determine," Keiko agreed.

"All right, here we go," Dax announced. "Electrostatic field engaged."

"Spectral index is well within parameters," Keiko confirmed. "Both waves and particles are being polarized away from the runabout."

"Prepare to enter the plasma field."

Dax maneuvered the runabout in a vector that would sharply intersect the edge of the storm. She didn't want to risk deflection, unsure of the effect that impact would have on the hull. She was also concerned about what might be concealed within the plasma. An ideal blackbody was theoretically impossible without a source of stabilized electric discharge. There was a distinct possibility that a comet-like pulsar or neutron star was at the heart of the storm, and if so, then the gravitational forces could easily overpower the runabout once they entered.

Dax glanced at Keiko, wondering if she should

share that nasty piece of information. She had included it in the burst transmission to DS9 because the station needed to be warned of the possibility. But it was too late for them to turn back now.

"Sensors at maximum sensitivity," Keiko announced. "Prepared for entry."

"You know . . . ," Dax said, "there is a chance the hull could be crushed by the internal turbulence. . . ."

Keiko held her gaze. "If the storm is that strong, then the station won't be able to withstand the pressure either. We need to find out."

"You're right about that. I'm taking us in." Dax hit the thrusters and held on.

But the runabout penetrated the storm without a shudder. Helm control remained steady, while navigational orientation began to swing aimlessly around the chart as if searching for some verifiable indicator to establish their position. Sensors were unable to penetrate the border of the storm.

Keiko switched the viewscreen to spectral/visual. "Look at that . . ."

Inside the blackbody, the plasma was alive. Constant reionization released photoconductive electrons, creating spectral colors within, and even beyond, humanoid sight. Other complex optical effects produced brilliant fluorescent streaks and luminescent flickers of light that twisted and swirled together in the hydrodynamic currents.

Dax slowed the runabout and released a dye marker to give their sensors a ground point. At first she was unsure if they were moving; then she realized the marker was cruising along at about the same speed they were.

She altered their course, concerned about the power spikes as particles and waves struck their electrostatic shields. She reminded herself to watch the relays to make sure the circuits didn't overload.

"I've narrowed the range on the sensors," Keiko announced. "But the interference is still too great to get anything beyond the most rudimentary readings."

"That's plasma for you," Dax said philosophically. "We need to isolate our targets."

Using the molecular beam, she released gas particles into the plasma. The computer would track the progress of their collisions and decomposition into charged electrons and photons.

"Keep an eye on the ternary collisions," Dax told Keiko, indicating the correct equation sequence. "Let me know if the cluster integrals get any larger."

"They already have," Keiko immediately replied.

"That fast?" Dax asked, having a look for herself. "This is some plasma storm. . . ."

She carefully recorded the thruster action against the movement of the released particles. They revealed an approximate reading of both longitudinal and transverse waves within the plasma, though the splitting of Alfven waves were recorded to the detriment of other variables, filling their data banks with random frequencies.

"Well, according to the gas particles, the plasma is rotating as a mass." Dax was glad to finally confirm one of her hunches about the storm. "It must be releasing huge amounts of rotational energy, approximately ten to the sixty-seventh power ergs per second. That's what supplies the relativistic particles and magnetic fields to sustain the storm."

"It's building on itself," Keiko realized.

"That's right, it's picking up particles through inverse Compton scattering. That keeps it moving in a steady vector." Dax returned to her readings. "I'll see if I can determine the oscillation distribution of the waves. That might give us a base frequency we can work with. But we'll need to isolate a sample of the plasma."

"How do you do that with charged particles that are in a constant state of flux?" Keiko asked.

"Usually we'd use the EGD converter. But the plasma is so dense that our power systems can't create a high enough electric field to contain the stuff." Dax grimly shook her head. "Maybe we should have brought the *Defiant* after all."

"Is there any other way to get a sample?" Keiko asked.

"Well, we could try a plasma trap," Dax decided.

She spent some time attempting to draw a sample of the plasma into a ring-shaped magnetic field. Despite the high temperatures of the trap, containment of the dense plasma was limited to fractions of microseconds. A bulge kept forming along the lateral surface, instantaneously extending tongues of plasma within the trap and disappearing on contact with the container walls.

"It's too unstable," Dax said. "Maybe I can create an open trap using two magnetic mirrors. That might contain the plasma long enough to get a sensor scan on it."

"Anything I can do?" Keiko asked.

"In a minute," Dax told her. "Let me just set this up. . . ."

Keiko got up to pace in the back of the runabout until Dax called her to return to the sensors.

"I'm establishing the trap in a vacuum field just outside the starboard hull. Look for patterns," Dax told her, ready to grasp at any straw. "Check number densities, temperatures, electric, and magnetic field strengths. We mainly need to determine the trajectory of relative particles."

"The ratio of negative and positive charges per unit volume are fairly equal," Keiko offered. "Though the numbers keep shifting."

"That's typical in high-density plasmas." Dax was preoccupied with the phase ratios. "That's why we get macroscopic readings rather than the motion of individual particles."

Keiko sighed and sat back in her chair. "Maybe I shouldn't have tried so hard to convince Captain Sisko to let me come. I'm not being much help."

"This isn't your part of the mission," Dax pointed out. "It's mine, and I haven't been very successful. You're here because you're the most qualified person to analyze the data once I've gotten it."

Keiko let out an exasperated sound. "Then why did I have to fight so hard to get the captain's permission?"

"Benjamin was just worried about Molly," Dax tried to explain.

"Oh, I don't blame him for asking about Molly.

How could he ignore her when she was practically jumping up and down on his feet?" Keiko turned to Dax. "But what does Miles have to do with it? I mean, really—does anyone call and ask me how I feel every time he crawls into a fusion generator?"

"No . . ." Dax hesitated, but it needed to be said. "Try to look at it from Captain Sisko's perspective. After all, he did lose his wife during a mission."

Keiko returned to her console. "That's true. Don't mind me; I've been like this ever since I left Bajor. I hate to be interrupted when I'm in the middle of a project."

"Well, then, let's get on with this one," Dax said, smoothing things over. "I'm taking us in deeper."

She engaged thrusters. Temperatures rose as the plasma became denser.

"Here's something," Keiko said. "Helix patterns."

"Where?" Dax demanded. She examined the readings. "Magnetic lines of force. That's consistent with synchronic radiation but . . ."

"But what?"

"Look at the total heat flux. And the thermal energy transported within the unit area. It's building, as if there's some other factor acting on the—"

The *Rubicon* lurched, and a blinding flash of light shorted the viewscreen. Dax squeezed her eyes shut, covering her face with her hands.

Even when the emergency lights came on, she could barely see through the red spots in her vision.

"Computer is off-line!" Keiko exclaimed.

Dax didn't breathe until the indicator signaled that the computer core was powering up again.

"Electrostatic field remains intact," Keiko added breathlessly.

That was exactly what Dax wanted to hear. The interior support systems came back on as indicators returned to normal—except for the viewscreen. She would have to replace the circuit buffer first. *And* increase the repulsion of the electrostatic guard to keep the same thing from happening again.

"What was *that?*" Keiko asked.

"I'm not sure. But, look—the sensors recorded the entire electromagnetic frequency range for the duration of the burst."

"Finally!" Keiko exclaimed. "That gives us the data we need to run a comparison against the biometric models."

Dax wasn't as pleased as Keiko. She wanted to know exactly what happened. She slowed the sensor logs and saw what she had been dreading—fifty nanoseconds before the burst of light, a faint luminous current on the order of several hundred thousand amperes had created a stepped leader between the runabout and the plasma. The runabout acted as the ground, releasing an outward discharge, short-circuiting the plasma that was in magnetic flux around them. The white flash had been just one of the secondary results.

"There was a direct energy discharge between the plasma and the runabout," she told Keiko.

"I thought the electrostatic field would prevent that."

"Apparently the magnetic currents are strong enough to override our power systems." Dax considered the readings. "In fact, there's no way we can compensate for the reaction unless we completely shut off the shields. And the radiation levels make that impossible."

"If the runabout can destabilize the plasma, what will the station do to it?" Keiko asked. "Will the shields hold?"

"It's not just the station—what about the wormhole?" Dax countered.

"They might both act as electrodes," Keiko realized. "That would mean . . ."

"A plasma arc as big as Bajor."

"With everything in between instantly ionized." A flicker of her eyes betrayed her immediate thought of Molly. "We have to get back to the station to warn them. Everyone should be evacuated."

Dax was already activating the helm. "Impact with the magnetic currents could burn out the wormhole permanently. Or the plasma could be caught in its gravitational flux, which means the entire system would be covered by a self-generating plasma storm for the next few centuries."

"Bajor . . ." Keiko whispered.

Dax couldn't understand the navigational sequence that she was getting. "We must have been thrown some distance by the discharge."

Keiko could tell something was wrong. Dax couldn't find the dye marker, and the angle of the transverse waves had altered.

"That wasn't just a magnetic field we ran into," Dax finally concluded. "The currents are being twisted into loops by the cyclonic turbulence. We've been transported deep inside the storm. I'm not even sure where we are."

"We couldn't have gone far," Keiko protested. "It lasted less than a second."

"I don't know . . . a reaction like that, involving high-intensity heat conduction and Coriolis forces from the rotation . . . it could have produced space-time variances within the magnetic loop."

Keiko was also checking the rudimentary readings of the sensors. "Particle and wave density is much higher in this area. And there's no sign of the dye marker or the gas particles we released."

"From the number of magnetic currents, I'd say we were much closer to the center of the storm."

"That can't be true!" Keiko insisted. "That would be faster than light—"

"Theory of relativity? You might as well forget about that. Our time scale depends on our frame of reference. Inside the blackbody, our only reference is this highly charged, high-temperature energy-matter."

"But the storm covers nearly half a sector!" Keiko looked as though she didn't know which way to turn. "It could take us a week to cross it at impulse."

"*If* we could figure out which way to go." Dax watched the particles perform their colored dance, flashing as if they were laughing at the runabout.

"What are we going to do?" Keiko finally asked.

"We're going to have to find a quicker way out of here. Unless you're willing to let a plasma storm get the better of us?"

Keiko's eyes flashed in return. "Never!"

Dax took a deep breath. "Then let's get to work."

STAR TREK
DEEP SPACE NINE™

24" X 36" CUT AWAY POSTER,
7 COLORS WITH 2 METALLIC INKS & A GLOSS AND MATTE VARNISH, PRINTED ON ACID FREE ARCHIVAL QUALITY
65# COVER WEIGHT STOCK INCLUDES OVER 90 TECHNICAL CALLOUTS, AND HISTORY OF THE SPACE STATION.
U.S.S. DEFIANT EXTERIOR, HEAD SHOTS OF MAIN CHARACTERS, INCREDIBLE GRAPHIC OF WORMHOLE.

STAR TREK™
U.S.S. ENTERPRISE™ NCC-1701

24" X 36" CUT AWAY POSTER,
6 COLORS WITH A SPECIAL METALLIC INK & A GLOSS AND MATTE VARNISH, PRINTED ON ACID FREE ARCHIVAL
QUALITY 100# TEXT WEIGHT STOCK INCLUDES OVER 100 TECHNICAL CALLOUTS,
HISTORY OF THE ENTERPRISE CAPTAINS & THE HISTORY OF THE ENTERPRISE SHIPS.

ALSO AVAILABLE:

LIMITED EDITION SIGNED AND NUMBERED BY ARTISTS.
LITHOGRAPHIC PRINTS ON 80# COVER STOCK (DS9 ON 100 # STOCK) WITH OFFICIAL LICENSED CERTIFICATE OF
AUTHENTICITY. QT. AVAILABLE 2,500